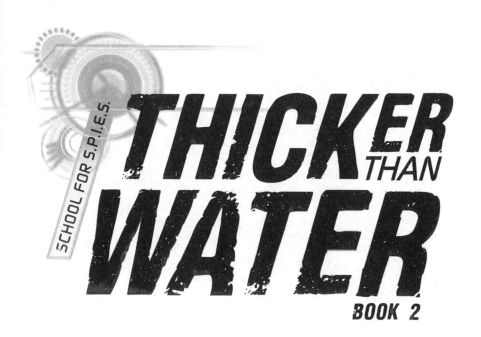

SCHOOL FOR S.P.I.E.S.

THICKER THAN WATER

BOOK 2

BRUCE HALE

WITH ILLUSTRATIONS BY

BRANDON DORMAN

Disney • Hyperion Books

Los Angeles   New York

First Edition
1 3 5 7 9 10 8 6 4 2
G475-5664-5-14091

Printed in the United States of America

Library of Congress Cataloging-in-Publication Data
Hale, Bruce.
Thicker than water/by Bruce Hale;
illustrated by Brandon Dorman.—First edition.
pages cm.—(School for S.P.I.E.S.; book 2)
Summary: "Max Segredo and the S.P.I.E.S. are on a mission
to steal a powerful mind control device and to keep the Merry
Sunshine Orphanage from closing"—Provided by publisher.
ISBN 978-1-4231-6851-5 (hardback)
[1. Spies—Fiction. 2. Stealing—Fiction. 3. Orphans—Fiction.
4. Identity—Fiction. 5. Racially mixed people—Fiction.]
I. Dorman, Brandon, illustrator. II. Title.
PZ7.H1295Tg 2014
[Fic]—dc23   2013046392

Reinforced binding

Visit www.DisneyBooks.com

For Ashley, who helped me find Max's heart

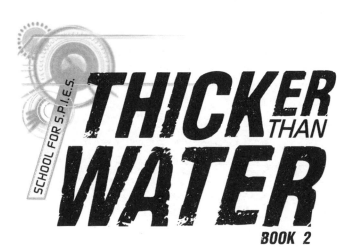

SCHOOL FOR S.P.I.E.S.

THICKER THAN WATER

BOOK 2

HIT AND POLISH

FOUR-THIRTY P.M., a shoeshine stand outside an office building in the financial district. Max Segredo was waiting to take out the ambassador of Gravlakistan, and he really, really had to pee.

If only he'd answered the call of nature, spent a penny, seen a man about a horse, made his bladder gladder half an hour before, when he'd had the chance.

Too late now. Everyone was in position, the mission was in play, and he'd just have to gut it out.

Max clamped his thighs together and tried thinking dry thoughts. This sort of thing never happened to James Bond or Jason Bourne. But then, ever since he'd landed at Merry Sunshine Orphanage—the cover name for the School for S.P.I.E.S.—Max had learned that much of what passed for spy life in the movies was absolute rubbish.

In his experience, espionage involved no glamorous lady agents, no dry martinis, no sports cars tricked out with gadgets. (And if it did, a thirteen-year-old agent trainee wouldn't be romancing, drinking, or driving them anyway.)

In his few weeks with S.P.I.E.S. (Systematic Protection, Intelligence & Espionage Services—honestly, could they have thought of a more obvious name?), Max had learned the truth about spying. It was dangerous, dirty, and occasionally dull work.

And he loved it.

Not only that, he was good at it.

Max shifted on the low wooden stool. "Shoeshine, get your shoeshine here," he called in a listless singsong. Impeccably dressed businesspeople strode past his alcove in the shade of the gleaming office towers, heading out to conduct their unbearably important business. No one spared him a second look.

Perfect.

With a glance to either side, he slid open a drawer in the wooden box before him, where normal shoeshine boys would store the tools of their trade. The waxy scent of polish intensified. He slipped a hand under the rags and checked his weapon.

Max patted it. He'd never taken out anyone before, but if you had to do it, this seemed like the perfect tool for the task. Now, if only his target would arrive before his bladder burst.

A chilly wind whipped through the concrete canyons of the financial district, carrying the smell of expensive exhaust from passing limousines. A blue-clad bobby crossing the little plaza slowed and gave Max the fish-eye.

Ever so casually, Max closed the drawer and snugged his heather-gray knit cap down over his ears, the better to cover his telltale earbud. "Shoeshine!" he cried, trying to keep his expression as bored-looking as a supermodel at a science lecture.

After a long minute, the cop moved on.

Max exhaled.

"Tremaine," he mumbled into the tiny microphone concealed up his jacket sleeve, "how's it look?"

On the other side of the lobby's glass wall, the teak-skinned art student took a break from sketching architecture, adjusted his spectacles, and muttered into his own sleeve. "Nothing yet, Maxwell." Tremaine was the lookout, monitoring the second-floor art gallery where Ambassador Potapenko and her party lingered at the reception.

"They're still up above," he continued, "talking and talking."

"It's Gravlaki art," Max complained. "What is there to say?"

"Awww, is widdow Maxi-Pad getting nerwous?" This jab came over the com system from the beefy red-haired girl sitting on a bench across the plaza. She was pretending to text on her smartphone. "Told you I should've been the triggerman."

"Right, Nikki," said the slender brown girl supposedly reading a book at the other end of the bench. She smoothed back her wiry hair. "You couldn't hit an elephant's bum with a banjo. Max is a much better shot."

Max felt a flush of pride at Cinnabar's remark. She'd been so distant lately, so wrapped up with her sister, Jazz; it was nice to know she still noticed him.

Or maybe she just loathed Nikki.

"Take that back, Brillo-head," Nikki Knucks snarled.

"Uh-oh," said Tremaine. "Say what you like to a fellow orphan, but you never insult a sister's hair."

Sure enough, Cinnabar whirled on the bigger girl. "You pigheaded—"

"*Oi!*" A sharp voice cut through the chatter. "*Damare!*" barked Hantai Annie Wong, orphanage director and mission leader. "Everyone shut you mouth. This is assassination; show some respect."

The com line went quiet. Cinnabar and Nikki turned away from each other. From his current position, Max couldn't see Hantai Annie's command post, but he could picture the lean Asian woman's scowl.

"This not gossip circle," she continued. "This is spy team. If you not serious, you gone. *Wakatta ka?*"

"Loud and clear," muttered Nikki.

Some would hear Hantai Annie's broken English and be fooled. They wouldn't guess that beneath that facade lurked a bright, highly trained spymaster who spoke seven languages and knew eight ways to kill a man with a ballpoint pen.

Their mistake, thought Max.

He nearly asked her for permission to make a quick trip to the loo, but he bit back the question. Max would only get one shot at the ambassador, and he didn't fancy missing it. He also didn't fancy the nickname Inky-Dinky Bladder, which Nikki would surely confer on him.

Max crossed his legs and shifted again on the hard stool.

He scanned the scene. Women in fur coats and men in power suits were beginning to leave the reception, joining the pedestrians on this glitzy downtown block in the capital city. A tall man in a camel-hair overcoat caught Max's attention, and his heart skittered a beat.

Was that . . . ?

No. The man turned, and Max could tell that it wasn't his long-lost father, Simon, who'd briefly reappeared in Max's life, nearly gotten him killed, and then vanished again. Max didn't know how to feel about the man. Right now he was only a distraction.

Max sighed and resumed his scrutiny of the street.

Three Mercedes sedans with diplomatic plates waited at the curb, heading a line of limos. Their drivers leaned against one of the cars, shooting the breeze.

A Gravlaki security officer stood with them, hands in his overcoat pockets, looking as gaunt and pale as a vegetarian vampire. He even had that Count Dracula haircut, slicked back and descending to a widow's peak on a high forehead. His ice-blue eyes missed nothing. When the man's overcoat gaped, Max glimpsed a pistol in a shoulder holster.

He gulped. Max hoped his team was ready to handle Gravlaki security, or his first hit would be his last.

Diagonally across the small square, the last of the sunshine illuminated a pale blond boy about Max's age and a deeply tanned older teen—Wyatt and Rashid—chatting with a news vendor at a pushcart. Hard by them, a tarp-shrouded bench displayed a sign: UNDER REPAIR. A savvy bystander might have observed that something under the tarp was creating a substantial bulge. Most paid it no attention at all.

When Wyatt noticed Max's gaze, he flashed a discreet thumbs-up.

"Good to go, mate," he murmured into the com link. Max gave a tiny nod. Someone, at least, had his back.

The other direction, past Cinnabar and Nikki, a man in a filthy hoodie sprawled on his own bench, taking frequent swigs from a bottle and muttering to himself. The mutters carried clearly through Max's earbud.

One of them was: "Heads up, my friends." Then the heavily disguised Victor Vazquez, the spy school's tech expert, continued, "Here comes the advance guard."

And sure enough, two bull-necked specimens wearing earpieces and dark suits pushed through the glass doors and spread out to secure the plaza's perimeter. Max had to look twice to tell that one of them was a woman. Forget blending in; the pair might as well have had the words *security guard* tattooed across their foreheads. But perhaps that was the point.

"Shoeshine," called Max, keeping up his cover. "Shoeshine here."

"Let's get jammin'," said Tremaine from his post inside the lobby. "The mongoose is on the wing. Repeat: The mongoose is on the wing."

"A mongoose isn't a bird, you git," said Nikki.

Tremaine's tone was mock incredulous. "No, really?"

"You know you don't have to speak in code, right?" said Rashid.

"I know," said Tremaine. "But I always wanted to say that."

"Focus!" growled Hantai Annie.

Max glanced over his shoulder and spotted the Gravlaki ambassador, Roza Potapenko, descending the escalator with her entourage. Finally, he thought.

Showtime.

"*Gambare*, everyone," said Hantai Annie. "Do your duty."

Max slipped a hand inside the wooden box. His heart hammered as his fingers closed around the weapon's grip, and he took a steadying breath. From the corner of an eye, he tracked the ambassador's group as it stepped off the escalator and started across the lobby.

Which was why he felt completely gobsmacked when someone's foot landed on the box in front of him.

"How much?" The man's voice was deep and posh.

"Er, sorry?" said Max. Standing before him was a barrel-chested geezer in a charcoal pinstripe suit, a real captain-of-industry type. The man's cordovan shoe rested on the sole-shaped stand atop the box.

Mr. Cordovan sniffed a haughty sniff and looked down his considerable nose at Max. He spoke slowly and loudly, as if addressing a two-year-old from another planet. "How. Much. Is. Your. Shoeshine?"

Irritation surged in Max's chest. This happened sometimes—people noticed his almond eyes, straight black hair, and golden-brown skin, and took him for a fresh-off-the-boat immigrant.

But this was no time to fight that fight.

He cut his eyes to the right. Ambassador Potapenko's party had nearly reached the tall glass doors. His bladder gave a painful twinge.

"Well?" said Mr. Cordovan. "Do. You. Speak. English?"

"Much better than I speak Mandarin," said Max. "But I can't shine your shoes."

The geezer looked as though a mangy wombat had just splashed down in his French onion soup. "Why ever not? Is this not a shoeshine stand?"

The ambassador's entourage pushed through the doors and past Max's alcove. "No, actually," said Max. "It's an art project."

"An art project?!" Mr. Cordovan huffed. He removed his foot from the box and drew himself up. "Dashed peculiar, if you ask me."

"I don't," said Max, watching his target move into the small plaza. "You can go now."

"Really!" said the man. "This country is going straight down the toilet!" He spun on his heel and marched off.

Hantai Annie's voice carried over the com line. "And . . . Victor-*san*, go!"

The scruffy man in the hoodie swigged from his bottle and staggered to his feet, weaving across the plaza on course to intercept the embassy group.

Max pulled his weapon from the box, making sure to keep the rags wrapped around it. He stood, holding it down by his leg, and began to pursue the ambassador.

Victor Vazquez lumbered into the path of a bulky bald man leading the entourage—Regional Security Officer Zigfrid Plotz, Max knew from his briefing. Plotz sidestepped. Mr. Vazquez stumbled into him, hunched his body once, twice, and yodeled his groceries all over the officer's chest.

Even knowing that the "vomit" was only cream-of-mushroom soup from Mr. Vazquez's bottle, Max felt a spasm of revulsion. Plotz was livid. As Vazquez apologetically smeared the mess across the man's chest with the tail of his ratty overcoat, the security officer cursed and cuffed him about the shoulders.

More importantly, he fell behind the ambassador's group.

"Nikki, Cinn-*chan* . . . go!" Hantai Annie barked.

The two girls accorded Ambassador Potapenko the sort of wide-eyed, shrieking reaction usually reserved for a boy band. "No way!" squeaked Nikki, in a passable surfer-girl accent. "It's Porta-Pot—uh, it's her!"

She and Cinnabar sprang from the bench and rushed the diplomat, producing little notebooks and pens from their purses. "You're so awesome!" squealed Cinnabar. "Like, fighting for freedom and stuff. Can I have your autograph?"

"Me, too!" trilled Nikki.

The ambassador took a step back, nonplussed. The security guards hustled forward to protect their leader from the two scary fangirls.

Head down, Max closed on his target. The weapon felt surprisingly light in his sweaty hand. He was a dozen paces off . . . then ten . . . then eight.

None of the ambassador's aides noticed him; the path was clear.

Then, from curbside, the Dracula-haired security guard spotted Max. His eyes narrowed. He uncrossed his arms.

Uh-oh.

"Rashid, Wyatt—go!" snapped Hantai Annie.

The two teens by the newsstand stepped over to the

covered bench and flung off the tarp. With a whoosh, a mass of turquoise, green, and red balloons—the colors of the Gravlaki flag—exploded into the sunset sky.

"Viva Gravlakistan!" the boys cried. Not the best language choice, perhaps—Gravlakis not being Italian or Spanish speakers—but their enthusiasm got the point across.

For a long moment, all eyes in the plaza, including Dracula Hair's, were riveted to those balloons.

All eyes but Max's.

He tossed aside the rags and brought up his weapon, thumbing the switch from safe to semiautomatic. Max closed the remaining distance in a rush.

Time seemed to stretch, as if in a dream.

He heard the *chuff-chuff-chuff* of his trainers against the smooth concrete.

He felt the cool curve of the trigger under his finger, the pebbly pistol grip in his right hand, and the ridged barrel grip in his left.

His target turned, alerted by some primal instinct. Behind wire-rimmed glasses, her eyes went wide. Ambassador Potapenko was short, Max's height, and her thick hair, cut into a bob, was as black as his own.

He had time to notice her pearl earrings and pale pink lipstick, slightly smudged.

Then he pulled the trigger.

CHAPTER 2

THE WRATH OF BUGGER-OFF

BAM-BAM-BAM! Even without a silencer, the shots sounded no louder than someone down the block hammering on wood.

Circles of purple paint sprouted across the ambassador's red-and-white blouse and brown jacket.

Bull's-eye!

In that moment, Max had time to admire his aim and to think that purple didn't really match the woman's clothes.

Faces turned in shock, reacting to the hit on their chief. More from surprise than from the impact, Ambassador Potapenko windmilled her arms and tottered backward, collapsing to the pavement. Her aides rushed to her side. Plotz and his security guards reached for their pistols.

Now *this*, thought Max, would be an excellent time to beat a hasty retreat.

He tossed the paintball gun into a planter of hardy orange flowers, dove across it, and rolled to his feet on the sidewalk. Then Max was off and running a zigzag between startled pedestrians.

A siren's wail followed by a two-tone *whee-oo whee-oo* echoed down the street. A screaming-yellow blur passed Max, heading for the plaza. Did the Gravlaki Embassy have an ambulance on speed dial?

First chance he got, Max ducked into an office building and visited the loo. Afterward, he strolled back down the block to rejoin his team.

As Max arrived, the ambulance was just pulling away from the curb. The other orphans clustered around Mr. Vazquez. Hantai Annie stood a few paces away from them, deep in conversation with a barrel-shaped man sporting the kind of white hair one might find on a cabinet minister or judge on the telly.

Max drew closer, and their voices reached his ears.

". . . our best effort, Mr. Deputy Chief," Hantai Annie was saying.

"Absolutely tip-top," boomed the white-haired man. "You certainly found the holes in our security operation—and with a team of teenagers, no less. Our RSO and I have plenty to discuss." He sent Plotz a steely glare.

The burly security officer looked sullen and bewildered, like a Rottweiler wondering how a family of skunks had managed to move into his master's house.

Hantai Annie offered the deputy chief a slight bow. Her lean body was sheathed in a midnight-blue business suit and her dark hair was neatly pulled back into a bun. "And when can we expect payment, Baghirov-*san*?"

"We'll send that off first thing in the morning." The man's upper-crust English accent seemed out of place, coming from a face that would've looked more at home on the steppes of Central Asia. "I say, nice touch with that ambulance. Made the whole affair seem very real."

"Not *our* ambulance." Hantai Annie frowned. "*Your* ambulance?"

By this time, Max had rejoined his comrades, who were riding their postmission glow. Rashid made a pistol with his finger and thumb and pretend-shot Max, smirking. Blond Wyatt clapped Max's shoulder.

"Well, if it isn't Deadeye Dick," he said in his sharp Australian accent. "Ace shooting, mate!"

Max grinned. "Fastest paintball in the West."

"Bull's-eye, Maxwell!" crowed Tremaine, bumping Max's fist.

At that moment, an electronic Beatles riff rang out. Mr. Baghirov fished his phone from his pocket, lifted a just-a-minute finger to Hantai Annie, and turned away to take the call.

Max tried to catch Cinnabar's eye. "Nice fangirl act," he said. "Scary-good."

She glanced up from texting on her phone—to her sister, Jazz, no doubt. "Um, right. Thanks," she said vaguely.

He felt unaccountably disappointed that she hadn't complimented his work.

"*I'm* the triggerman next time," growled Nikki. "This girlie stuff bites. What use is it being a spy if you don't get to shoot and blow stuff up?"

Max let his attention wander across the square. Not far off, Security Officer Plotz was chewing out Dracula Hair and the two beefy guards. Max felt some sympathy, but this *was* a security audit after all. Someone was bound to suffer if everything wasn't up to snuff.

"Plotz!" Mr. Baghirov barked. He jammed the phone back into his breast pocket, his broad face red as a beetroot. *"Now!"*

"Something is wrong?" asked Hantai Annie.

"Wrong?!" said Baghirov mock-sweetly. "What on earth makes you think something is *wrong*?"

Hantai Annie pointed at his face. "Veins standing out on you forehead."

Wyatt snickered. Mr. Vazquez shot him a warning glance.

"Yes, sir?" said Plotz, joining his boss.

"Nanda?" Hantai Annie asked the deputy chief. "What is problem?"

Baghirov got right up in Hantai Annie's face. His bulk dwarfed her, but she didn't yield an inch. "The bloody *problem*," he said, "is that my ambassador has been kidnapped."

"Kidnapped?" repeated Plotz, his face ashen. Max and his friends exchanged uncertain looks.

"And on *your* watch," growled Baghirov.

"Mine?" Plotz cringed.

"Not yours, you prat," snapped Baghirov. *"Hers."*

Hearing that, Max, Cinnabar, and Nikki pushed forward simultaneously. "You're bonkers," said Max.

"Dead wrong," Nikki snarled.

"We were hired to do an audit, *not* protect your boss," said Cinnabar.

Hantai Annie's hand chopped down. *"Oi! Chotto mate!"* Turning back to the Gravlakis, she said, "They are rude, but they are right. Guarding not our responsibility."

The rest of the embassy security team drifted closer, drawn by the argument.

"Nevertheless," said Deputy Chief Baghirov, in a voice colder than four months of Finnish winter, "I'm holding *you* responsible."

"But, Chief," Dracula Hair began, "they—"

"Nyet, Dobasch." The deputy chief cut him off.

The rest of the S.P.I.E.S. team stepped up behind Hantai Annie, faces grim and shoulders tense. The spymaster herself was as still as a sculpture, but her dark eyes glinted dangerously.

"Explain yourself," she said.

"Ambassador Potapenko was taken by one of *your* competitors," said Baghirov.

"That's crazy," Max blurted, but he fell silent at a glance from Hantai Annie.

"Excuse me," said Victor Vazquez, pushing back the hood of his sweatshirt, "but why is that our responsibility?"

Plotz raised a finger to him. "Butt out, you tramp."

"I'm no tramp; I'm on the team," said Vazquez.

"Oh," said Plotz. "Butt out anyway."

Baghirov wore the expression of someone who'd bitten into a teacake and discovered a dead mouse. "Apparently this is some sort of dispute between your two organizations, and we've just been caught in the cross fire."

"What you mean?" said Hantai Annie. "Who took ambassador?"

"LOTUS Security Systems," said the deputy chief.

Dracula Hair's eyebrows climbed his forehead. He shot Plotz a sharp look, and the security officer made a tiny head shake.

Hantai Annie spat several curse words in Japanese.

Max gasped, but not at her swearing. He had helped rescue several of his fellow orphans from LOTUS's headquarters not two weeks ago. Since then, that unscrupulous group had taken several jobs away from S.P.I.E.S., trying to put the school out of business—but they'd never done anything this extreme.

"What do they want?" asked Victor Vazquez.

"Your fee," said Baghirov. "And if we refuse to pay, they'll sell Ambassador Potapenko to the rebels." Max knew that the Kreplachi separatist movement back in Gravlakistan had been the whole reason for the embassy's security audit.

"So," said Hantai Annie, "job costs you twice as much, then."

The deputy chief offered a smile as sincere as a get-well card from a poisoner. "You mistake me, madam. They stipulate that we can't pay *you*—only LOTUS."

"That's not fair!" Max exclaimed.

"Nevertheless," said Baghirov, with an expressive shrug.

Hantai Annie planted a fist on her hip. "We will rescue ambassador."

"Certainly not!" Mr. Baghirov huffed. "Any rescue attempts and the ambassador dies. That's their promise."

Wyatt had been following this whole exchange with great interest. In the pause that followed the deputy chief's remark, he raised a hand.

"Can I ask a question?"

Baghirov glowered at him.

"How did LOTUS find out about all this in the first place?" asked Wyatt.

Security Officer Plotz flushed wine-dark. "It doesn't matter. Shut your mouth, little boy."

Max bristled at the insult to his friend, but the orphanage director spoke first.

"He's right," said Hantai Annie. "How they know ambassador's schedule? How they know we stage fake assassination to test security?"

"You have a leak," said Plotz, avoiding her eyes. "Nothing more."

Dracula Hair had been looking more and more like someone had slipped spiders down his shirt. At last he burst out, "No! I'll tell you how they knew."

"Zip it, Dobasch," growled Plotz.

"*He* told them." Mr. Dobasch hooked a thumb at the security officer.

"Ridiculous!" Plotz spluttered.

A bitter smile lit Dobasch's gaunt face as he spoke to Annie. "You see, Comrade Plotz put the audit job out to bid. He left all four bidders with a copy of the ambassador's itinerary for the week. Sheer brilliance."

"That'll do, Dobasch," Baghirov chided.

But the security guard was on a roll. "I told him not to, but does this bear-faced son of a ratcatcher ever listen to me? Never! *I'm* only a decorated KGB veteran who—"

"That's enough," said Baghirov.

Dobasch's upper lip drew back from his teeth. If looks could fry, Plotz would have been a grease spot. "Better hope LOTUS paid you in advance, Plotzkin."

"Why?" said the beefy security chief. "Would they—?" Belatedly, he clapped a hand over his mouth.

Hantai Annie Wong crossed her arms, leveling her gaze on Mr. Baghirov. "So," she said, "leak is from your embassy, not my school."

Max, Cinnabar, and Nikki sneered at the embassy crew, who looked embarrassed.

"Enough!" Deputy Chief Baghirov's black eyes burned, and his jowls quivered with rage. "Dobasch, you're fired."

"Me?!" said the Dracula-haired man. "It's not my fault; Plotz was the one."

Baghirov wagged his finger in Dobasch's face. "But Plotz didn't air our dirty laundry in front of outsiders."

"But they—"

"I don't care!" snarled Baghirov. "Pack your things tonight. You're gone."

Cinnabar frowned. "That's not right."

"That's none of your business, girl." The deputy chief unleashed his scowl on her. "Trot along and buy some lip gloss."

"Hey!" said Max.

"And you . . ." Baghirov swung on Hantai Annie. "Take your ruddy orphans and go."

"Our payment—" she began.

"—is going to LOTUS. Be thankful I don't bill you for the ransom amount."

Hantai Annie's face went hard and motionless, as if it were carved from old bone. Energy crackled behind her still facade, and for an instant it looked as if she might punch the diplomat in his jowls and pop him like a party balloon. Instead, she called out to the fired security officer, who had stepped away from the group.

"You, Doughboy . . ."

"Dobasch," said the bony man. "Stanislav Dobasch."

"You like job?"

He turned a contemptuous eye on the deputy chief and Plotz. "As long as it's not with Mr. Bugger-off here, yes."

"Come work for me." Hantai Annie Wong plucked a business card from her pocket. "I know value of decorated KGB veteran."

Dobasch took the card and met her gaze. "And they said it would rain today," he recited with an odd little smile.

"You don't need weatherman to know which way the wind blows," she answered. Max thought this sounded suspiciously like some kind of password. Either that, or bad song lyrics.

"I'll call tomorrow." Dobasch glided off toward the embassy cars.

The diplomat and his security chief had their heads together—discussing ransom procedures, Max guessed. Baghirov glanced back at Hantai Annie.

"I'll be spreading the word about you," he said coldly.

"Me, too," said Hantai Annie, "about *you*." With great dignity, she led her team away from the plaza and down the street to the parking garage.

"Cho!" said Tremaine. "After all that work, we're not even getting paid?"

"Apparently not," said Rashid.

Tremaine spat. "Blackheart buggers."

"Stupid embassy gits," Nikki sneered.

The other team members chimed in with some choice words, but Max's attention was fixed on Hantai Annie and Victor Vazquez, walking ahead of the group and conferring in low voices. He had noticed that the adults at the orphanage often kept matters, vital matters, from the students, as if they all were little kids incapable of understanding.

Max was heartily sick of this. After years of misery in the foster-care system, he'd finally found a home at Merry Sunshine Orphanage. So if something threatened his home and surrogate family, he wanted to know about it—bang off the mark. He fell in behind them, listening closely.

"—not saying that," Mr. Vazquez said. "But where will we find the money to pay him with?"

"I will find," said Hantai Annie.

"But, Director, we can't lose another job. Government payments don't cover all our expenses, and—"

"*Chotto mate,*" said the director, catching sight of Max. "You have question?"

"Me?" said Max. "Sure. How bad are our money troubles?"

She waved a dismissive hand. "Not your worry. We handle it."

"Really?" said Max. "'Cause it sounds pretty bad. Don't you think the orphans have a right to hear if something big is—oh, I don't know—threatening the orphanage?"

"*Baka yarou,*" scoffed Hantai Annie. "Of course not. We . . ."

But her explanation trailed off as a tall figure in a brown overcoat stepped from the alcove of a boarded-up storefront. The director and Vazquez separated, hands reaching for concealed weapons.

The figure raised its own hands as if surrendering. "A word?"

Hantai Annie Wong squinted at the man's features, shaded by the brim of a battered hat. *"You?"*

"You've got some nerve," Mr. Vazquez said. A wicked-looking knife suddenly appeared in his fist.

"I only want to talk. Please." The mystery man shifted, and a stray beam from a streetlight spilled over his long jaw and thin lips.

Recognition struck Max like a bucket of ice water.

What he wanted to say was *Dad!* but he turned it into "Simon?"

CHAPTER 3

DAD ON
THE RUN

SIMON SEGREDO had been at large for nearly two weeks—ever since Max's daring rescue mission at LOTUS headquarters. That whole time, LOTUS agents had been hunting everywhere for the man, with orders to shoot him on sight.

Max's relationship with his father was complicated, to say the least. Simon had duped him into trading S.P.I.E.S. secrets to LOTUS, and then locked him up when Max had a change of heart. Clearly a minus, relationship-wise. But then, Simon had also Tasered the double agent who was about to shoot Max, thus allowing Max and his mates to escape. That had to be a plus, right?

Max hated him, he loved him, and he deeply mistrusted him.

On second thought, complicated didn't even begin to describe it.

Simon Segredo's eyes flicked over to his son, but he addressed his words to Hantai Annie. "I can help you."

She snorted. "Help *yourself*, you mean."

Max's father held out his palms in a conciliatory gesture. "Help all of us." Max noticed that Simon's cheeks were hollowed, dark smudges ringed his eyes, and beard stubble dusted his jaw.

"*Doushite da?*" Hantai Annie demanded. "Tell me why I should talk to you?" Her fists rested on her hips and her chin pointed up at the tall man. The orphans fanned out in a loose semicircle, eyeing the elder Segredo with varying degrees of suspicion, hostility, and curiosity.

Simon's gaze darted up and down the sidewalk, but none of the passersby spared them a second glance.

"We have a common enemy," he said.

"Duh," said Max. "Your old employer."

"Or maybe they're *still* your employer," said Nikki. "And you just want us to *think* you're on our side."

"Take that back," Max snapped, although he'd been thinking precisely the same thing. He and Nikki traded sneers.

Simon Segredo appealed to Hantai Annie. "Join forces with me. I know their weaknesses."

"And if we let you in," she said, "you'll know *ours*."

The rogue agent shook his head. Urgency touched his gaze, like the sharp bite of an arctic blast. "It's not like that. Use me as bait. We'll draw them out, then hit them full

force"—his fist smacked into his palm—"and kill them all."

Hantai Annie's lips drew into a narrow line. "*Tondemonai.* Never."

"But they'd kill you without batting an eyelash," argued Max's father. "Why not kill them first?"

The orphanage director stared at him for a few breaths. "To stop them, yes. Is my goal for many years. But ambush and kill?" She shook her head. "*Dame da.* That is LOTUS's way."

"Spot-on," said Simon. "Fight fire with fire."

"I want to stop LOTUS," she said. "Not *become* LOTUS."

Simon winced and rubbed his stubbly cheek. "At the end of the day, you may not have that choice. They mean to destroy you utterly."

Max felt for his father, but at the same time doubted him. He wanted to say something, but he had no idea what. Hantai Annie motioned for the orphans to follow her, and the group flowed past Simon, toward the car park up the street. Max started to trail after them.

Simon caught Max's arm. "Max."

"I, uh . . ." Max's throat was tight with unsaid words.

The rogue spy dug in his overcoat pocket and fished something out. "I don't know when I'll see you again."

Max held up a hand warily. "That's okay. You don't need to—"

"No. I—I know you don't trust me. I wasn't there for most of your early years."

"Try *any*," Max blurted.

Simon grimaced. "That's fair. But . . ." He pressed an object the size of a book into Max's grasp. "Maybe this will remind you of happier times."

Max glanced down. In his palm lay a photo in a simple black frame. It showed a lovely Asian woman with a blinding smile, holding a chubby toddler. A long-jawed man grinned up at the camera, one arm flung about the woman's shoulders.

"It's the only shot ever taken of the three of us," said Simon. "Spies don't much fancy being photographed."

Max found the snapshot oddly touching. He possessed very few artifacts of his long-ago life before becoming a foster child, and his mother's smile beamed straight to his heart. "How—" He cleared his throat. "No one ever told me. How did she die?"

Sudden pain etched his father's face, as if someone had slipped a knife between his ribs.

"Max," called Hantai Annie. *"Ikuzo!"* She stood at the parking-garage entrance in a wash of yellow security light, the last of the orphans filing past her.

"How?" Max asked again.

"It was . . ." His father swallowed, caught in an undertow of strong emotion.

"Max! *Now!*" yelled Hantai Annie.

Reluctantly, Max took a step toward her, his eyes still glued to his father's face.

"Next time," promised Simon Segredo. "Next time, I'll tell you everything."

Max choked down his disappointment. "Right. Sure you will."

"Be safe, son."

Max hunched his shoulders and headed up the sidewalk. As he went, he thought he heard Simon say, "Family is hard for spies," but when he glanced back, his father had melted into shadows.

Merry Sunshine Orphanage stood on a quiet city street, an unremarkable four-story redbrick structure like its neighbors. Unremarkable, that is, save for the spikes on the roof edge, the bars on the windows, and the captured spy in the basement. This last was the result of a mission to interfere with LOTUS's operations. Max had yet to see the prisoner.

The next morning, after news of the botched assignment spread, the mood at the orphanage was as sober as a surgeon in scrubs. Thanks to his new awareness of the school's financial troubles, Max surveyed his home with fresh eyes. For the first time, he noticed that the exercise mats were wearing thin, the porridge far outweighed the meat at breakfast, and the computers were what could most charitably be described as senior citizens.

How had he missed all this before?

At midmorning, Hantai Annie granted the students a free

study period and summoned the teachers to her office for a meeting. Something felt off. Max had a strong suspicion that the agenda of this meeting involved the future of the orphanage, and when the director wouldn't let him take part, he silently vowed to listen in by any means necessary.

After a quick trip upstairs, Max caught Victor Vazquez outside the office just as he was about to join the other teachers. "Almost forgot," Max said, handing him a device. "I borrowed one of your calculators."

"Oh?" said the tech teacher. "Thanks, Max." He absentmindedly tucked it into his shirt pocket and stepped into the director's office. The door swung closed behind him with a solid click.

"Riiight," said Wyatt, who had been watching from the staircase. "You borrowed Mr. V's calculator, 'cause you're mad about maths."

Max signaled his friend to keep his voice low. "Cynicism is so unattractive in one so young."

Wyatt offered a lopsided smile. "And yet, so necessary. Whatcha got up your little sleevies, mate?"

"Nothing but my little armies." Max crooked a finger. "Join me?"

He poked his head into the library and found the room unoccupied. Dropping into a chair at one of the sturdy oak tables, he withdrew a compact silver device from his pocket.

"Well, well, a receiver," said Wyatt, flopping into a chair

across from him. "And why, exactly, are we snooping on our teachers?"

Max arched an eyebrow. "Have you ever noticed how none of the grown-ups ever tells us anything about what's really going on here?"

"Since God's dog was a pup."

"Sorry?" said Max.

Wyatt smirked. "For a long, long time. Don't you speak English?"

"Yeah, but I'm not so sure about you." Max plugged a set of mini-headphones into the receiver, flipped the ON switch, and handed an earbud to Wyatt. "Have a listen."

A moment later, Hantai Annie's voice came through as clear as well water: "—going to do about problem."

"That makes four jobs now that LOTUS has stolen from us." Madame Chiffre's voice was nasal and sharp. "Ze under-bidding was bad enough, but this? This eez vile."

Max grimaced. Things were worse than he knew.

Mr. Vazquez's smooth tenor chimed in next: "My friends, I don't wish to alarm you, but if we don't bring in some new revenue by next week, we may have to close down the school."

Close down the school?

Max's eyes met Wyatt's. Things were *much* worse than he knew. Their home was hanging by a thread.

"Blimey," breathed Wyatt. "No more Merry Sunshine?"

Max pictured leaving his new friends, his new home, and

returning to the life of an unwanted foster child, shuttled from family to family, from bad to worse. His stomach clenched. Seven years of that life was enough—no more, he vowed.

"There must be some other way to raise money," said Madame Chiffre. "We could sell something, surely?"

A rustle like a hurricane in a willow grove was followed by a crunch like a Buick landing on a barn. Max and Wyatt recoiled. Mr. Vazquez must have set the bugged calculator on the table.

"And what do you suggest?" This voice with the lilting Indian accent belonged to Chandrika Moorthy, the third teacher. "A bake sale? I can see it now: Buy a tart; help an orphan learn to spy."

"Well, we can't simply give up," said Madame Chiffre, with an edge to her tone.

Hantai Annie's voice sliced through. "No one is giving up. We find way to keep school going. Victor-*san*, why don't—"

The front-door chimes cut her off with a riff from the James Bond theme.

"See who is there," said the director. "And take this."

Another deafening rustle, and the *shoosh-shoosh* of footsteps on carpet.

Max met Wyatt's gaze. They wanted to hear the rest of the discussion, but visitors to the orphanage were as rare as lipstick on a bullfrog.

"We won't miss much," said Wyatt.

"Let's take a peek."

Just to be on the safe side, Max pocketed the receiver and earbuds before joining Wyatt at the library door. The blond boy eased it open a crack, and they peered into the entryway.

At the front door, a gray-haired woman in a chic moss-green jacket and narrow black skirt spoke into the intercom. "Yes? Who eez there?"

From where they stood, the visitor's response was garbled, but on the entryway's grainy security monitor Max could make out the image of a man with a wispy goatee. Whatever he said must have done the trick, because the woman, Madame Chiffre, swiped her key card, pressed her thumb to the biometric lock, and opened the front door. She disappeared into the narrow passage between inner and outer doors.

"Well?" said Wyatt. "Who do you reckon?"

"Not a salesman, anyway," said Max. "She'd put the dog on them."

Presently, Madame Chiffre led the visitor into the entryway. The first thing Max noticed was that there were actually three visitors: the bearded man and two bodyguards—one huge, mustachioed, and mahogany brown; one lean, ponytailed, and paper white. Max was just guessing about their duties, but the men's six-foot-plus frames packed with muscle and their snake-mean expressions made *bodyguard* more likely than *nanny*.

The bearded man stopped in the center of the entryway, his hands held close to his chest, as if he didn't want to touch anything. With his chiseled cheekbones and chocolate-drop eyes, he resembled a Chinese Johnny Depp. Of course, the movie-star effect was spoiled somewhat by the greasy locks of thinning hair that hung to his shoulders.

"Annie Wong?" he said.

"In her office," said Madame Chiffre. "Who shall I say wants to see her?"

"A man with a job." The visitor smirked. "A spy job."

Wyatt whispered, "He looks familiar."

"One of your old foster dads?" Max whispered back. Wyatt elbowed him.

Madame Chiffre folded her arms and pointed her blade-like nose at Chinese Johnny Depp. "Men with jobs are welcome, monsieur. But may I tell her your name?"

"Reginald Demetrius Elbow," said the man, in tones as round and ripe as a BBC broadcaster's.

"The crackpot billionaire," said Wyatt, just a little too loudly.

Four heads swiveled his way. The bodyguards stepped forward, shielding their boss. Ponytail Man slipped a hand under his jacket, as if reaching for a weapon.

"Mr. Elbow prefers the term *eccentric*," said Mr. Elbow.

NEVER MENTION THE G-WORD

CHAPTER 4

"COME OUT from there, both of you," ordered Madame Chiffre.

With a heavy sigh, Max and Wyatt pushed the door wide and stepped into an entryway filled with tense bodyguards and mysterious visitors.

"Sorry about the crackpot crack," said Wyatt.

Seeing that the threat to their boss was only two teenage boys, Ponytail Man snickered and relaxed. Mustache Man rolled his boulderlike shoulders and gave them a my-hands-are-lethal-weapons-so-don't-try-anything glare.

"And what are these?" said Mr. Elbow, eyeing Max and Wyatt as if they were a particularly disgusting species of bug.

"Students," said Madame Chiffre. "*Nosy* students."

"No hard feelings, sir," said Wyatt, extending his hand for a shake.

Mr. Elbow shrank back, as if Wyatt had offered a rabid badger instead of a slightly grubby palm.

"Mr. Elbow don't shake," rumbled Mustache Man, in a voice that came from the subcellar.

"Really?" said Max.

"Germs," said Ponytail Man.

The bearded billionaire shuddered at the word. "Purell for Mr. Elbow," he snapped.

Ponytail Man hastened to whip out a pocket-size dispenser of hand sanitizer and spritz it into his boss's palms. Mr. Elbow scrubbed his hands together as if he were trying to remove DNA evidence after a crime.

"Told you never to mention the G-word," muttered Mustache Man to his comrade.

"Mr. Elbow is a busy man," said the billionaire. "Take him to Mrs. Wong."

"Certainly," said Madame Chiffre, ushering them toward the office door. She stopped abruptly, patted her jacket pocket, and turned to Max. "This, I believe, eez yours."

Her palm held the calculator listening device.

Max rolled his eyes and reluctantly reclaimed it.

"Go," said Madame Chiffre. "Study."

"Yes, ma'am," said Wyatt brightly. "Flat out like a lizard drinking."

She handed him a peculiar look, and the office door closed behind the four adults, leaving Max and Wyatt alone.

"Now I *really* want to know what's going on in there," said Max.

"Too bad the Mighty Mole isn't ready yet."

"Mighty Mole?"

"My latest gadget." Wyatt shook his head ruefully. "But until I finish it, I'm afraid you'll have to learn what's happening the way the rest of us do."

"How's that? On Facebook?"

"By waiting for Hantai Annie to tell us."

Max grimaced. "That," he said, "is my least favorite way."

Too restless to study, Max changed into a ratty T-shirt and sweatpants and headed for the exercise room to see if anyone was up for sparring. Maybe some controlled mayhem would distract him from obsessing over what was happening in the director's office.

Stepping through the doorway, he nearly bumped into Cinnabar Jones.

"Oh," he said. "Hi."

"Hi."

Her golden eyes met his, then slid away. Max couldn't help noticing the graceful curve of her neck, the way sweat beaded on her smooth, milk-chocolate cheek. His heart stumbled, and his throat felt drier than a bath mat in the Sahara.

An awkward moment passed as both of them froze in the doorway, temporarily tongue-tied.

"So, uh," he said, "haven't seen you much lately."

"Been busy." Cinnabar tucked a stray curl behind her ear. "With Jazz and all."

"Right." Max had thought he and Cinn were friends— maybe even something more. But ever since her sister's rescue, Cinnabar had seemed . . . different somehow. Distant. "So how's Jazz doing?"

Cinnabar made a noncommittal move with her shoulder and head. "The same, pretty much." *The same* was not good news, as Jazz was wrestling with a crippling case of posttraumatic stress after her ordeal as a captive of LOTUS.

"Oh." Max looked down at his hands, as if they might give him a clue what to say. His hands held no bright ideas. "Um, if there's anything I . . ."

She nodded rapidly. "Yeah. We'll, um . . ."

"Okay," said Max.

"Okay, bye."

Before he could untie his tongue, Cinnabar had slipped past him and out into the hall, leaving behind the sweet fragrance of orange blossoms.

Max raked a hand through his hair, temporarily baffled. Well, that could've gone better, he mused.

"Mighty mighty Maxwell." Tremaine's scratchy voice broke into his thoughts. "Fancy a little wind and grind?" The Jamaican teen and Nikki Knucks were running several of the younger kids through punching drills.

"That's why I'm here." Max stepped out onto the thick mats with a smile. Tremaine always cheered him up—plus, the older boy had some serious martial-arts abilities.

"Crucial, mon!" said Tremaine. "Nikki could use a challenge."

Max's smile wilted.

The redheaded girl's grin showed off tiny square teeth like a bracelet of white beads. "A match with him?" she said. "No contest. You're going down, Maxi-Pad!"

Max sighed. He would've preferred practicing with Tremaine—heck, he would've preferred French-kissing a skunk—but if he backed out now, she'd think he was chicken.

Tremaine chuckled and said, "Don't break anything, you two."

Nikki followed Max to an open stretch of mat. They donned sparring gloves, bowed, and began circling each other.

"So," said Nikki. *Jab-cross-uppercut.* "Hantai Annie's given you all the plum assignments lately."

"I guess," said Max. *Block–jab–hook–roundhouse kick.*

"You grotty wazzock." *Duck-jab-snap kick.* "You must think you're hot stuff."

"Only compared to you," said Max. *Block–jab–side kick.*

She dodged back and her small blue eyes narrowed. "You're here less than a month, you bloody teacher's pet. And look what you get to do." *Back fist– side kick–jab–snap kick.*

"Jealous?"

"Of a bloody traitor? Who's still conspiring with his traitor dad to help LOTUS? Dream on."

"*Who's* a—"

Bam! Her jab snapped his head back.

Max danced away, a coppery taste on his tongue. He shook his head, as if to clear it of his father's image.

"You're short on loyalty, you're a spoiled little prat, and you got one of our teachers killed," Nikki sneered. "What's to be jealous of?"

Though the crack about causing Roger Stones's death rattled him, Max kept a bland face. "For starters? My mad skills and good looks."

He rained a combination of kicks and punches on his taller opponent. Although Nikki claimed to be a black belt, Max found that they were fairly evenly matched, thanks to his attack-play training from Foster Parents No. 3, the Dickensons.

All part of the built-in spy lessons his absent father had so thoughtfully arranged for Max to have—instead of a normal family.

Pow! A side kick sneaked past his guard and punched into his gut. Max's air went out in a *whoosh*. Get Simon out of your head, he scolded himself, ducking to avoid her spin kick.

"Kids who have been here longer—better-trained kids— might not fancy you getting special treatment," Nikki said. *Feint—hook—side kick.* "They might want to teach you a lesson."

Max dodged her kick and grinned. "They're welcome to try."

The next several minutes were a blur of punches, kicks, and the occasional judo throw, made clumsier by the sparring gloves. At last, they stepped apart, panting.

"I *almost* broke a sweat," sneered Nikki. "But know this, dimwat: I've got my eye on you."

"You fancy me?" said Max, openmouthed in mock shock. "Now I'm worried."

She glowered. "You don't care about this place; you're only out for yourself."

"Oh, and you're not?" said Max, but he had to admit that she was right, just a little behind the times. He *had* been pretty self-absorbed during his first week at the orphanage. But things changed after the LOTUS rescue.

Nikki chomped down on one glove's Velcro fastener and savagely ripped it open. She wedged the glove under her other arm to pull it off. "When you betray the school again," she said, "I'll be there to bring you down."

Pointless though it might be, Max had a sudden impulse to tell her he was doing his level best to keep the school together. But he was interrupted by the appearance of Madame Chiffre.

"Older students, report to Classroom Two in five minutes," she said. When the kids stared at her blankly, she clapped her hands. "*Vite, vite!* I cannot wait all day. Change your sweaty clothes and join me."

Nikki pointed a finger at Max. "To be continued."

"Can't wait."

Not all spy training is fascinating and deeply cool, Max had learned. In fact, much of the tradecraft required hours of dull, painstaking practice, and this next session was as dull and painstaking as it got. Observation class.

Classroom Two felt muggier than a giant's armpit. The overstuffed chairs encouraged sleep. And it didn't help that today's lesson involved gazing at a mess of random objects on a desktop, then trying to list them from memory. After ten minutes, Max was biting his cheek to stay awake.

"I can't believe it—the fate of the school hangs in the balance, we're stuck doing *this*," he muttered to Wyatt.

"Too right," Wyatt replied. "I'm a hands-on bloke, not an observer."

Max tried to focus on the latest display. Spool of thread, thumb drive, fork, comic book, pencil . . .

Madame Chiffre whisked a purple velvet cloth over the tabletop, concealing the items. "Tell me, someone," she said. "What's under this cloth?"

"Boredom on a stick" would've been Max's first guess. He welcomed Hantai Annie's arrival like a desert wanderer welcomes a cooler full of Coke.

"*Oi, küiterunoka!*" said the director. "Listen up. We have new mission."

Suddenly the flushed, sleepy faces became alert. Wyatt

glanced over at Max, waggled his eyebrows, and mouthed, *Here we go.*

Hands behind her back, Hantai Annie Wong surveyed the students like a general reviewing fresh recruits. When she felt she had their full attention, she nodded once. "We have new client."

Max and Wyatt shared a look of relief. This would definitely help the orphanage keep its doors open.

"New client wants us to steal something from RookTech— from very secure building," Hantai Annie continued.

"How secure?" asked Rashid, leaning forward onto his elbows.

The director ticked off points on her fingers. "Many guards, biometrics, maybe key cards, maybe passwords."

"Brilliant." Rashid grinned.

"Is—is it dangerous?" Jazz asked, her brown eyes wide as a startled deer's. Cinnabar reached over from the next desk and laid a hand on her sister's arm.

Hantai Annie grunted assent. *"Mochiron da.* Some of you go on away-team; some stay here, work on support team." Her pitying expression made it clear which group she felt Jazz belonged with.

"What are we stealing, then?" asked Wyatt. "Government secrets? Gold bullion?"

"Is a . . ." The director scowled and looked to Madame Chiffre. *"Douiunda?"*

"Electroneuromanipulator," said the teacher.

Blank faces greeted this pronouncement.

"Uh, wuzzat?" mumbled Dermot, a weasel-faced boy who sat with Nikki.

"Mind-control device," explained the Frenchwoman.

At this, murmurs rippled through the classroom. Kids traded skeptical, puzzled glances. Nikki chuckled. "Yeah, right."

"This eez no laughing matter, mademoiselle," said Madame Chiffre. "It eez an extremely valuable, unbelievably powerful device. Whoever possesses it could affect politics, finance, even ze course of history."

"Crikey," said Wyatt, his eyes alight. "How's it work?"

Hantai Annie shook her head. "We don't know."

"And we're stealing it?" asked Cinnabar. "That doesn't seem right."

"Client doesn't want it to fall into the wrong hands."

Solemn looks stole across the orphans' faces as they absorbed the importance of their task. And most of them, Max reflected, didn't even suspect that the entire future of the orphanage rested on the mission's outcome.

"If it's all that and a bag of chips," he asked, "why is this electro-whatsit just sitting around?"

"It's not," said Madame Chiffre. "It's about to be auctioned off by ze inventor."

"And we're not the only ones trying to steal it," said the director.

"Let me guess," said Max. "LOTUS?"

Hantai Annie nodded. The room was quiet now, as loaded with tension as a sprinter on the starting blocks.

"So let me get this straight," said Max. "We're meant to go up against an evil organization that has unlimited resources, break into a heavily guarded building, and steal a device that could change the course of history."

"*Souda*," said the director. "And we have only three days to do it."

"Three whole days?" said Max. "Why didn't you say so? Count me in."

CHAPTER 5

THE MARSHMALLOW MAN COMETH

FOR A MISSION of this complexity, the S.P.I.E.S. staff was shorthanded, what with Alfred Styx turning double agent and assassinating S.P.I.E.S. teacher Roger Stones on the rescue mission at LOTUS headquarters. Two men gone: one good, one bad. Ready or not, the older students would have to pick up the slack. Max relished the thought.

Because time was so short, much of the prep work would take place during their regular classes, Hantai Annie informed the group. And as if the job wasn't challenging enough already, there was another wrinkle to contend with.

"We have new student," the director announced.

"Hopefully not a total cheese log," Nikki told her friend Dermot. They snickered together.

Hantai Annie fixed them with her icy glare until they subsided. "As usual, we cannot tell her this is spy school. She must work out for herself, prove she is worthy. *Wakatta ka?*"

"Understood," said Rashid.

"Why now?" asked Cinnabar. "Why not wait until after the mission to let him in?"

"Her," said Hantai Annie. "Because we turn away no one."

Because we're dead broke, more like, thought Max.

The director nodded brusquely. "I bring her now." She left the room, and the students buzzed like a barrelful of mosquitoes at a bikini contest.

"Dig a hole and bury me—it doesn't get any better than this." Wyatt rubbed his palms together. "An impossible mission? High-stakes spying? I bet we'll get to use some of my new gadgets."

"Even better," said Max, "we'll be able to keep Merry Sunshine open."

"Uh, right," said Wyatt. "That, too."

Max noticed a shift in the crowd's energy, and he glanced toward the doorway. His mouth fell open.

"Who's *that*?" someone muttered.

Hantai Annie Wong marched to the front of the room, leading the orphanage's newest orphan.

And what an orphan.

The lithe blond girl was maybe a year or so older than Max. Her huge, toffee-colored eyes were set far apart over a snub nose and full lips. Even in the depths of fall, her tan was dark and even. Her curvy shape belonged on an older girl, and it was draped in a black cashmere sweater over faded blue jeans.

She looked like every surfer boy's dream.

"*Jya,*" said Hantai Annie. "Introduce youself."

The blonde's smile stretched from ear to ear. "Hello, sports fans! I'm Vespa da Costa." Her throaty voice was like honey poured over fur—sticky, sweet, and impossible to ignore. "I've been in three foster homes, but this is my first orphanage." Her dimples deepened as her gaze landed on Max. "I hope we'll be good friends."

Max swallowed.

The director took Vespa's arm. "You can make nice at lunch. Now, back to office. *Oi, koi.*"

They slipped out the door and the classroom erupted into a hullabaloo. It took Max a while to realize that Madame Chiffre was slapping her ruler on the desk to catch their attention.

"This eez still Observation class, not a gossip circle," she said, frowning. "Quickly, before your memory fades—describe ze new student, Vespa."

"Sweet," said Wyatt.

"Stuck-up," said Nikki.

The Frenchwoman's mouth twisted in a wry smile. "Not her personality; her voice, her looks—only what can be observed."

"Cute," said Rashid with a grin.

"Spray-on tan," said Jazz.

"Um, blond," said Max. His mouth was dry.

"Dead sexy," said Tremaine.

Jazz swatted him on the arm.

Cinnabar's lips pursed. "She wore a fake cashmere sweater. Black."

"And what else?" asked Madame Chiffre.

"Um," said Max.

Shan, a Chinese girl with spiky green-streaked hair, said, "A bad knockoff of prefaded Lucky Brand jeans, and coffee-colored suede Dallas boots—suede, in this weather?—with three-inch heels."

The teacher nodded approvingly. "Excellent, Shan. And what about her voice, class?"

"Sweet," said Wyatt again, his blue eyes slightly glazed.

"A little scratchy," said Max. Cinnabar shot him a look.

"She had a fake-y foreign accent," sneered Nikki. "Like she was trying to be all mysterious."

"'Da Costa'?" said Tremaine. "Maybe the sister's Brazilian or Portuguese."

"Oh, sure," said Nikki. "That's what she'd like you to think. Bloody poser."

Madame Chiffre wielded her ruler as if she might not be averse to using it on Nikki's knuckles. "*Ça suffit.* Enough. The more you practice your powers of observation, the stronger they will grow." She booted up her laptop. "Rashid, ze lights, please. Wyatt, ze projector. Now I will turn your attention to ze building we'll be breaking into. . . ."

But as the teacher began calling up images on her computer, Max found that his mind kept returning to a different image—that of a blond Brazilian with a killer smile.

Lunch was . . . interesting, to say the least. While Tremaine and Rashid monopolized Vespa at one end of the table, the debate over the new girl percolated down the line over spaghetti, garlic bread, and salad. But on a more serious note, some of the orphans were openly wondering whether the S.P.I.E.S. team could pull off their new mission.

"It's not that I doubt our abilities," drawled weasel-faced Dermot. "It's just that I doubt our abilities."

"How's that?" said Jensen Swensen, a beefy boy with wheat-colored bangs.

"I mean, we've got only *three days*—that's including casing the building, sorting out how to beat a top-notch security system, stealing their passwords or whatever, and actually doing the job. *Three days*, people."

Wyatt helped himself to a second slice of rhubarb crumble. "Don't get your knickers in a twist, mate. Me, Cinnabar, and Max pulled off that rescue at LOTUS HQ completely on the fly."

"And you're lucky you didn't get everyone killed," said Nikki Knucks.

"Jealous much?" said Cinnabar, wiping her mouth with a napkin.

Nikki snorted.

Dermot leaned across her and jabbed a finger at Wyatt. "And that's the other thing: LOTUS. If they want this whatsit so bad, they'll be going after it tooth and nail."

"So?" said Max.

"They're way out of our weight class," said Dermot. "Only five minutes ago, I got a text from them."

"Sure you did," said Max. "Saying what? 'OMG, Dermot! You're a totally hot love god'?"

Wyatt and Cinnabar chuckled. Under his sarcasm, though, Max felt a tingle of alarm. Could Dermot somehow be working with LOTUS? Maybe through the captured spy in the basement?

The scrawny boy sent Max a sour look. "It said S.P.I.E.S. can't possibly pull off the job, and that we should just give up."

"They know we got a new mission?" Wyatt's forehead creased in a worried frown. "And they know what it is?"

"That's what I'm saying," said Dermot, slouching over his spaghetti. "We're gonna get creamed."

"Speak for yourself," said Max. He pushed aside his own concerns about how LOTUS had learned of their plans. "I can't wait to snatch that gadget first and then rub their noses in it."

Normally Max didn't think of himself as vindictive, but

LOTUS *had* kidnapped his friends, used his father to persuade Max to spill secrets about S.P.I.E.S., and lit his last foster parents' house on fire. Those kinds of things tended to get on a guy's nerves.

Wyatt grinned. "That device sounds so *cool*! I can't wait to see how it works."

Cinnabar glanced over at Vespa, then sent Wyatt a knowing look. "And I can imagine who you'd like to test it on, Tech Boy."

Wyatt blushed.

The noise level in the dining room had swelled, so at first Max and the others didn't notice the new arrivals. But when Hantai Annie strode to the head of the table and raised her hands, conversations died out.

"*Oi, shizuka ni shiro,* everyone," she said. "I introduce you to somebody." At her gesture, a pale, puffy-looking man with a clipboard stepped forward. Max's first impression was that scientists had finally found a way to bring marshmallows to life.

Of medium height, the man was snowy white, and soft and swollen all over. His belly bulged within his suit coat, and his head was shaped like a block. All his features huddled together in the middle of his face, as if they were afraid of his ears.

"Hello, children. I'm Henry Krinkle," said the marshmallow man in a fussy, nasal voice.

"Mr. Krinkle is from government," said the director, looking like "government" was someplace where flatulent warthogs went to die. "From Ministry of Health. He inspecting Merry Sunshine. Give him full cooperation."

Mr. Krinkle tugged on his too-tight jacket. "Quite right," he said. "We've had a complaint about this facility, so I'm here to follow up and get to the truth of the matter."

"A complaint?" Max echoed. "From who?"

His fellow orphans surveyed each other with suspicion.

The inspector straightened his skinny tie. "I'm not at liberty to say. And besides, it was anonymous." His gaze fell on the tureen in the center of the table. "I say, is that Bolognese sauce? And real cheese on the toast?"

"You hungry?" asked Hantai Annie. At Mr. Krinkle's eager nod, she told Cinnabar, "*Omae*, make plate for our guest. Bring to my office."

Max caught Wyatt's eye, and the blond boy lifted his eyebrows meaningfully. They were thinking the same thing. After the director and her visitor left the room and Cinnabar had begun loading pasta onto a plate, Max and Wyatt approached her.

"Cinn," said Wyatt, under his breath, "take your own sweet time getting that tray together."

She narrowed her gaze at them. "Why? What're you up to?"

"Nothing much." Max offered her a sunny smile. "We'll

simply nip up to the electronics closet and find the proper bug to go with that meal."

"You're mental." She gave him a look that was half distracted, half affectionate. "Now's not the time, anyway. I've got enough going on without adding your schemes to the mix."

Max's temper flared. "You'd do it for Jazz."

"Maybe I would," Cinnabar fired back, her cheeks flushed. "But *she* would never ask." And with that, she banged her plates onto a tray, picked it up, and swept out of the dining room.

"Am I the only one who gets how fragile this whole place is?" Max griped. "Merry Sunshine could be shut down any minute, and then where would we be?"

Wyatt touched his arm. "I get it, mate. And that's why I'm gonna break out the Mighty Mole."

Max gave him a dubious look. "Is it ready?"

"Ready as a rooster at sunrise," said Wyatt with a grin. "This'll be her maiden voyage. I'll just go and fetch her."

Max didn't much like the sound of *maiden voyage*, but as he didn't have any better ideas, he followed Wyatt from the room.

A short time later, they squatted in the entryway beside the office door, examining Wyatt's invention. The device consisted of a dome-shaped object a bit bigger than half a grapefruit, with a chunky, ten-inch metal handle. A clear plastic tube led from the dome into a bag, and a pair of earbuds dangled from the end of the handle.

"You realize this looks less like a mole, and more like a toilet plunger?" whispered Max.

"Poetic license," Wyatt whispered back. "It *works* like a mole."

He placed the open end of the gizmo against the wall by Hantai Annie's door, an inch or two above the baseboard. Then he twisted a knob on the handle until the device stuck to the wall on its own.

"And how exactly does this work?" said Max.

Wyatt smirked like a mischievous baby. "Once the seal is nice and tight, like so, we activate the drill." He flipped a toggle switch, and a faint whirring sound began. "The vacuum sucks all the dust and plaster bits down the tube into this bag so there's no evidence, and then—"

"Hang on," said Max. "Can't they hear that drill?"

Wyatt flapped a hand. "Never in a million years."

"*I* can hear it," said Max. "They're only ten feet away—why can't they?"

Wyatt switched off the device and chuckled nervously. "Heh. Don't fret your freckle; it's only a minor snag."

"What we need is a noise to cover it up." Max scanned the entryway. Just then, Pinkerton, the orphanage's immense dog, ambled in from the back hallway, licking his considerable chops. Pinkerton was allegedly some kind of Bernese-mountain-dog mix, but Max thought he looked more like a mountain and less like a dog.

"Perfect," he said, approaching the creature. "Pinkerton, speak!"

The massive black-and-brown dog blinked doubtfully up at him.

"Maybe he doesn't know that command," said Wyatt.

Max snapped his fingers in front of the dog's nose. "Speak, boy!"

A low rumble like a distant avalanche emanated from deep in Pinkerton's barrel chest. He didn't much care for snapping.

"That's the stuff," said Wyatt, switching on the device. "More of that."

Again and again, Max snapped his fingers around the dog's head, even blowing into his face for good measure. Pinkerton's growl revved up to the level of jet aircraft, and he threw in a few short *whuff*s for good measure. He *really* didn't like face blowing.

Wyatt made the okay sign, and Max left off tormenting the dog before he decided to snack on Max's fingers. Shooting the boys a haughty look, Pinkerton turned and padded back down the hallway. Max made a mental note to give him a treat later.

"And now," whispered Wyatt, "we activate the bug." He

pushed a button, then passed an earbud to Max while nestling the other one in his own ear.

"—mmn nnggmfn bbn mffnb."

"Nngmf mmbn?"

The voices coming through the tiny headphones sounded like a couple of ants having a conversation under a mattress.

Wyatt's face fell.

"Can't you make it any clearer?" Max whispered.

"Maybe I didn't drill far enough," said Wyatt. "I'll give her one more go. . . ."

He and Max removed their earbuds and Wyatt drilled again, just a short burst. When they put the buds back in their ears, the voices were much clearer.

"Several days, perhaps." Mr. Krinkle's fussy tones came through. "I shall need to review *all* your operations. These are serious allegations, after all."

"They say I mistreat *kodomotachi*?" Hantai Annie's gruff voice hardly needed amplification. "Never. I *never* hurt children. Who says this?"

"That's immaterial," said Mr. Krinkle. "What counts is whether the charges are accurate. Whether—"

The hiss of static interrupted the conversation. Wyatt fiddled with the wires and tapped his invention. The voices resumed.

"—not true," snapped the director.

"They'd better not be," said Mr. Krinkle. "Because if they

are, I am empowered by the government to discontinue your operations."

"Nandatte?" said Hantai Annie. "Speak English. What you mean?"

"I can shut down Merry Sunshine Orphanage. Clear enough?"

Max's jaw dropped open. *Close the orphanage?*

But he didn't hear the director's response to this threat, because the Mighty Mole chose that moment to start up on its own and drill all the way into Hantai Annie's room, where the drill bit fell off with a clatter.

CHAPTER 6

LITTLE LETHAL SNOOKUMS

THE OFFICE DOOR banged open. *"Nanka you ka?"* snapped Hantai Annie Wong. "What you doing to my wall?"

"We, uh, that is . . ." Wyatt fumbled with the Mighty Mole, trying to loosen its grip.

"It's a . . . science experiment," Max improvised. "We were meant to invent a drill that could tidy up its own mess."

Wyatt's smile was closer to a grimace. "Still a few bugs to be worked out."

"Omaetachi . . ." the director growled. Her eyes flicked over to Mr. Krinkle, and she seemed to reconsider what she was about to say. A borderline-scary smile found its way to her lips. "Good idea, but needs work. We talk later."

Max and Wyatt goggled at her response. They'd been expecting a tongue-lashing at the very least. But Max could tell they weren't off the hook—the glint in Hantai Annie's eyes promised that their later discussion might not be a pleasant one.

"Unsupervised science experiments?" huffed Mr. Krinkle, peering past her shoulder and scribbling on his clipboard. "Humph."

With a significant look at Max and Wyatt, the director steered her guest back into the office and shut the door.

"As ready as a rooster, huh?" said Max, helping Wyatt collect the parts of his invention. "Come on, let's go find Cinnabar. Time for a powwow."

They found Cinnabar in the library—for once, without Jazz—practicing her computer-hacking skills. She favored them with a doubtful glance.

"What, another bugging?" she said. "I'm kind of busy just now."

"It's important," said Max.

Cinnabar sighed. "Make it snappy, Spy Boy. Mr. Vazquez says he needs someone to help him hack the RookTech computer system, and that someone's going to be me."

"Over my dead body," said Wyatt.

"Never mind the mission," said Max. "We've got bigger problems."

Together, he and Wyatt brought Cinnabar up to date on everything Hantai Annie hadn't told them—the latest threats from LOTUS and the Ministry of Health's Mr. Krinkle.

Cinnabar leaned back in her chair and folded her arms. "That's awful," she said. "But there's nothing we can do about it."

"'Nothing we can do'?" Max tossed up his hands. "So you won't even try?"

She rolled her eyes. "What do you suggest? Assassinate Mr. Whatchamahoozie?"

"Krinkle," said Wyatt. "And no, I think someone might notice."

Max paced. "I don't know what to do. But I can't just sit around eating bonbons while this place goes up in flames. Can you?"

Cinnabar bit her lip and looked from Max to Wyatt. "No, of course not," she said. "But I'm not sitting around. I've got my hands full here, what with the mission . . ."

"And Jazz," Max said, maybe a touch sarcastically. "All Jazz, all the time."

Cinnabar bristled. "Yes, *and Jazz*. My sister needs me, and family comes first."

"Exactly," said Max. "That's why we've got to do something."

Eyes locked, they both fell silent for a moment, bursting with hot words left unsaid. The atmosphere in the library felt as fragile as a dragonfly wing.

"Hey," said Wyatt, breaking into the staring match, "maybe we can't do much about this inspector—apart from making sure he doesn't catch us in full-on spy mode. But what about LOTUS?"

"What about them?" said Max.

"Look, it's clear as bird farts on a sunny day that they're trying to put S.P.I.E.S. out of business, right?" said Wyatt.

Max suppressed a smirk. "The way you talk."

"And we know they're planning to steal that doovalacky before we do."

"Doovalacky?" Cinnabar asked.

Wyatt rolled a hand impatiently. "The electro . . . neuro . . . mind-control thingo. They've got to come up with a better name."

"Okay . . ." said Cinnabar.

"But what if we could learn more about their plans?" asked Wyatt. "Wouldn't that be helpful?"

"Well, yeah . . ." Max interlaced his fingers atop his head and paced the room, thinking. "So you want to . . . what? Hack their computers? I think LOTUS's cyber security might be too tight even for you."

"Too right, mate. But there must be another way."

For a minute or so, the library was as quiet as dreaming trees, with only the barely audible hum of the computers and the whisper of the heating system to be heard.

"Ooh," said Wyatt, breaking the silence. "We could ask that information broker you guys went to—what's her name?"

"Tully," said Max. "But she might not know what we need

to know, and besides, she always wants something in trade."

Cinnabar gazed up at a corner of the room. "What we really need," she mused, "is someone on the inside."

Max and Wyatt gaped at her.

"Bloody brilliant!" crowed Wyatt. "Get someone from LOTUS to spill secrets."

"I wasn't serious," said Cinnabar. "I was only thinking out loud. Where would we ever find someone from LOTUS who's willing to turn double agent?"

Max smiled. "Oh, I think I may know just the place," he said. "And it just so happens that one of us holds the key."

Cinnabar quirked an eyebrow at him. "Which one of us did you have in mind?"

Five minutes later, the three of them stood outside the door that led down to the basement, the door marked OFF-LIMITS. This part of the house was shabbier, with stained wallpaper and frayed carpet. The faint odors of mildew and cooked cabbage blanketed the corridor with a funky-homey feeling.

Cinnabar hesitated, one hand on the doorknob, the other holding a fat ring of keys. "I don't know if I should be doing this. . . ." she said.

"No worries," said Wyatt. "We won't let him out or anything."

She sucked air through her teeth. "Yeah, but Hantai

Annie trusts me. She only lets Catarina and me take him food—nobody else."

Max rested a hand on her shoulder. "It's for the good of the school. For all of us."

"This bloke's dangerous—you've got to watch yourself every second," she said. "You know that, right?"

"Sure, sure," said Max. "We'll be careful."

At last, Cinnabar shook her head, muttered something under her breath, and slipped the key into the lock. The door opened onto a cramped landing at the top of a flight of rough wooden stairs, which descended into darkness. As they stepped inside, Cinnabar pulled a chain dangling from a bare lightbulb, and Max blinked in the sudden brightness.

"Well, it won't make the cover of *Better Homes & Hideouts* magazine," he said.

The weathered steps led down past a pair of rust-spotted water heaters to a bare concrete floor. Cobwebs big enough to snare a condor stretched from the beams, all but swallowing some rickety chairs and a stack of cardboard boxes. On the far side of the drab space, just visible at the edge of the light, stood a forest-green door, triple-locked.

Cinnabar removed a smaller loop that hooked into the larger key ring. "These three will open that door," she said. "And this one's for the outer door. You've got ten minutes."

"Aw, come on," Max protested. "That's not nearly long enough."

Her eyes narrowed. "You're lucky I'm giving you that much. This could land me in big trouble." Something buzzed, and Cinnabar pulled her phone from a pocket to check a text. "That's Jazz. Gotta go. Find me in ten." Then she trotted up the stairs and stepped out the door, closing it behind her.

Wyatt arched an eyebrow. "After you, mate."

Together, they crossed the basement. The cold, damp air raised gooseflesh on Max's bare arms. They paused at the door and peered through the peephole, but the inside of the room was as dark as a ditch digger's bathwater.

"She did say this bloke's behind bars, right?" asked Wyatt, his voice a little tighter and higher than usual.

"Right," said Max. "Nothing to worry about." He flipped on a light switch beside the door, fit the keys into their locks, and turned the knob. "Well, here goes nothing."

The door opened into a concrete-floored room neatly bisected by a set of jail bars. On the near side of the bars sat two straight-backed wooden chairs. On the other side: a simple cot, a metal toilet, a sink, and a man.

Max stared. He didn't know which LOTUS agent Miss Moorthy had captured at the museum a couple of weeks ago, but he hadn't expected it to be one he would recognize.

"Gorilla Man?" he blurted. That was what Max had dubbed him.

"What'd you say?" The spy stood, shielding his eyes against the glare of the overhead lights. He was thickly muscled across the chest and arms, with olive skin and a brow heavier than a murderer's conscience. Although he was wearing a cheap tracksuit rather than the five-hundred-dollar business suit Max had last seen him in, it was definitely the agent who had pursued Max's team on his first mission to the capital.

"Uh, nothing," said Max.

"Come to gape at the big bad, have you?" Gorilla Man rumbled. He lowered his thick paw and checked out his visitors. "Get a good look, sonny-me-lad. I won't be here long; LOTUS is about to tear your little playhouse down."

"What a coincidence," said Wyatt, with a nervous chuckle. "We've come to talk about LOTUS." He dug into his brown paper sack and held up an apple and cookies. "And see, we've brought you a snackie."

"How thoughtful," the man sneered. He gestured at the bed. "Toss it there."

Wyatt complied, while Max sized up the burly spy. This had seemed like such a good idea when it had first come to him, but now he wasn't quite sure how one went about turning an enemy agent into an asset.

Oh, well. When in doubt, start by building rapport.

"What's your name?" Max asked.

"You don't know?" Gorilla Man gave a sardonic chuckle. "You must really be insiders, then." He shrugged a massive shoulder and strolled up to the bars. "Some call me the Knife of Nanjing, some the Death Ape, and some Little Lethal Snookums." At the boys' disbelieving expressions, he growled, "Don't ask."

"Wouldn't dream of it," said Max.

The prisoner gripped the bars in his huge, scarred fists. "But you can call me Mr. Ebelskeever."

"Evil skeever?" A chortle escaped Wyatt's lips before he clamped a hand over his mouth.

The big man scowled. "E-*bull*, not E-*vil*."

Wyatt held up his palms, still trying to contain his giggles. "Sorry, sorry. It's just—never mind."

"So . . ." said Max, searching for a way to gain the man's trust. "Are we treating you all right?"

Ebelskeever's contemptuous glance took in his cell. "I've known worse."

"How's the tucker?" asked Wyatt.

Max and Ebelskeever both swiveled their heads and asked, "What?"

"The tucker," Wyatt repeated. "You know, food?"

"It's no three-star Michelin restaurant." The spy leveled a skeptical gaze at them. "You from the Health Department?"

"No," said Max. "Only wanted to make sure everything was A-OK." With a sudden twinge, he thought that S.P.I.E.S. wasn't much better than LOTUS, keeping their captive in such conditions.

"Of *course* it's not bloody okay!" the prisoner roared, face against the bars, spittle flying. "I'm locked up!"

Max and Wyatt jumped back.

"Ooh, did I startle you?" Ebelskeever said mildly. He snickered. "Ever so sorry. Apologies all 'round."

Max sucked in a deep breath. Perhaps a different tack was called for here. "How is it," he said, "working for LOTUS?"

"Why?" Ebelskeever sneered. "Thinking of joining the team?"

Wyatt chuckled. "That'll be the day. Oh, wait." He eyed Max. "I guess you technically *did* join them for a little bit."

"All in the past," said Max. "I'm just curious." He indicated the cell. "You don't seem to have any pressing appointments. Humor me."

The prisoner cocked his head, considering. "Right, then. Best kind of job for a bloke like me."

"Really?"

"Oh, yeah." Ebelskeever spread an arm expansively. "Plenty of travel, I make good bank, and of course I get to kill people regularly. That the kind of intel you were after?"

Max nodded. "And do they treat you well, Mrs. Frost and the rest? Do they give you the proper respect?"

A dark cloud crossed the man's face, and he squinted with sudden suspicion. "You trying to turn me, boy?"

"I, uh . . ." Max didn't know whether it would be better to confess or deny.

"You green little milksop. You think I'd give up my own people, my own family, for you, like bloody Ben Singh?" He barked a laugh. "You're a regular riot."

"Who's Ben Singh?" asked Wyatt.

"A blip," snarled the big man. "A zero. A bloody turncoat who went over to your side last month, that's who. If you think I'd flip, and give up everything for—" He broke off, staring at Max's face. "Half a tick. I know you, don't I?"

"I doubt it," said Max.

Ebelskeever waggled a thick finger. "Yes, I do. You're the Segredo brat, aren't you?"

Max tried to keep his face blank. "What if I am?"

"Yeah, we nearly got you at that train station. Your old man works for us—that must make family reunions a mite touchy."

"*Worked*," said Max. "He quit, and now he's on the run from your . . . so-called family."

"Is he now?" Ebelskeever folded a pair of arms as thick as nesting anacondas. He smiled a dark smile. "Maybe that's exactly what he wants you to think."

"You don't know a thing about my father," said Max. He felt his voice wobble a little.

The spy's heavy brows lifted in mock innocence. "Maybe not," he said. "But I know what he did to his own wife, and I know he's a poxy traitor."

Max stepped closer. "Take that back," he snapped.

"Ooh, touchy-touchy," said the spy. "Does it bug you that Simon Segredo is still working for us, and he just didn't care to let his little boy know?"

"My dad's not a ratbag like you!" Max cried, his face inches from the bars. "He only worked for LOTUS because you threatened my life."

Suddenly one of Ebelskeever's meaty hands shot out and grabbed Max by his T-shirt, slamming him forward against the steel bars.

Hot, fishy breath blew into Max's face from only inches away.

"Gotcha now!" the big man growled.

CHAPTER 7

FLIRTY DEEDS DONE DIRT CHEAP

EBELSKEEVER'S other hand slipped between the bars, fumbling for the key ring that dangled from Max's fingers. Barely in the nick of time, Max tossed the keys behind him.

"Gimme those!" snarled the prisoner.

In a flash, Max saw two ways this situation could play out—he could either be strangled or used as a hostage—and he didn't care for either option. His senses sharpened. Peripheral vision showed no weapons within reach and Wyatt frozen in shock. The horizontal bars kept him from kicking the man. He was too close to punch.

But Ebelskeever's grab had placed his face nearly at Max's level and right between two vertical bars.

Before the spy could bring his free hand into play, Max leaned forward and bit down on Ebelskeever's nose like he was crunching into a ripe pippin apple.

74

"Eeuarrgh!"

With an incoherent cry of rage, the big man released the T-shirt and clapped a hand to his maimed nose.

Max danced back out of reach. His body buzzed with adrenaline. Sudden sweat beaded his brow.

"Yeah!" cried Wyatt, punching a fist in the air. "Serves you right, you wacker!" He drew closer to Max. "You all right, mate?"

"Just peachy," said Max. He bent to retrieve the keys. "Never underestimate the power of fighting dirty."

"Oi!" Ebelskeever cried. His hand still cupped his nose. "You can't bite a prisoner."

"I just did."

"That's not cricket!"

"Then I guess I'm no gentleman spy," said Max. "Come on, Wyatt. We're done here."

"But I'm not done with *you*, boy," snarled the big man. "Not by a long shot."

As Max shut and triple-locked the door behind them, he caught one last glimpse of Ebelskeever's angry eyes, burning like barbecue coals. A chill danced across his shoulders.

I don't want to be anywhere nearby when that guy gets free, he thought.

Max and Wyatt had just secured the outer door and pocketed the keys. They were turning around, when a familiar voice from down the hall brought them up short.

"Well, well, look who's creeping about where they shouldn't be. If it isn't Greedy Guts and Maxi-Pad."

"Hello, Nikki," said Max.

The red-haired girl strutted closer, eyeballing them up and down, as if they were a particularly useless example of modern art. "If I didn't know better, I'd say Golden Boy and his mate were visiting the prisoner. Planning a little jail break, were you?"

For a nanosecond, Max considered letting Nikki in on their scheme, but just as quickly he rejected the idea. No way would she understand. And even if she did, she'd only mock him for how it had failed so utterly.

"Wrong as usual," said Max. "We were doing a bit of exploring, and we found a locked door. So our prisoner's down there?"

"Come off it, barmpot," said Nikki. "You know just as well as I do."

But Max and Wyatt maintained their innocent expressions, and when she saw she didn't have enough rope to hang them with, Nikki switched on her familiar sneer. "No matter. I don't have time for you losers anyway—I'm on a special assignment from the director."

With a final evil grin, she swaggered back down the hall.

"Special assignment?" Wyatt muttered. "Doing what, fetching toilet paper?"

Max shook his head. "I don't know, but I don't trust her as far as I could throw her."

"Not a bloke alive could throw Nikki," said Wyatt.

"Exactly."

As they headed back to the main part of the house, Wyatt said, "Back to the drawing board, eh?"

"Not quite," said Max. "We did learn one thing from the prisoner."

Wyatt smirked. "Stand well back from the bars?"

"Two things, then. He mentioned a LOTUS agent who went turncoat."

"Bloody Ben Singh," Wyatt recalled. "Lovely name."

"I'm sure it's a big hit with the ladies," said Max. They turned a corner and entered the hall that led to the front of the house. "But I'm more interested in what Bloody Ben knows about LOTUS's plans."

Wyatt squinted. "You reckon he knows what they're up to now?"

"Only one way to find out. Do you think you could—"

"Hack a few databases and try to get a fix on this Mr. Singh?" said Wyatt. "One step ahead of you, mate."

Max grinned. "Brilliant. Meanwhile, I'll sort out a way for us to go talk with the man."

"Good plan," said Wyatt. "One might almost think you were a spy."

"On my better days," said Max.

But before they could make any headway with their extra-curricular activities, Max and Wyatt had other duties to contend with, namely preparing for the RookTech mission. The older students assembled in the computer room, where Victor Vazquez challenged them to hack into RookTech's VPN, or virtual private network.

Max scanned the room, but didn't see the new girl, Vespa, anywhere. Maybe Hantai Annie was keeping her away from the mission prep work. The students clustered in twos and threes around the computers, and Max found himself sitting with Jensen and Cinnabar.

She shot him a significant glance. "How was your . . . free time?"

"Fairly productive," said Max. He asked Jensen, "Which program should we use for this, do you know?"

"Sure," said Jensen, booting up the software. While the other boy was distracted, Max slipped Cinnabar the keys and mouthed *later* to her questioning look.

"So, what do you guys reckon?" Jensen said, pushing back his floppy bangs. "Should we try ClickJacking and pirate someone's e-mail ID, or see if we can overwhelm their servers and get in that way?"

Max and Cinnabar stared at him.

"What?" said Jensen. "Why does everyone think I'm a total wally, just because I'm fit and I got nice hair? I can read, you know."

"Of course," said Max.

"I got a brain."

"No one thinks you're stupid," said Cinnabar quickly.

"'Course not," said Max. "Why don't you get us started on the clickety-jack thingy?" Truth to tell, Max was probably the worst in the class at computer-related activities, as his previous foster parents had rarely allowed him access to electronic devices.

They poked around with the program for a while. To Max's untrained eye, it looked like they were making about as much headway as a guppy climbing a glass staircase. Mr. Vazquez prowled the computer bank, checking everyone's progress. Max guessed that most of the other groups were equally unsuccessful, for just minutes later, the teacher called a halt to their hacking.

"My friends, you have made a valiant effort." He ran a hand over his slicked-down hair and beamed a movie-star smile that inspired sighs from several girls. "But time is of the essence. Now, I need a volunteer."

Instantly, all the girls' hands shot up, followed by Wyatt and Jensen's.

Mr. Vazquez's dark eyes roamed over the group, twinkling with delight. At last, his gaze landed on one student. "Wyatt, come. Let us show them how this digital dance is done."

Cinnabar pouted, and Jazz fired a jealous glare at the blond boy.

Max rolled his eyes.

With a sense of ceremony, Victor Vazquez smoothed the front of his bloodred silk shirt, settled his iPod into a dock beside his laptop computer, and clicked PLAY. Some kind of electro-Arabic tango music filled the room, and he and Wyatt sat down to work. Clattering keystrokes beat a counterpoint to the music's rhythms.

As one, the rest of the class came to stand behind them, drawn by the spectacle.

"First, we access the RookTech employee records," purred Mr. Vazquez. "Wyatt?"

The blond boy's fingers flew over the keyboard. A singer wailed from the iPod dock, and Wyatt and the teacher leaned closer to the screen.

"Yes, yes," said Mr. Vazquez. "Now we locate a couple of likely victims . . . ah, Timothy Hu. And . . . Jay Ruttmiller." He scanned their vital statistics. "Perfect, they're both single."

"Why are you only picking on blokes?" asked Nikki.

"You'll see."

Wyatt cracked his knuckles. "So how do you want to land him?" he asked. "Phishing?"

The teacher put a finger to his chin dimple. "Mmm, how about online dating? Here, let me. . . ." He pulled up several Web sites—one of which was called GeekyLove.com, Max noted—and began searching for the employees' names.

"Got him," said Mr. Vazquez.

"Who?" asked Max.

"Yes," said the teacher.

Max frowned. "I mean, what's the guy's name?"

"Hu."

"The employee you're trying to catch?" asked Max.

"Hu."

"That's what I'm asking y—" Max broke off and shook his head. "You know what? Never mind."

In record time, Wyatt and Mr. Vazquez had set up an online profile using a photo of the teacher's sister, Anita. "She's hot," said Tremaine, which earned him a sharp elbow from Jazz.

"She is a *lady*, not a plate of chorizo," said the teacher. "She's beautiful." Then, pretending to be Anita, Mr. Vazquez struck up an online chat with Timothy Hu while Wyatt piggybacked on the conversation, seeking the IP address of the man's computer.

> *Anita: What do you do for fun?*
> *Tim: Oh, you know, luv. The usual.*
> *Anita: Walks in the woods, going dancing, seeing movies?*
> *Tim: Playing World of Warcraft and watching football.*
> *Anita: Oh.*
> *Tim: Maybe we're not such a good match?*

A warm breath tickled Max's cheek as someone leaned over his shoulder to peer at the screen. The scent of some tropical flower teased his senses.

"Hacking the poor man's computer, are you?"

It was Vespa da Costa, the new student.

Wyatt gave a guilty start and Mr. Vazquez coughed. "No, of course not," the teacher said. "We were, uh . . ."

Vespa chuckled throatily. "I knew you guys were up to something at this orphanage."

The other students eyed her warily. Nikki clenched her fists.

"We're not. . . ." Wyatt said.

The new girl tossed her wavy blond hair, and Max got another whiff of flowers. "It's okay by me," she said. Her toffee-brown eyes found Max's own. "What are you learning to be? Criminals? Spies?"

"Um, spies," said Max, despite himself. He realized he was staring at her and tore his gaze away.

"Sounds fun," she said. "Better than studying to be a beautician, or the other silly rubbish they teach you at trade schools."

Max half smiled. This girl was definitely more than she seemed.

"Cor . . ." Wyatt marveled. "No one's ever tumbled to it this fast. She's good."

"Wyatt . . ." Cinnabar's tone held a warning.

"I'm just saying," said Wyatt innocently.

Mr. Vazquez cleared his throat. "Yes, Vespa, you've guessed correctly. We'll talk more of this later, but now—"

"Now you need some lessons in flirting," said Vespa.

A collective gasp emerged from all the female mouths in the room.

"My dear," said Victor Vazquez, offering a patronizing smile, "I am from Argentina after all, and I believe we know a thing or two about flirtation."

"I'm sure you do, señor," said Vespa with a wink. "But if you're pretending to be a girl, you need to play things a little differently."

"He knew that," said Cinnabar hotly.

Max was thinking that he'd never before met a girl who winked.

Vespa held up her hands. "I don't want to step on anyone's toes here."

"No, please." Mr. Vazquez suppressed his irritation. "How would you play it?"

Twirling a lock of her hair around a finger, she gazed up at the ceiling. "Say something like . . . 'Football? You must be very fit, then.'"

Mr. Vazquez typed her suggestion and received an immediate reply:

Tim: You guessed it, luv. And how about you?

"I like to use my body," purred Vespa. "I stay active."

Max's mouth hung open. Wyatt glanced back at her incredulously, blue eyes nearly bugging from his head.

After the teacher entered her response, the RookTech employee replied:

Tim: Better and better. What say we get our bodies together sometime?

Mr. Vazquez growled, "That's my sister you're talking to, you pig!"

"Actually, it's you," said Max.

"Actually, it's Vespa," added Tremaine.

The teacher ground his teeth.

Wyatt tapped a few keys. "Hang on," he said. "Almost got the IP. Keep him chatting."

Mr. Vazquez fumed.

"Tell him he's a cheeky monkey," said Vespa. "That usually works for me."

Cinnabar looked disgusted. Nikki muttered, "I bet it does, you tart."

The exchange lasted long enough for Wyatt to accomplish his goal. Mr. Vazquez wrapped up his chat by telling the disappointed Tim that he, Mr. Vazquez, was a nice girl, and that he didn't think their relationship had a future.

Tim, predictably, sent him a frowny-face emoticon in reply.

Vespa chuckled. "Heartbreaker."

All the girls glared at the new student, offended by her

attitude toward their favorite teacher. The boys looked slightly stunned.

She's not making many female friends at Merry Sunshine, Max thought.

"Now that we know the employee's IP address," said Mr. Vazquez, "we can access his computer remotely whenever we please. So the next—"

A fussy, nasal voice broke into their discussion. "I say, what sort of class is this?"

CHAPTER 8

A DATE WITH BLOODY BEN SINGH

EVERYONE FLINCHED. Heads swiveled to stare at the doorway. Standing just inside it was Mr. Krinkle from the Ministry of Health, wielding his ever-present clipboard like a shield. He eyed the bank of machines suspiciously.

"This, oddly enough, is computer class," said Mr. Vazquez, hiding the hacking window they'd been working in. "Hence the computers. I was just giving the students a few tips about online security."

"Is that a dating Web site?" The puffy inspector peered at Mr. Vazquez's screen. "I hardly think that's appropriate."

The teacher closed his Web browser. "I disagree."

"Yeah," said Nikki, staring at Vespa. "It was right enlightening. He was showing us the dangers of flirting." Vespa met her glare, unruffled.

Mr. Krinkle pursed his thin lips. "Well, that's true enough,

I suppose. But I still don't believe online dating is a proper subject for orphans."

"And where do you think baby orphans come from," said Max, "if not online dating?"

This brought a few chuckles from the group. Mr. Krinkle frowned at Max, then scribbled a note on his clipboard. "I can see that proper respect toward one's elders is not being taught here," he snipped. The inspector strolled about the room, peering curiously at everything.

Cinnabar casually set her spiral notepad atop a book entitled *The Art of Intrusion: Hacking Made Easy* before the visitor had a chance to notice it.

"RookTech?" Mr. Krinkle squinted at an unattended computer screen. "What's that?"

Jensen blasted over to the workstation on his wheeled chair and closed the Web browser. "It's, uh . . . a chess Web site."

"A high-tech site," said Cinnabar simultaneously.

The inspector frowned, looking back and forth between them. "Well, which is it?

"It's a chess site *and* a tech site," said Wyatt.

Krinkle's brow smoothed out. "Capital," he said, raising a finger as if lecturing. "Chess teaches one to think, and high tech is the wave of the future."

Behind the inspector's back, Max and Cinnabar traded an is-this-guy-for-real? look.

"So, students," Mr. Vazquez continued, with one eye on the interloper, "how do we make sure our password is strong enough? What's one thing to avoid . . . Jazz?"

Cinnabar's sister blinked and glanced about, as if her mind had been a million miles away—and not focusing on anything pleasant, Max thought.

"I, um . . . sorry?" she said.

"Don't pick your birthday or your phone number as a password," Cinnabar said. She cast a worried look at Jazz.

"That's correct," said Mr. Vazquez. He kept up this innocuous line of questioning until the inspector left the room and Jensen confirmed that he wasn't eavesdropping from the hallway.

"My friends, we must all stay alert," said Victor Vazquez. "This project is vital to our school's survival, but so is making sure that that man goes away happy."

"He hasn't been happy since Buddha was in baby clothes," said Wyatt.

"If someone here hadn't spread lies about Merry Sunshine," said Nikki, glowering at her fellow students, "we wouldn't even have to worry about Mr. Marshmallow Head."

"How do you know it was one of us?" said Max. "It could've been anyone—a teacher, LOTUS, even you."

"*Me?!*" Nikki snarled. She rose from her seat. "You filthy little—"

"Enough!" Mr. Vazquez's voice froze the redheaded girl midgrowl. "Sit down and be civil to each other."

Blushing furiously, Nikki took her seat. Max raised his hands innocently.

"We have enemies enough on all sides," said the teacher, "without making enemies of each other."

After class ended, Wyatt stayed on to help with the hacking. Several girls lingered to toss their hair, giggle with the teacher, and generally make it harder to get any work done. And Max turned his thoughts to how he and Wyatt could sneak off and see Ben Singh.

Fortunately, Max had observed that Mr. Vazquez kept his key card in the pocket of his leather jacket. *Un*fortunately, however, the jacket hung on a wall hook directly behind the girls, smack-dab in the man's line of sight.

Max sidled up to Cinnabar. "Lend a spy a hand?" he asked.

"Maybe." Her eyes slid past him and onto Jazz, who stood off to one side, watching Mr. Vazquez with a preoccupied expression. "What is it this time?"

"Just distract him—get him looking away from that jacket so I can borrow his key."

"Borrow?" said Cinnabar. "For how long?"

Max looked offended. "I'll give it back. We're only using it for a side mission tonight."

"Well, I might. . . ." she began. But when Jazz slipped out

the door with her notebook clasped to her chest, Cinnabar stepped around Max to follow her sister. "Sorry. Find yourself another helper."

Max ground his teeth. Wyatt was too close to the teacher for Max to fill him in on the plan, and the giggling girls were no assistance at all.

"Need help with something?"

Max turned. It was Vespa da Costa. "Were you listening in?" he said.

She shrugged sheepishly. "None of the girls will talk to me, but you seemed friendly, so . . ."

Max couldn't take his eyes off her. Her face was so achingly lovely. Her eyes were luminous, and a little . . . melancholy?

For the first time it struck him that, despite her beauty, it might be hard for Vespa, being the new girl. He'd certainly been the new kid in enough schools and foster families to know what a delightful and heartwarming experience that was.

"Actually," said Max, "I, um, wanted to borrow something from Mr. Vazquez without his, uh, knowing it."

"His key card?" She leaned closer.

Max's face felt warm. He thought she might be a bit *too* close. "Well . . ."

Vespa's eyes sparkled with mischief. "Don't worry. I used to break out of my last group home, too. I won't tell. Where are you going—joyriding?"

"Not quite."

"You can trust me," she said in a husky voice.

Her lips, Max thought. They looked so soft, so . . . He found himself saying, "We're off to see a bloke called Ben Singh."

"Beats staying in." Vespa inclined her head at Mr. Vazquez. "You need me to distract him?"

"Only for a minute."

She gave a low chuckle. "Distraction is my specialty."

Max gulped.

Vespa sauntered up behind the teacher, opposite from where the other girls stood. Max couldn't make out her words, but in short order, Mr. Vazquez had shifted around to look at her, and all the girls wore indignant expressions.

Max ambled over and lifted the key card without anyone noticing.

He knew the teacher lived in the house now, in Mr. Stones's old room. Max only hoped that Victor Vazquez wasn't planning to go out on the town that night.

Max and Wyatt waited until after eleven P.M., when the house was quiet, to make their move. Creeping downstairs, they paused outside Hantai Annie's office. No light showed under its door.

"You sure we shouldn't let her know where we're going?" said Wyatt. "She might give us the thumbs-up, you know."

Max sent his friend a wry look.

"Right, right," said Wyatt. "What was I thinking."

"Besides," said Max, "she's got enough on her mind."

They huddled by the biometric lock that secured the front door, and Max produced the key card.

"So how do we beat the lock without Mr. V's thumbprint?" asked Wyatt.

"Did you bring those gummy bears?"

Wyatt dug a small bag from his coat pocket and held it out. "I don't see what my private emergency stash has to do with anything."

"Watch and learn," said Max, taking one of the candies from the sack.

He swiped the key card through the slot, breathed hotly onto the thumbprint reader, and mashed the gummy lozenge into it.

A quiet buzz, and the door clicked open.

"Cor . . ." Wyatt marveled. "And I thought they were only good for snackies. Where'd you learn that?"

"From every spy's best resource," said Max. "YouTube. Shall we?"

Leading the way into the holding corridor, he repeated the procedure on the outer door, and then Max and Wyatt stepped out into the chilly embrace of night. Fog clung to the houses, cars, and fences like a fearful child, turning the familiar into the eerie.

Max flipped up his coat collar and cat-footed it down the

path and through the gate. Glancing back, he noticed only two lit windows in the house. Luckily, no one was peering out of them.

With their hands jammed into their pockets for warmth, Max and Wyatt hurried down the road toward the tube station. Traffic was light. The occasional car rumbled by, swathed in a cocoon of diffused light.

Tonight, their trip would be a short one. Through a little creative hacking, Wyatt had learned that Ben Singh was living under an assumed name in the same town as the orphanage—only four tube stops away.

The underground station was nearly deserted. A transit employee yawned. Somewhere, a steady drip plopped into a puddle, and a faint rumble down the tracks told of a recently departed train. Max and Wyatt didn't have long to wait, and they boarded behind three ruddy-faced businessmen who smelled like the aftermath of an explosion in a brewery.

"Wait, wait, wait," slurred Ruddy Man No. 1. "So how is Miss Poofington related to the grandmother again?"

"Cousin once removed?" said Ruddy Man No. 2.

"Removed?" said Ruddy Man No. 3, whose nose resembled a ripe strawberry. "You mean she's off the show? Aw, poor wee thing." He staggered toward a seat and bumped into Max on the way. "Sorry, sonny."

"Hollingberry Line for Left Owl, Chortleyton, Craigside,

and beyond." The conductor's voice buzzed through the speakers. "Stand clear of the doors!"

As the train jerked into motion, Wyatt and Max swayed on the cracked vinyl seat. The businessmen continued their in-depth discussion of some TV program Max had never heard of. He stared out the window at the dark tunnel walls, thinking of the orphanage, Vespa, Cinnabar, and his father.

"So," said Wyatt at length, "do we ring this bloke first, or just drop in on him?"

Max recalled the last time they'd dropped in on someone late at night. They had ended up dodging bullets and climbing out of a Dumpster. "Let's ring first."

"Here's the number."

Max pulled out his phone and dialed. His friend leaned close to hear.

"Hullo?" came a groggy voice. An artificial laugh track chattered from a television in the background.

"Um, hi," said Max. "Is Sarah Quimby there?"

"No," said the voice. "You've got the wrong number, lad."

"Ah, sorry." Max hung up.

Wyatt produced a gummy bear from his pocket and popped it into his mouth. "So far, so good."

Three stops passed without conversation. As the train started up from the third platform, Wyatt turned to Max. "Could it really happen?" he asked. "Could they really shut down Merry Sunshine?"

"Who?" said Max. "LOTUS, or Mr. Krinkle's lot?"

Wyatt shrugged. "Either one, I guess. I just can't imagine it."

"Me neither," said Max.

Wyatt's blue eyes grew round and full of concern. "Where would we go? They'd break us all up, wouldn't they?"

Max gently bopped his friend's knee. "Don't worry—it's not going to happen. Not if I have anything to say about it." But to Max, his bravado felt as hollow as a kettledrum. He was just as worried as Wyatt.

Maybe more so. Because if it came down to it, being in the foster-care system was the devil he knew, and being with his dad was the devil he didn't know. Which would he choose? Would he even *have* a choice?

On top of that, he had no idea whether Ben Singh would provide any useful tips on stopping LOTUS—or whether they'd be able to act on them if he did. Max vowed to do his best not to think.

Exiting the underground at Craigside station, they stepped into a ghostly, fogbound landscape. The businessmen wobbled off in the opposite direction, still rattling on about their TV show.

Max and Wyatt followed their phone's map down misty roads, past curry shops, Indian grocery stores, and vendors of international phone cards—all shuttered tight. The fog swallowed even the echo of their footsteps, as if the boys were fading from existence.

Not another soul roamed the empty streets.

Sackville Road appeared on their left, a middle-class avenue of redbrick duplexes crowding right up to the sidewalk like hogs at a feeding trough. Most of the houses stood dark, but in number 212, a yellow light shone from the small window by the front door.

"Lucky for us he's a night owl," said Wyatt.

They opened the wrought-iron gate between two brick columns that served no useful purpose and headed up the minuscule walkway. Max was raising his hand to knock, when he noticed a pair of dark eyes staring at them from the door's fan-shaped window. He turned the knock into a wave.

"Hello," he called. "Are you Ben Singh?"

"Don't use that name," came the man's muffled voice.

"What, you mean Ben Singh?" said Wyatt.

The dark eyes widened in alarm. "Shhh!"

"But that's your name, isn't it?" said Max. "Ben Singh?"

Locks clicked and the door swung open to the length of a security chain. "I'm not saying it's my bloody name," hissed the caramel-skinned man peering through the gap. "But I'll thank you not to shout it down the block."

"Why?" asked Max. "Are you afraid LOTUS will hear?"

Singh's hand dipped into the pocket of his khaki trousers and emerged bearing a small silver pistol. "Who in blazes are you?" he said.

Max knew—he *hoped*—that the man wouldn't shoot them

out of hand, but he couldn't be sure. He lifted his palms slowly.

Wyatt smiled his innocent-baby smile. "We're from S.P.I.E.S."

"I always thought that was a rubbish name for an intelligence agency," said Singh.

Max lifted a shoulder. "No argument here. Look, your enemy is our enemy. We just want to talk."

For a few breaths, Singh just stared at them. Then he shut the door.

"Aw, hard cheese!" Wyatt whined. "After we came all this way."

Max bit his lip in frustration.

Then the security chain rattled, and the door opened wider. The pistol, however, remained pointing at them. "Nice and easy," said the man. "Hold open your coats and turn around slowly, one by one."

Max and Wyatt complied. Mr. Singh's free hand patted under their arms and at the small of their backs, searching for weapons. When he was satisfied, the man stuck his head out the door and surveyed the street. Then he motioned them inside with the gun.

The sitting room was simple but cheery, not at all what you'd expect from a turncoat spy's hideout. A pair of healthy ficus trees framed the bricked-in fireplace, some classical piano music burbled out of hidden speakers, and a fat paperback lay facedown on a comfy armchair.

"Sit," said Singh, indicating a fawn-colored leather sofa.

They sank onto the cushions, and Max took the chance to size up their host. He was short and broad-shouldered, with an oversize head that gave him the appearance of a doll—Sidney the Spy, maybe. A neatly cropped black beard covered his lower face; his eyes were large, black, and full of ghosts.

"How did you find me?" Singh demanded. "I go by the name Gurtaj Gupta now; no one knows me as Singh."

Max hooked a thumb at his friend. "Wyatt, here, is a bit of a wizard on the computer. I'm Max, by the way."

"You're certain you were not followed?" the spy asked.

"Positive," said Wyatt.

"Then explain yourselves." Singh crossed his arms and leaned against a chair, the pistol still loosely gripped in one hand.

Max took the lead, telling how LOTUS had been trying to put the orphanage out of business, and how they were intent on stealing a certain invention (Max didn't say what) from RookTech. When he finished, the spy blew out some air in a sigh and returned his gun to his pocket.

"I left that pit of serpents weeks ago," said Singh, sinking into the armchair. "I'm on the straight path now. What do you want from me?"

Max leaned forward on the sofa. "An angle," he said. "Some insight on their plans or their weaknesses. Anything that'll help."

Singh squeezed out a bitter chuckle. "Weaknesses?"

"Exactly," said Max.

"You're mad as a box of frogs, both of you. They've got no weaknesses. LOTUS has an army of agents, cash and kit coming out their ears, a worldwide network. Hantai Annie's a tough old bird, I grant you that, but you're just a pack of kids with a handful of babysitters. You're like a pesky mosquito to them."

Wyatt spoke up. "Just a mozzy, eh? Well, Max and Cinn led a mission smack into LOTUS HQ. Rescued our hostages and got clean away, right under their noses. How's that for just a mozzy?"

Singh's eyes widened. "Max? *You're* Max Segredo?"

"Yeah," said Max, a little uncertainly.

The spy shook his head. "I wouldn't want to be you, boy. Not for all the naan in Punjab."

"Why not?"

"They want you something fierce."

Max spread his hands. "Hey, I didn't start that fire in the mansion. Everyone thinks I'm a pyro, but I'm not."

"No, not like that," said Singh, resting his elbows on his knees. "They want you working for them."

"Wha-at?" Max sat back, temporarily gobsmacked.

"Why?" asked Wyatt. "I mean, Max is good, but he's not exactly James Bond Jr."

"Thanks a lot," said Max.

The spy shook his head. "The why I don't know. I left LOTUS just after your little escapade, and I didn't work at HQ. I only know—"

An electronic chime interrupted him.

"More visitors?" said Singh. The pistol reappeared in his hand, and he motioned the boys to join him in the kitchen. There, a closed-circuit screen revealed two men stepping up to the front door.

Two ruddy-faced businessmen.

"The geezers from the tube," said Max.

"You said you weren't followed," Singh snapped.

Wyatt shrugged. "We rode with them, but they went the other way. They seemed okay—you know, just regular blokes."

A hard fist rapped on the front door.

"LOTUS?" whispered Max.

The turncoat spy nodded and motioned to them.

Singh stepped into a pair of muddy gardening shoes, lifted a key ring off a hook, and peered out the kitchen window. The pocket-size garden stood empty, wreathed in mist.

Singh eased the door open and, pistol at the ready, crept outside. Max and Wyatt followed. Just as they closed the door, the sound of hard kicks and splintering wood carried from the front of the house.

"You know what I'm wondering?" whispered Wyatt as they hustled toward the spot where a stepstool leaned against the yard's back wall.

"Let me guess," said Max. "Where's Businessman Number Three?"

Singh trotted up the steps and peeked over the six-foot barrier. A pistol coughed. He ducked down again.

"Got it in one guess," said Wyatt.

CHAPTER 9

COUNTDOWN TO A CAPER

MAX SIZED UP the situation in a flash. They had only seconds to make their getaway, and the man with the gun was apparently not too keen on their making it. Max cast about for a weapon, and his eyes landed on a steel bucket half full of potting soil.

He tapped Singh on the shoulder, indicated the bucket, and motioned that he was going to throw it over the wall. The ex-spy caught on immediately. He crouched on the stool's top step, ready for action.

With Wyatt's help, Max hurled the bucket, which made a satisfyingly loud thump on the other side. Singh popped his head up, fired twice, and boosted himself onto the wall. "Let's go!" he hissed.

Max and Wyatt scrambled over, landing heavily in the neighbor's scraggly bushes. Singh was already halfway across the yard, heading for a side gate. The tang of gunpowder hung in the air.

Max stumbled on something. He glanced down to discover the form of the third agent sprawled facedown across a flower bed. He didn't know if the man was alive.

Max's stomach flipped.

A memory flashed through his head—that of his teacher, Roger Stones, lying on a plush carpet, shot dead. Guilt and remorse froze Max in his tracks.

Wyatt tugged sharply on his arm. "Down!"

From his spot by the gate, Singh fired three times, right at them! Max and Wyatt hit the dirt.

Answering shots echoed from the wall. Male voices cursed.

Singh motioned to Max and Wyatt. They dashed across the yard while the ex-spy squeezed off another round to keep the LOTUS agents at bay.

Hurtling through the wooden gate, they found themselves in a narrow passage between two houses. A streetlight shone ahead, wearing a smudged halo in the mist.

"I knew it was too good to last," muttered Singh. "I knew it. You don't just rat out LOTUS and walk away. Everyone knows that."

They hustled down the alley and crouched behind a rubbish bin, scanning the street. Nothing but parked cars and fog.

The turncoat spy hurried to the nearest vehicle. "Drop you boys somewhere?" he asked, opening the driver's-side door.

"If it's not too much trouble," Max said shakily.

They piled into the battered Volkswagen. The engine turned over, and just then, one of the LOTUS operatives raced from the alley's mouth, gun raised.

"Down!" cried Singh.

Wyatt and Max hit the seats as the car peeled away from the curb, tires screeching. The enemy agent's bullets shattered the passenger-side window. Glass fragments rained onto Max's back like hail.

Singh fired one shot in return. They heard a cry, and then the Volkswagen carried them down the street away from danger.

None of them spoke as Singh drove the teens to an underground stop different from the one they'd arrived at, just in case.

"I'm sorry we led them to you," said Max as the lights of the station entrance emerged from the mist. "I don't know how that happened."

"I do." The spy's face was grim. "You've got a security leak."

"Stuff a duck!" blurted Wyatt.

Singh nodded. "Either they've bugged your place, or they've got it under visual surveillance. Take your pick."

And with that cheerful thought, he dropped them at the curb and disappeared into the mist.

Under the fluorescent lights, Wyatt's face looked a little green around the edges. Max touched his shoulder.

"All right, then?" he asked.

Wyatt nodded. "So LOTUS wants you for their own, eh?" He fumbled some coins from his pocket, trying for a casual tone.

"Seems like," said Max. His limbs felt shaky now that they'd reached a safe haven.

"Why, do you reckon?"

"Dunno." Max lifted a shoulder. "Must be my winning personality." But secretly, he'd been brooding over the same question.

As he paid for his ticket, the blond boy's hand trembled. "Why is it, every time we go on a midnight walkabout, it ends in gunfire and getaways?"

"Dunno," said Max. He could feel the tremor in his own voice. "Just lucky, I guess."

Later, after they'd sneaked back into the orphanage and crept off to bed, Max tossed and turned on his mattress, too wired for sleep.

His mind hopped about like a cricket on a hot plate. The image of the fallen LOTUS agent kept returning. And that thought, of course, led to poor old, dead old Roger Stones, which led in turn to thoughts of LOTUS getting their hands on a mind-control device, and then to Max's father, Simon.

For the twentieth time, Max rolled onto his side. Reaching out for the framed photo on his nightstand, he examined it in the night-light's bluish glow. His mum, beautiful and smiling, holding him so lovingly. And his dad, grinning up at the camera without a care in the world.

What exactly did Ebelskeever mean when he mentioned that Simon had done something to his own wife? Something bad?

Max gazed at the younger version of his father. What's going on in your mind? he wondered. Whose side are you really on?

And, still gripping the photo of a happier family, he drifted at last into a troubled sleep.

"Dokero!" barked Hantai Annie Wong. "Everyone into dining room. Fast."

It was six forty-five on yet another drizzly morning, and the director had just cut short her Morning Warm-ups class for an important announcement. Dripping with sweat and curiosity, the orphans stowed their exercise mats and flocked into the dining room for toast, eggs, and porridge.

A yawning Max noticed Vespa down at the far end of the table. When their eyes met, she smiled broadly. Max's heart did a little flip. He ducked his head, feeling awkward. Then she raised her eyebrows and gave him a thumbs-up sign, asking, *Did your mission go all right last night?*

It hadn't, in fact. But still, he favored her with a waggly sideways thumb—*It wasn't a total loss*—and a wry smile in return.

"Sending signals to your little blond friend?" asked Cinnabar. Her tone was so sharp, it could've sliced bread all day and still given a man a close shave.

An answering prickliness rose up in Max. "She helped me with something you didn't have time for."

"Lovely," Cinnabar spat, eyes narrowing. Her tawny cheeks flushed wine-dark. "I'm so glad you two are getting along famously."

"Me, too," snapped Max. "She's brilliant."

At that, Cinnabar clamped her lips tight and turned her shoulder on him.

Max was spared any further girl-related unpleasantness by the arrival of Hantai Annie and Victor Vazquez. *"Minna, yoku kike!"* the director yelled. "Listen up now."

The mealtime chatter quickly subsided, and heads turned to watch. Hantai Annie stood ramrod straight, fists planted on hips and glittering black eyes surveying the students.

"You know we have important mission," she said. "Most important mission ever for this school. After today, only two days left. So we split you, *betsu-betsu*, into teams. Victor-*san*?"

The teacher lifted an eyebrow and smiled a closed-lip

movie-star smile, as if to acknowledge that this was indeed a serious occasion. Cinnabar clasped her hands and stifled a sigh.

"My friends," said Mr. Vazquez. "We have much hacking to do, and not much time to do it. On my team: Wyatt, Jazz, Tremaine, Dermot, and Catarina."

Jazz sent an anxious glance at her sister. Cinnabar reached out to pat her hand.

"My team goes to capital," said Hantai Annie. "We set up surveillance on target. Rashid, Nikki, Cinnabar, Shan, Max—we leave in one half hour."

"Why so soon, Chief?" asked Rashid, his dark eyes serious.

The director's mouth pursed as if sucking on a spoiled lemon. "Inspector Krinkle," she spat. "We go before he comes. Less trouble that way."

Vespa raised her hand. "What about the rest of us—the ones you didn't mention?"

Hantai Annie favored her with a kindly look. "You very new. Stay here with Madame Chiffre and others, help distract inspector."

The blond girl smirked. "I can do that."

"I'll say." Tremaine chuckled.

Under her breath, Cinnabar echoed "I can do that" in a mocking tone.

"Jealousy is such an ugly emotion," Max said.

The director clapped her hands. "Well? Why you wait? *Ikuzo!* We go."

Chairs scraped back from the table as the go-team headed out. Wyatt stuffed the remains of a scone into his mouth and rose with Max.

"Why the rush?" said Max. "You're staying here."

Wyatt pointed to the ceiling and mumbled something that sounded like "upstairs" in scone talk.

When they reached their room, Max peeled off his sweaty T-shirt and began changing into warmer clothes. Wyatt dug under his bed for a shoe box, which he handed over with the air of presenting a rare treasure.

"Er, thanks," said Max, "but I've got shoes."

"My latest invention," said Wyatt. "Go on, open it."

Removing the lid, Max discovered a fat paperback book of the sort someone would buy for an epically long plane ride. "Genius," he said. "It'll revolutionize reading."

"Don't be a dill," Wyatt scoffed. "Look."

Max flipped open the first pages to reveal a cutout space inside. Nestled within lay a gray-and-silver device the size of a fist, sporting two buttons and a dial.

"And this is . . . ?" he asked dubiously.

"The Great Disruptor." Wyatt's chest swelled like a bag of microwave popcorn under maximum heat.

"Very nice," said Max, handing back the box.

Wyatt held up his palms. "You don't get it, mate. I'm loaning it to you for your mission."

"Oh. Well, the thing is . . ." Max searched for a way to let his friend down gently. "I'm sure it's brilliant. But

I doubt Hantai Annie would fancy me drilling through a wall or blowing something up when we're supposed to be all stealthylike."

Wyatt shook his head, blond curls bouncing. "No, no, no. This one's different."

"Right."

"Works like a dream. Just press this red button, and it disrupts all electrical devices within twenty feet. Careful to turn off your cell phone first."

Against his will, Max was intrigued. "And the other controls?"

"Black button turns it off, and the dial sets the amount of disruption—from just a bit of static here"—he touched the left side of the dial—"to full-on malfunction over here."

"I don't know. . . ." said Max.

"Take it," said Wyatt, his blue eyes intent and serious. "A spy should always be prepared."

"All right, then," said Max.

He stowed the book in his rucksack, along with a change of clothes, his gold-plated lighter, and the photo of him with his parents. Living the erratic life of a foster kid had made him value his special things. He hated to be without them, even for a short trip.

"Luck, mate." Wyatt slapped Max's palm.

"You as well."

As Max reached the doorway, Wyatt said, "Hey."

"Yeah?" Max turned.

"What that Ebelskeever bloke said," Wyatt mused. "You don't really think your dad is still working for LOTUS, do you?"

Max hesitated only a moment before answering. "No. 'Course not."

"Just what I thought," said Wyatt. "Cheers, mate."

"Cheers."

But Max wished he felt half as sure as he'd made himself sound.

The recon team gathered in the entryway, slipping into raincoats and heavy jackets. Most carried small rucksacks like Max, but Hantai Annie and Miss Moorthy toted long gear bags, which bulged suspiciously.

"Chan-*kun*," the director told Miss Moorthy, "bags to car. Hurry."

"Yes, Director," said the teacher, in her musical Indian accent. Although a slender woman, she hefted the two carriers with ease. As the school's martial-arts instructor, she packed quite a punch.

Hantai Annie surveyed her little group. "Well? You both legs broken? Go, after her—*isoge!*"

One by one, the students filed through the doorway and into the outer passage. Tall Rashid went first, sporting a blue tracksuit for the occasion. Nikki Knucks stomped along after him, her flyaway red hair sprouting above her coat collar like the tattered end of a burst firecracker. Chatting together in low tones, Shan and Cinnabar followed. Last of all came Max with Hantai Annie.

"You learn something on mission last night?" she asked.

Max winced. No matter how sneaky he tried to be, she always seemed particularly well informed about his extra-curricular adventures.

"Not much," he sheepishly admitted. "We may have a security leak, and LOTUS wants me on their team."

Hantai Annie's eyebrows rose, but she merely grunted. As they stepped out into the morning drizzle, she said, "You good spy, Max-*kun*. Disobedient, but good."

Max bumped into Shan and Cinnabar, who had stopped dead on the walkway. "What's the holdup?" he asked.

Cinnabar pointed a finger toward the gate. "Him."

"I say, are you having a field trip?" said Mr. Krinkle. "Good thing I arrived early." The pudgy man closed the gate and waddled toward them, green umbrella lifted against the sprinkle.

Hantai Annie pushed through her students. "We leaving now. Go see Mr. Vazquez inside."

"Wouldn't dream of it," said the inspector.

"*Doushite da?*" she said. "Why not?"

Henry Krinkle's tiny mouth offered up a smug little grin. "Because I'm going with you, of course."

WAR AND CHEESE

NO MATTER HOW Hantai Annie argued, cajoled, and blustered, Mr. Krinkle was dead set on accompanying the go-team to the capital. Max had a sudden mental picture of the fussy inspector observing their surveillance at RookTech and scribbling comments on his clipboard. *Full marks on the recon*, he'd write.

Yeah, like *that* was going to happen.

Mr. Krinkle climbed back into his tan Toyota and followed their Range Rover down rain-slicked streets. During the brief drive to the train station, Miss Moorthy and Hantai Annie worked out a plan, despite plenty of more or less helpful comments from the orphans.

"Lose him in the backstreets," suggested Max.

"Tell him we're going somewhere deadly dull," said Shan, tossing her rainbow-colored hair, "and maybe he'll bow out."

"Unless he's so dull that he *likes* dull places," said Cinnabar.

Nikki grunted. "Just knock him in the head and have done."

By the time Mr. Krinkle joined them at the station's ticket machine, their strategy was set.

"So, where are we off to?" he said, shaking droplets from his umbrella.

"Museum," said Hantai Annie.

Miss Moorthy offered Krinkle a warm smile. "For cultural enrichment."

"I see," he replied, and jotted down a note on his clipboard. "Culture."

"Mmm-mm, can't get enough of it," said Nikki, with one of the phoniest smiles seen outside of beauty-contest runners-up.

The train ride seemed to take ages. Apparently, Cinnabar was still nursing a grudge, as she stuck close to Shan and gave Max the cold shoulder. Deprived of her company, Max kept an eye out for any LOTUS agents who might want to interfere with their mission. But the biggest danger turned out to be death by boredom.

As it transpired, Mr. Krinkle was one of the world's dullest travel companions. He was a terrible storyteller, a dismal conversationalist, and his favorite topic was the various types of cheese he'd had the opportunity to taste.

"As they say," he chortled, "Camembert is to share, but the Brie is all for me!"

Fortunately for Max, Krinkle mostly chose to bore the adults. But during the last half hour of the ride, the inspector began taking the students aside one by one to ask how they were treated at Merry Sunshine Orphanage. Max's turn came last.

When the man beckoned, Max plopped down into the open seat beside him.

"So . . ." Mr. Krinkle looked up from his clipboard, peering at Max as if he was a new species of insect. "Max Segredo. Tell me, how long have you been at the orphanage?"

"Almost a month," said Max, stone-faced as a sphinx. He was determined to give the man as little information as possible.

"How do you like it?"

"Best group home ever," said Max.

Scribble-scribble-scratch went Mr. Krinkle's pen. "Have you any complaints?"

"Yeah," said Max. "One."

The inspector sat up straighter, eyes shining and pen quivering. "Go on."

"I wish my caseworker had sent me there earlier, instead of placing me with all those wretched fosters."

Mr. Krinkle cleared his throat. "Ah, I see. . . ." His face fell, and Max almost burst out laughing. "And they treat you well at the orphanage?" the inspector asked.

Max flashed on the healthful meals, the camaraderie of

the group, and his sense, for the first time he could remember, of actually *belonging* somewhere. At the thought of this man shutting it down, a hot spike of anger rose in him.

"*Very* well indeed," he said.

"How about the other children—do you hear any complaints from them?"

"Never," Max said. "Everyone loves it."

Mr. Krinkle's eyes narrowed, almost disappearing in his puffy marshmallow cheeks. "Are you *certain* you're not leaving anything out?"

Like classes in martial arts, code breaking, lock-picking, and computer hacking? Like orphans training to become spies?

"Absolutely nothing," lied Max, his gaze as bland as a three-course tapioca dinner.

The inspector's lips pursed tightly. He wore his irritation like an ill-fitting suit, but there was nothing he could do about it.

"That is all, young man," he said. "But if I find you've been lying to me—"

"Yeah, yeah, you'll drag me in chains to the Tower of London," Max snarled, shooting to his feet. "Why don't you leave us alone and go help some kids who really need it?"

Mr. Krinkle's mouth popped open. "Well!" he said. "I can see that however much you enjoy this orphanage, they are not teaching you proper manners."

In a split second, Max considered and rejected three replies: a rude gesture, an eye jab, and several unprintable words. Instead, he bowed stiffly like a British gentleman, said, "Good day, sir," and returned to his own seat.

One transfer and a short tube ride later, the group found itself trudging through light rain toward what looked like some Roman emperor's summer palace plunked down in the middle of a modern city. But Max had bigger concerns than gawking at classical architecture.

"Sure you can keep him occupied long enough?" he muttered to Miss Moorthy. Max nodded at Mr. Krinkle, who was negotiating the steps just ahead of them while still managing to annoy the director. The man was gifted that way.

"Silly boy." The lovely teacher patted her glossy hair, so black it was almost blue. "He won't present a problem. I know his weakness."

"Not . . . uh, women?" said Max, feeling a little squirmy at the thought.

Miss Moorthy indicated Krinkle, who'd stopped to peruse a placard just inside the entrance, listing the museum's restaurants.

"Food," she said.

Once the group was inside the museum proper, Hantai Annie Wong hustled them up and down stairs, marching through the halls with grim determination, as if they were competing in some kind of cultural marathon. They tramped past displays of ancient Greek towns, Asian teacups through the ages, Sumerian fertility totems, and one devoted entirely to The Warthog.

With each new hall, Max's impatience swelled, until it felt like he was trying to keep a fully inflated blimp earthbound. Hantai Annie's jaw was clamped so tightly, she seemed in danger of crushing her teeth. And with each exhibit, the overweight Mr. Krinkle looked progressively more whey-faced and winded.

"I say," he called out as the director trooped them toward a display of ancient Welsh wind instruments. "I must admit I'm feeling a mite peckish. Would anyone mind if I—"

Miss Moorthy took his arm. "I've heard that the restaurant here has the most divine sesame-crusted salmon. Why don't we go and find out?"

Mr. Krinkle's expression was that of a drowning man who spots a rescue boat.

"Such a sensible woman," he said.

Giving the go-team a finger wave, Miss Moorthy said, "Ring me when you're ready, and we'll meet up. Cheers."

As soon as the pair was out of sight, Hantai Annie changed course, making a beeline for the exit at quick-march speed. The orphans trotted after her like a flock of oversize ducklings. *"Isoge!"* she urged. "This *baka* leaves us no time. Hurry!"

Fortunately, RookTech's headquarters lay no more than ten minutes' walk away. Hantai Annie had them there in five. But instead of taking the orphans directly into the building's lobby, she led them toward a car park across the street.

"Um, hello?" said Nikki. "Wouldn't it be easier to check out the security if we're actually *in* the building?"

"This is why *I* lead mission, not you," said the director.

Nikki pouted. Hantai Annie headed into the car-park stairwell, which reeked of fresh petrol and stale urine. Wrinkling their noses, the orphans followed. At the second level, the director paced along the outer wall—a series of interlocking concrete triangles that offered a view of the street from their openings—until she found the perfect spot.

"Here," said Hantai Annie, setting down her gear bags and unzipping them. She began barking out orders like a drill sergeant. "Rashid!"

"What do you need, Chief?" he said.

"Set up camera here, focus on lobby security."

Rashid helped her remove equipment from the bag. "Disguise it?"

"*Mochiron da.* Of course. Cinn-*chan!*"

"Yes, ma'am?" said Cinnabar.

Hantai Annie passed her a laptop computer and some other equipment, along with a key and a slip of paper. "Take Shan, go to safe house. Set up computer and relay."

"We have a safe house?" asked Max.

The director grunted. *"Nice* safe house. Our client is very rich."

Cinnabar and Shan hurried off, mapping out the route on their smartphone.

Max still felt awkward around Cinn; she'd barely said a word to him all day. But he still called after her, "Good luck!"

She glanced back, offering a tight-lipped half smile.

Not exactly what he'd hoped for.

"What about me?" asked Nikki, her face still sullen. "What do I do?"

"You lookout," said Hantai Annie. "Keep watch for Rashid. Then, when he finishes, go to bus stop." She indicated a shelter with benches just down the street. "Watch out for me and Max. If LOTUS or police come, call me."

Nikki's scowl deepened. "Why does Maxi-Pad get to go? Why not me?"

"Baka yarou!" Hantai Annie barked. "Time is short. You do what I say."

The red-haired girl flinched. Her pout grew so pronounced you could've balanced a set of teacups on her lower lip. But she stomped off a few paces and took up her post, leaning on a pillar with arms crossed.

"Now, Max-*kun*,"—the director dug in her bag for a plastic container—"you and me get dirty."

"Sorry?" said Max, not sure he'd heard right.

"Dirty." Hantai Annie popped the lid off of a Tupperware

bowl to reveal that it was full of half-dried mud. "We get dirty." She dipped three fingers into it and began painting her face and hands. "What's the matter, you? I speak English."

Max shrugged and began smearing his own face. When they'd finished, she handed him a greasy watch cap and overcoat that smelled like they'd been fished out of a rubbish bin and dragged along the docks by a seasick sea otter.

"Really?" said Max.

"Really," said Hantai Annie.

As Max suited up, she bent and wiped some mud on his tennis shoes for good measure. The director donned her own raggedy coat, cap, and even trousers, right over her own clothes. Then she stuffed their good coats into plastic grocery bags, along with some old T-shirts. Max stowed his rucksack in the gear bag, trying not to smear mud on everything.

Nikki hooted. "You make it look so natural, Maxi-Pad."

"Me?" said Max. "If *you* were any more natural, they'd put you back in the ape cage at the zoo."

With a snarl, the redheaded girl unfolded her arms and clenched her fists.

"Enough!" snapped Hantai Annie. "We wasting time. Come, *ikkou-ze*."

On a last-minute impulse, Max lifted Wyatt's paperback and its hidden cargo from the gear bag, nestling it in among the old T-shirts in his grocery sacks. He hoisted the sacks, feeling grimier than if he'd spent a weekend at the bottom of a rubbish bin. The director pulled one more thing from her gear bag—a hand-lettered cardboard sign:

HOMELESS — ANYTHING HELPS

She tucked it under his arm, hefted her own sacks and a blanket too ratty even for a nag on its way to the glue factory, and led the way downstairs.

"Homeless?" asked Max. "How do you figure?"

Hantai Annie glanced back at him. "Nobody looks at homeless. It's shameful. But we not here to fix society. We here to spy."

Getting into character, they slouched and shambled across the street, making for the recessed entrance of the RookTech building. Max saw that Annie had been right; passersby gave them no more than a cursory glance and a wide berth. She spread their blanket on one side of the alcovelike space, in a spot where they had a clear view of the guard desk as well as the door's security devices.

The director propped their sign against the plastic bags and set an empty coffee cup beside it. Then she and Max slumped down and began their watch. People walking down the street avoided their gaze; employees entering the building pretended that the "homeless" spies were invisible.

Max caught Annie fiddling with a top button of her overcoat.

"Problem?" he mumbled.

"Turning on camera," she replied. Then Hantai Annie angled her coat to record the entrance security procedures and eased back into position.

Pretty slick, thought Max. Although he would've felt slicker if he didn't smell like yesterday's fish-and-chips wrapper. With a sidelong gaze, he scrutinized a RookTech employee returning to work. The woman scanned her key card and looked directly into a rectangular metal box mounted at head height beside the door. A brief pause, and the door buzzed, letting her inside.

"What you notice?" muttered Hantai Annie.

"Key-card lock and some kind of camera," Max replied.

The director pretended to scratch at fleas. (Or maybe authentic fleas came with her coat—Max wasn't sure.) "Face recognition," she said.

Max nodded. "Also, the guards at the desk keep a watch on visitors." Those guards, in fact, were eyeing Max and Hantai Annie through the glass at that very moment. Max guessed maybe they were the exception to the rule that nobody notices the homeless.

"What else you see?" asked the director.

Letting his gaze take in everything, Max said, "Um . . . no outside wires."

"*Souka,*" said Hantai Annie. "System is self-contained. We cannot cut power. So, how we break in?"

"Through a window?" Max guessed. A gust of wind whirled leaves and dirt around their alcove, and he lifted a hand to shield his eyes from the grit.

She shook her head. "Window sets off alarm and brings guards. Camera is key. We must hack into system." Hantai Annie glanced at Max's plastic bags. "Maybe we try your friend's invention?"

Max gaped. "Do you know *everything* that goes on at Merry Sunshine?"

Though her face remained blank, her eyes twinkled. "Almost."

Pulling the sack closer, Max slipped a hand inside and removed Wyatt's invention from the paperback while still keeping it hidden from view. His finger found the red button.

"Um, just so you know," he said, "this might not work as advertised."

"*Daijoubu da.* Wait one minute." Hantai Annie made a quick call, then turned off her phone. Max followed suit. She watched two employees approach the door, one of them a pinched-faced woman who was gabbing nonstop on her cell phone. "Good spy uses every asset she has. Push button, Max-*kun.*"

Max said a silent prayer to the gods of espionage, and he pushed the button.

WHEN DIJON CAN'T CUT THE MUSTARD

CHAPTER 11

GGGZZZZUTCHHHH!

With a harsh crackle, the high-tech lock system spat blue sparks.

"Hello? Hello?" said Cell-Phone Woman into her phone. "It cut off," she told her coworker.

Her companion, a balding white man with wire-rimmed glasses, swiped his card through the lock, then swiped it again. He stared up at the camera. "Blast. It's not working." Mr. Chrome Dome hammered on the thick glass with his palm. "You there! Open up; the lock's malfunctioning."

From her desk in the lobby, one of the guards held a hand beside her ear and shook her head to indicate that she couldn't hear him.

"I said, *it's not working!*" the man bellowed. He pointed at the key-card lock and camera, then gestured for her to come to the door.

125

The guard, a heavyset, walnut-skinned woman with a bulldog jaw, rolled her eyes expressively. As slow as honey in winter, she pushed a button on her console, waited, and pushed it again. The bald man glowered.

Max glanced over at Hantai Annie. "It's working," he said, surprised.

With the air of doing Mr. Chrome Dome an enormous favor, the bulldoggish guard stood, sauntered around her desk, and approached the door. She fiddled with the locking mechanism from her side and rattled the door handle. At length, Mrs. Bulldog shook her head.

"Well, really!" said the man. "I have a meeting, you know!"

Mrs. Bulldog did the I-can't-hear-you act again, and Mr. Chrome Dome fumed. She held up a finger and then mimed making a telephone call.

"Oh, for heaven's sake," he complained to Cell-Phone Woman. "Can you believe this?"

The female guard tried to place the call with her cell phone. From her reaction, Max guessed that it wasn't working either. Way to go, Wyatt, he thought.

Then Mrs. Bulldog returned to her desk outside the disruption zone, used her landline, and held a brief conversation with someone on the other end.

"What do we do now?" Max whispered. "She just called the repairman."

"We wait," Hantai Annie replied. "Thank you, sir," she

called to a passerby who'd just dropped some coins into her paper cup.

Within five minutes, a white van pulled up to the loading zone and parked, disgorging a skinny repairman in light blue coveralls. Two more RookTech workers arrived to join the line. The entryway was growing crowded, but somehow all four employees managed to avoid looking directly at Max and Hantai Annie.

"Turn off jammer," the director whispered.

Max reached a hand into the bag and snatched it back. "Ow!" Wyatt's Great Disruptor had grown as hot as a slice of jalapeño pie. More carefully this time, Max found the OFF button and pressed it.

"Coming through." The repairman pushed his way between the workers, toting a tool kit and some sort of handheld electronic device. "What seems to be the trouble?" he asked in a Russian-accented voice.

All the workers replied at once, griping that they couldn't get inside. The repairman quieted them. "Not to worry," he said. "I will fix it." As he passed by Max and Annie, he nodded.

Max blinked. With those gaunt cheeks and that high forehead under the blue cap, the repairman seemed awfully familiar. "Dracula Hair?" he asked Hantai Annie. When she sent him a strange look, he explained, "The Gravlaki guy?"

"Now he is S.P.I.E.S. guy," she said. "He works for us."

Dracula Hair, who Max recalled was named something like Dogswash, set down his tool kit and scanned the electronic lock up and down. Then he unwound a cord from his handheld gizmo and plugged it into a port on the face-recognition device.

"What's he doing?" Max mumbled.

Hantai Annie leaned closer, the funk from her grimy clothes enfolding him like a fog. "Downloading database," she whispered.

Max squinted at the street. "But what happens when the real repairman shows up?"

"*We* do," she said.

After a few minutes, another van, this one silver, parked just behind the white one. The logo emblazoned on its side read HERCULES SECURITY.

"Um, that would be her." Max tipped his head at the blond driver peering through her windshield at the scene.

"*Jya,*" said Hantai Annie. "Showtime." She climbed to her feet, patted her coat pockets, and glowered down at him. "You! You steal my money."

"What?"

"You. Steal. My. Money." The director widened her eyes at him, in a get-with-the-program look. In a flash, Max tumbled to her plan.

"I never stole nothin'," he cried, jumping up. "You lost it."

"Low-down, stink-eyed, lying boy," she growled. "Where

is it?" Hantai Annie began rooting through one of his bags. "Push me," she whispered.

"Oi!" Max cried, slamming her shoulder. "Get out of my stuff, old witch!"

The director staggered back theatrically, caroming off one of the RookTech workers and straight into the path of the real repairperson. The woman in green coveralls shrank back, like she might catch some particularly loathsome disease. Trying to avoid the fracas, the four employees pressed up against the building. No one wanted to get involved—except perhaps for the five security guards standing helpless on the other side of the glass.

"You push me?" Hantai Annie snarled, eyes popping. "*You* no push *me*!"

She windmilled her arms like a cartoon boxer and stomped toward Max. Getting into the spirit of their act, Max rushed forward and grappled. Arms locked together, the two cursed and spat as they staggered about the sidewalk, effectively blocking the repairperson's attempts to bypass them.

"Fight! *Fight!*" screamed Cell-Phone Woman.

From the corner of an eye, Max noticed the Gravlaki spy finishing his download and picking up his gear. "Almost there," he muttered to Hantai Annie.

She gripped Max's forearms and swung him about in wild circles. On one rotation, they smacked right into the repairperson, knocking her onto her duff in the gutter. Mr.

Doughwash, or whatever his name was, slipped past them and around the front of his van, tipping his cap to the stunned repairperson.

Hantai Annie released Max and stopped her attack. For the benefit of the onlookers, she said, "You really don't have my money?"

"No," said Max. "I *really* don't have it."

"Oh." She scratched at a flea, suddenly calm. "Okey-dokey."

"Okey-dokey?" Max whispered. Hantai Annie shrugged.

The white van accelerated away from the curb and drove down the street. Mission accomplished.

Max and Annie brushed themselves off, turned, and began shuffling back to collect their bags and blanket. Just then, Mr. Chrome Dome cried, "Look! Something's smoking."

Sure enough, oily brown smoke was rising from the grocery bag that held Wyatt's invention. Before Max could reach it, the bald man extended his foot and nudged the bag, causing the silver gizmo to roll partially free of the T-shirts.

Oh, Wyatt, Max thought. What now?

"Bomb!" screamed Cell-Phone Woman. "The bums have a bomb!"

Instantly the small knot of employees backed away, gaping at Max and Annie. Max made a move to reclaim their belongings, but one of the women cried, "He's trying to set it off!" and Mr. Chrome Dome stepped into his path, arms spread wide.

"Oh no you don't," he growled. "Not at *my* workplace. Bloody terrorist."

"Terrorists!" screeched Cell-Phone Woman. "Call the police!"

Max gritted his teeth. This lady was growing awfully tiresome.

"Oitoke," muttered Hantai Annie. "Leave it. We go."

She pivoted and stepped into the street. Just then, a jet-black SUV screeched to a halt, blocking their way. A svelte woman in black and silver who looked like the world's most ruthless supermodel glided from the passenger seat.

Alarm flooded Max. This was no ordinary evil supermodel, but Dijon, a LOTUS agent he'd encountered during his rescue mission at their secret headquarters.

Dijon's eyes widened in recognition. "You!"

"LOTUS!" cried Max. "Run!"

Hantai Annie planted her left foot and delivered a devastating side kick to Dijon's solar plexus. With a grunt, the spy tumbled back against the car.

As more agents piled out, Max and Annie dashed through the gap between the rear of the SUV and the Hercules van.

"We're from MI5!" Dijon shouted. "Stop and surrender yourselves!"

MI5? thought Max. Oh, *please*. More like MI-ever-sick-of-these-people.

Max and Hantai Annie sprinted for the car-park stairwell.

"How'd they know we were here?" he panted.

"Just like us," she said. "They doing surveillance."

Up the street, a blur of movement caught Max's eye—Nikki Knucks, leaving her post by the bus stop to join them. Max held out his hands in a why-didn't-you-warn-us? gesture, and Nikki responded by pointing at her phone and scowling.

Ah, of course. He and Annie had both turned off their phones. Duh.

"Halt!" a man yelled behind them. Then they were inside and pounding up the steps.

"Rashid!" called Hantai Annie.

"Got you covered," came a reply from the floor above them.

They burst through the stairwell door and onto the second level, narrowly missing Rashid, who was hefting a steel rubbish barrel. "This'll slow 'em down," he grunted as they sped past.

Glancing back, Max saw him hurl the barrel into the stairwell, presumably at the pursuing agents, then slam the door and wedge a two-by-four against it. Rashid snagged the gear bag, and they fled across the car park, between rows of gleaming Peugeots, BMWs, and Renaults.

Max hoped the structure had another entrance or three.

Sure enough, they spotted a green fire-exit sign in the far corner. The team blasted past a surprised attendant. "Keys, please?" he called after them. The three orphans and Annie hustled over to the stairs and down, to emerge on a street parallel to the one they'd left.

The director led them across the road, through a brick alleyway, into the back of a department store, and out the front of that building before she slowed to a walk.

"Enough . . . running," panted Nikki. Her face was as red as an angry sunset.

Max smirked. Black belt she might be, but Nikki Knucks was not a huge fan of aerobic exercise.

Hantai Annie placed a quick call, instructing Shan and Cinnabar to meet them outside the museum. Then she peeled off her outer layer of rags and stuffed it into a nearby rubbish bin. Max tossed his grimy watch cap in after, but kept his funky overcoat. The cold drizzle was threatening to turn heavy, and his own warm coat was probably being tested for explosives at that very moment. Luckily, his family photo and other valuables were stowed safely in Rashid's gear bag.

The director's phone chimed. *"Hai,"* she barked. After listening for a few seconds, she replied, *"Jya,* okay, okay," and disconnected. Her face was grim.

"What is it, Chief?" asked Rashid.

Nikki frowned with concern. "A problem at the orphanage?"

"LOTUS again?" guessed Max.

Hantai Annie grunted. "Worse than anything you can imagine." Her mouth drew into a tight line. "Mr. Krinkle has finished his lunch."

THE ONLY THING WORSE THAN VAMPIRES

CHAPTER 12

ONE MIGHT THINK that after a stretch of surveillance
and a close call or two, an orphan would fancy a refreshing
cup of tea and a quiet ride home. But such, Max discovered,
is not the life of a junior spy.

After coaxing a nonstinky overcoat from the employee at
the information desk who handled the lost and found, Max
and the rest of the group left the museum and headed down
a tree-lined street toward the tube station. Hantai Annie
led them, and Miss Moorthy, with the chatty Mr. Krinkle,
brought up the rear. Max never stopped scanning the street
for another appearance of the LOTUS-mobile.

But the first surprise came from a different quarter.

As they passed a stately plane tree a half block from the

station, a tall policeman stepped out from behind it. "Please listen," he said.

On reflex, Hantai Annie dropped into a defensive karate stance, fists raised. The other orphans stepped back, but Max froze in his tracks, pinned by a rush of conflicting feelings.

The cop was Simon Segredo.

His father looked as haggard as he had a few days earlier, but at least he was clean-shaven now, and his navy-blue coat and helmet were spotless. He glanced at Max, then reached out to the director.

"Please, you must—"

"No," she said, lowering her fists. "You already have my answer."

"But don't you see?" Max's father pleaded. "Whatever mission brings you here, LOTUS is onto it. They're running rings around you, and if you keep on this path, someone"—his eyes cut over to Max again—"will get hurt."

"You don't know that," said Hantai Annie. "You just—"

"I say," Mr. Krinkle interrupted, barging through the orphans. "Why are you arguing with this fine police officer?"

"*Baka yarou!*" snapped the director, scowling at him. "He—uh . . ." She seemed to recall the need to keep Krinkle happy and clueless. "We not arguing. He is giving directions."

"Really? Because it looked like . . ." Mr. Krinkle made a face and waved his hand vaguely.

"No, no," said Max, with a forced chuckle. "We needed directions to the, um . . ." He glanced over at Cinnabar.

"Tube station," she said.

Krinkle frowned. "But it's right there."

"Different tube station," said Hantai Annie. "For our *next* visit, yes, Officer?" Her eyes drilled into Simon's.

"Yes, that's right," the fake policeman assured Mr. Krinkle. When the marshmallow man looked away, Simon turned to Max and hissed, "Who is this git?"

"Just play along," Max muttered under his breath.

"Sorry to interrupt your duties, Officer." The pudgy inspector lifted his cap. "I'm Henry Krinkle, from the Ministry of Health. Pleasure to meet you."

Max had just turned to stare at the oblivious Mr. Krinkle, when he saw it beyond the man—popping up like an ever-present monster in a horror movie—surprise number two.

The black SUV.

Brakes screeched, and it stopped dead, blocking the lane. The car doors flew open.

Oh no, Max thought, not again. "LOTUS!" he cried. "Look out!"

After that, everything seemed to happen at once.

Dijon lunged through the passenger-side door, followed immediately by a bearlike man from the backseat.

"Down!" cried Simon.

He drew a silver pistol from his coat with one hand and swept his other arm to the side, pushing Max out of the line of fire. The gun barked twice, and the LOTUS agents ducked back.

"Oh, I say!" cried Mr. Krinkle. "Are those gangsters?"

"Worse," said Cinnabar.

The marshmallow man frowned as she tugged him behind the tree. "What's worse than gangsters?"

"Um, evil ninja gangsters?" said Rashid.

"It's me they're after," murmured Simon Segredo.

"No, it's me," Max whispered, recalling what the turncoat Singh had told him. Another thought struck him. "And by the way, how did you just happen to be here?"

His father drew a breath to speak, but, realizing this was perhaps not the best time for a chat, whirled and dashed down the sidewalk.

"I say, why is he fleeing the scene?" said Krinkle. "Shouldn't he be chasing them?"

"*Dokero!*" cried Hantai Annie. "Move it!" She caught Max's arm and shoved him toward the nearby tube station. Recovering from their shock, the other orphans hustled after him. Miss Moorthy followed last, dragging a befuddled Mr. Krinkle behind her.

"What on earth is going on?" he kept demanding. "Are they filming a movie?"

"That's it exactly," said Miss Moorthy. "How did you guess?"

Glancing back, Max saw that the SUV had turned and was pursuing Simon the wrong way up a one-way street, to a chorus of honking horns and screaming pedestrians.

His father was right; LOTUS really did want to get their hands on him. Max only hoped Simon could keep it from happening.

He pushed through the doors to the tube station and waited in the ticket lobby for the rest of the group. Cinnabar arrived first.

"Bloody LOTUS," she griped. "They're worse than vampires—nothing keeps them down."

"I can't believe that cop shot at them," said Shan, stepping inside with Rashid. "He could have hit an innocent bystander."

"That cop was Max's dad," said Rashid.

"And he had his reasons," said Max. "Like, they want him dead."

Nikki banged open the door, catching his comment. "All a ploy," she said. "I bet he's meeting with them right now, plotting their next move."

Heat rushed into Max's face. Without thinking, he stepped forward, grabbed two fistfuls of Nikki's coat, and slammed her against the door. "Take that back!"

Nikki clapped her palms together and drove them up between his arms, breaking Max's grip. "I've had a bellyful of you, Segredo," she snarled. They stepped apart and raised their fists, squaring off.

Hantai Annie entered just at that moment. *"Yamerou!"* she barked. "Knock it off!"

"But he—" Nikki began. She faltered as she saw Miss Moorthy and Mr. Krinkle pushing through the door to join them. When the inspector frowned at her raised fists, she faked a smile and playfully cuffed Max on the shoulder. "And that's how you do it, Max, old buddy."

Max's answering smile was phonier than a birth certificate for Bigfoot. "Thanks, Nikki, old pal."

The inspector gave them a vague nod and resumed complaining to Miss Moorthy.

"As I was saying—completely unacceptable," Krinkle huffed. "For orphans to be placed in this kind of danger. Who *were* those people?"

"Bad actors," said Hantai Annie grimly. "Capital is full of them. Like rats. But we only extras in movie, so what can you do?"

Mr. Krinkle harrumphed. "I'm not certain that those actors were firing blanks," he said. "And I don't know what business orphans have being in a movie of this nature. You can be sure this is going in my report."

Miss Moorthy and Hantai Annie exchanged a dour look behind the inspector's back. It would not be a pleasant ride home.

The mood back at the orphanage was as gray as the day. It had dawned on the S.P.I.E.S. crew that stealing a mind-control device from under LOTUS's nose wouldn't be as easy as scarfing down a steak-and-kidney pie. That is, assuming the orphanage stayed open long enough for them to even attempt the task.

To top it off, more students had received threatening texts from LOTUS, and no one knew how they'd learned the orphans' phone numbers. Vespa in particular was rattled by the text she'd gotten, which she described as "deeply creepy." Anxious glances traveled up and down the dinner table.

After a simple supper of roast chicken, brussels sprouts, beans, and mashed potatoes, the kids on kitchen duty cleared the dishes and the recon team compared notes with the hacking team. Max was relieved to see the food go; despite the stress of the day, he found he didn't have much appetite. He sat beside Wyatt and gnawed at a fingernail.

Hantai Annie Wong went first. She sketched out what the go-team had discovered and what they hoped to learn from their surveillance camera—namely, the timing and movements of the guard shifts. She also mentioned the spectacular malfunction of Wyatt's Great Disruptor.

"Heh." The blond boy turned as red as a fistful of cherries. "Back to the ol' drawing board," he mumbled, tracing his finger along a puddle of spilled gravy.

Hantai Annie finished by telling the group about LOTUS's attack. "They keep close watch on RookTech," she said. "And we must assume they are working on plan like ours."

"But why haven't they snatched this thingummy already?"

asked Cinnabar, who sat across from Max with her sister, Jazz. "They must've heard about it before Mr. Elbow hired us."

"Shiranai." The director shook her head. "We don't know. But they have same deadline we do—two nights from now."

"Too bad you don't have someone inside their organization," said Vespa, who'd been sitting quietly beside Rashid. Max and Wyatt swapped a yeah-we-already-thought-of-that glance.

"Too right," said Rashid.

He gave Vespa a thumbs-up, but she missed it, because she was gazing at Max. Her attention made Max antsy, and though he wanted nothing more than to gaze back at her, he brushed some imaginary crumbs off the table. Cinnabar's eyes narrowed.

Sitting back down, Hantai Annie addressed Mr. Vazquez. "Victor-*san*, what did your team learn?"

Victor Vazquez sipped his espresso. His dark mane, usually as slick and immaculate as a helmet, was sticking up in random spikes. After hours of staring at a computer screen, his eyes looked bloodshot and as glazed as a doughnut.

"Director," he said, "my friends, we have good news and bad news."

Hantai Annie snorted. "We need good news." To Max, her usually ageless-looking face seemed lined and careworn.

"Good news it is, then," said Mr. Vazquez. "After much effort, we were able to hack into the RookTech system."

The director smiled a weary smile. "*Yoku yatta*, Victor-*san*. Is good."

"And believe you me, it wasn't easy," said Wyatt. "First-rate firewalls—tougher than rhino jerky and twice as nasty."

Mr. Vazquez continued the tale. "We downloaded the building's layout, and what do you know? We discovered a secure room inside the premises."

"*Ah, souka.*" Hantai Annie studied him over steepled fingers. "And this is where they keep mind-control device?"

The teacher shrugged. "Best guess? Yes. But to know what kind of protection it's got, we'd have to deal with the company that installed their system—"

"Hercules Security," Max cut in. At Mr. Vazquez's quizzical look, he said, "We sort of ran into one of their repair people."

"That's the outfit," said the teacher. "Top-notch. Unfortunately, all the system specs are in *their* files, not at RookTech."

"So that means . . . ?" said Nikki.

Cinnabar grimaced. "We'll have to crack Hercules before we can break into RookTech?"

Mr. Vazquez nodded. "I'm afraid so. And you can bet that *their* computers will be ten times harder to hack."

"How about doing a physical break-in?" asked Tremaine. "A bit of the old bash-and-grab?"

Victor Vazquez sighed. "Like I said, ten times harder. Alarms on windows and doors, cameras out the yin-yang, guards, biometrics—your basic burglar's nightmare."

A long minute passed in which nothing was heard but the ticking of a clock, the creaking of the old house, and the air being let out of everyone's hopes and dreams.

Max looked around the table at all the glum faces. "But apart from that," he said to Mr. Vazquez, "what's the *bad* news?"

A TIGER IN THE BASEMENT

IF RESEARCH WERE an Olympic event, the S.P.I.E.S. team would have at least qualified for the semifinals that night. Most of the orphans, along with Mr. Vazquez and Madame Chiffre, dove into learning all they could about Hercules Security—its workers, its products, its cyber security, even its employee football team (go, Fighting Bagels!).

Cinnabar and Jazz sequestered themselves to review the day's footage from the surveillance camera outside RookTech. They hoped to discover a clue as to how LOTUS was monitoring the tech company, and when the rival agency was planning to make its move.

Max didn't think much of their chances. LOTUS was far too slick to give away its game.

Right in the midst of this anthill of activity, Stanislav Dobasch arrived with no fanfare. The gaunt Gravlaki spy promptly found a corner, plugged in his laptop, and went straight to work analyzing the data he'd downloaded from the RookTech face-recognition system.

Max, however, felt far too twitchy to play research boy with the rest of them. He paced the halls, grappling with the distinct feeling that he was missing something. Some random thought, some half-noticed detail nagged at his mind, like an itch in that spot on your back where your arms can't reach.

So much had happened these last few days. His father's sudden reappearance, and oddly, only when Max was in the capital. The new mission. Mr. Krinkle's anonymous complaint, and his threats to shut down the orphanage at any second. And the offhand clue from their LOTUS captive that led to the near assassination of Singh, the turncoat spy.

If some kind of thread connected these events, it was harder to find than a truant officer's sense of humor. One thing Max could see, though: their prisoner, Mr. Ebelskeever, had played him for a chump.

Impulsively, Max sprang into action. First, he talked Cinnabar into telling him where the keys were kept, and then he went to pay another visit to their reluctant guest.

The cramped basement cell was as clammy and chilly as ever. Ebelskeever rolled off his cot, blinking in the sudden brightness of the overhead light.

"Come to clear the dishes, have you?" he rumbled. Then he saw Max. "The nose biter."

Max stopped a good five feet short of the steel bars. "You must think you're pretty clever, pulling strings from inside a jail cell."

A vertical crease appeared between the spy's thick eyebrows. "What are you on about?"

"You oh-so-casually mention the name of a turncoat spy, knowing that we're trying to get some intel on LOTUS. Then, when we go visit him, your little hit squad comes to call."

Ebelskeever's coffee-bean eyes lit up. "They nailed the ratbag?"

"Mr. Singh got away, no thanks to you."

"Pity." The prisoner glowered. "He had it coming."

Max jabbed an accusing finger at him. "So you admit you tipped off LOTUS that we were going to Singh's house."

"Pssh." Ebelskeever waved his hand dismissively. "You think I had something to do with setting up the hit? You're living in Narnia, boy."

"I know you used us," said Max, stepping closer.

The burly man spread his arms. "And how did I send word about it, eh? With ESP? With a secret transmitter hidden in my bum? You lot have got me locked up tighter than a newt's nostril."

Max folded his arms and stared at the man. His anger had carried him in here, but now that it was cooling, he felt woefully underprepared for squeezing a confession from a hardened field agent.

Ebelskeever's dark eyes sized him up. "Are you so grass green you don't think we've got this place under surveillance? Any semicompetent agent could've followed you little boys playing at spies." The prisoner's smile was as full of evil as a devil's to-do list. His voice dropped to a near whisper. "I can't wait till my lads come bust me out. You'll be crying like a baby."

"Will I really?" Max drawled. "Actually, I heard that LOTUS wants me on their team."

The spy's statement of disbelief rang just a little false, like an out-of-tune bell. "LOTUS wants *you*? First I've heard of it."

"Aren't you the insider, then?" said Max.

If a gorilla-like superspy could be said to sulk, Ebelskeever's face might have been called pouty (though not to his face). He didn't speak.

"And why haven't your lads busted you out already?" Max continued. "Could it be you're not worth the effort?"

Doubt flickered in Ebelskeever's eyes, so quickly Max almost missed it.

"Nonsense," said the prisoner. "I'm a top agent."

"Of course you are," said Max. "That's why it's been two weeks and no one's come after you."

The big man paced in his steel cage, irritation rolling off of him in waves. "The reason I'm still *here*," he snarled, "is that your precious Hantai Annie has a tiger by the tail and can't work out how to turn him loose."

"Maybe," said Max. He turned and sauntered off, paus-
ing in the doorway. "Or maybe everyone's just"—he flipped
the light switch, plunging the cell into blackness—"forgotten
about you."

Max turned the locks on the prisoner's curses. As he
secured the outer door, the scuff of a footstep came from
around the corner. But when he reached the intersection of
the corridor, the hall was empty.

Feeling at loose ends, Max returned the keys and made
his way up to the bedroom he shared with Wyatt and Jensen.
A great lump sprawled in the latter boy's bed, snoring like a
fleet of single-engine aircraft. Wyatt's mattress was vacant.

Max prepared for sleep, but despite being totally knackered, he ended up lying on his back, mind whirring away.
The questions wouldn't leave him alone. If Ebelskeever wasn't
the mole, then who was? Why was LOTUS so on top of their
every move? And how were they able to learn the orphans'
phone numbers? Had someone planted bugs inside Merry
Sunshine?

Max snorted. Preposterous. Mr. Vazquez swept the school
for bugs every day, and the building was a miniature fortress.
Nobody could get inside to plant something unless they'd
been invited.

His father hadn't been inside. In fact, nobody new had
entered the orphanage lately, except for their client Mr. Elbow;
his bodyguards; and the obnoxious government inspector,

Mr. Krinkle. Oh, and Vespa. But it couldn't be her—she was receiving threatening texts like everyone else.

Could one of the others be working for LOTUS?

A ripple of pure cold shimmied up Max's spine. After that, sleep was slow in coming, and he lay staring at the ceiling for a long, long time.

Stanislav Dobasch's formal introduction to the orphans came the next morning, during a brand-new class: Elements of Disguise. Students filed into Roger Stones's dingy old classroom, which had been set up with rows of folding chairs and a long table at the front. It still smelled faintly of sweat socks and machine oil, even though the ex-instructor's gear had been hauled off somewhere.

An image of the cheerfully sarcastic teacher sprang to Max's mind. With a pang, he realized he still missed the man, despite having known him only a few days before he was gunned down at LOTUS headquarters. Worse, the guilt Max felt over his death lingered like the stench of decay at a rubbish dump.

He eyed the new teacher—gaunt and taciturn, where Stones had been burly and talkative.

No, Mr. Dobasch couldn't replace Mr. Stones, Max thought. Never in a million years. But maybe, just maybe, he could help the school survive.

"Greetings, comrades," said the Gravlaki, his manner as

somber as an undertaker on a blind date. "We have much work to do, and little time. But isn't that always the way in the spy biz?"

When the orphans continued to stare at him blankly, Mr. Dobasch cleared his throat and went on. "Disguise is the art of confusing your enemy, of seeming to be someone you're not. For this mission, disguise is crucial."

Wyatt raised a hand. "Will we get to wear wigs and rubber faces and talk in funny accents?"

The Gravlaki spy arched an eyebrow. "You have, perhaps, been watching too many movies."

"He should *be* in a movie," muttered Dermot, loud enough to be heard. "Something about freaks whose faces look like a monkey's bum."

Nikki Knucks snickered and bumped fists with Dermot. Wyatt blushed. Seeing their snide expressions, Max wondered if Nikki or Dermot might be the mole.

"But you have a point, comrade," said Mr. Dobasch. "Not the weasel-faced boy, but you, with the curls . . . ?"

"Wyatt," said Wyatt, turning to grin at a sullen Dermot.

"Ah, yes." The bony teacher unsnapped two clasps on a wooden box and folded down the sides to reveal trays of greasepaint, spirit gum, and other mysterious items. "At least two of us will need a thorough disguise for this job."

Hearing that, most of the orphans shot their hands into the air. Clearly, they'd woken up in a Halloween-y mood.

Which was appropriate, Max thought, given that today was October 31.

Mr. Dobasch waved down the raised hands. "I'm not looking for volunteers. Yes, I will teach you simple tricks to change your appearance. But for this mission, I have already decided who will wear disguises."

"Who is it, mon?" asked Tremaine.

"Patience," said the Gravlaki spy. He switched on a projector linked to a laptop computer and snapped his fingers. "Lights!"

After a student near the door had darkened the room, the teacher brought up a slide showing row upon row of faces— men and women both, from a range of ethnicities. Almost all had the glamour-challenged look of driver's-license photos. Almost all looked nerdy enough to be charter members of GeekyLove.com.

"These are the employees of RookTech," said Mr. Dobasch.

"And a sorry-looking lot they are," said Nikki. Some of the kids chuckled.

The teacher gestured at the images covering his wall. "They are also the ones whose faces are stored in the recognition bank, the ones who are approved to enter the building."

"Ahhh," said Vespa, awareness dawning. "Then the disguises will go to whoever looks the most like these workers."

Dobasch nodded. "Just so. The problem, of course, is that most of you are still children. Therefore, too short, too young . . ."

"Too obnoxious," said Tremaine, with a wink at Nikki. She sneered in reply.

"Nevertheless," said Mr. Dobasch, "I did not lose all my skills while working for those mental defectives at the embassy. I have found two close-enough matches. The first"—he advanced the slide to show a photo of Ivan Medved, a hollow-cheeked man with dark eyes—"is me."

Mr. Dobasch clicked again, and his own image appeared next to Medved's.

"Not bad," said Cinnabar. "With different hair and eye color, you could almost be twins."

The teacher sniffed. "As if I would be brothers with this walrus-kissing Ukrainian. Still, it works. And for the second match . . ."

Up flashed a slide of a teenage boy with spiky dark hair and cool-nerd glasses. The caption read: *Addison Rook.*

"Cute," said Vespa, "for a nerd. Who's he?"

"The son of the company's founders, and something of a boy genius," said Mr. Dobasch.

"But who here looks like this bloke?" asked Wyatt, glancing about the room.

The next slide showed an orphan's photo beside that of the boy genius.

"Me?" said Max. He shook his head. "You've got your work cut out for you."

CHAPTER 14

CHITTY CHITTY FLASHBANG

THE NEXT HOUR passed pleasantly enough in a crash course on fabricating a disguise. Of course, crafting a partial latex mask (for Max) and a wig (for Mr. Dobasch) would take them only halfway toward beating the RookTech security system. They also needed to steal or copy a key card.

But just as Mr. Dobasch was about to adjourn the class so he could grapple with that problem, Madame Chiffre rushed into the room.

"*Eh bien,*" she said, "I am glad you are all here. It will make ze announcement easier."

"What announcement?" asked Max.

Madame Chiffre beamed and patted the string of pearls around her neck. "We have found a way into Hercules Security." The gray-haired teacher approached Mr. Dobasch's laptop computer. "May I?"

He nodded, and Madame Chiffre quickly booted up a Web browser, opening it to the Hercules Security Web site. On the employees-only page, she entered a user name and password.

"It took us all night, but we found one employee who didn't change the default login," she said.

"So now their system's wide open to us?" asked Wyatt, eyes brightening. His avid grin reminded Max of a dog accidentally locked inside a butcher shop.

Madame Chiffre pursed her lips. "Sadly, no. That employee eez ze janitor."

Wyatt's face fell.

"But," she continued, "he did have enough access for us to find this."

She opened a Web page covered with cheesy clip art of vampires, black cats, and pirates. The headline read A HERCULES HALLOWEEN BASH.

"Brilliant," said Nikki. "So we know they celebrate Halloween."

Madame Chiffre lifted a finger. "Ah-ah-ah, mademoiselle. That eez not all we know."

"Oh no?" said Nikki.

"*Pas du tout,*" said the teacher. "If you will use ze eyes that God gave you, you will see that they are throwing a costume party tonight."

"Big whoop," said Dermot. He dug a finger into his ear and then sniffed it.

"Yes," said Madame Chiffre. "It will be, as you say, a big whoop—particularly for ze team that crashes ze party and steals ze information."

Now the class broke out in excited murmurs. "My kind of bash," said a beaming Wyatt. "Treats *and* illegal spying."

"Monsieur Dobasch," said Madame Chiffre. "Do you think perhaps you could help us with some costumes?"

The Gravlaki rubbed his neck and released an exasperated sigh. "Why not?" he said. "It's not like I've got anything else on my plate."

By lunchtime, Merry Sunshine resembled a three-ring circus more than an orphanage (except, of course, for the lack of big cats and clowns). Multiple projects hummed along in multiple locations, Hantai Annie barked commands like a ringmaster, and the staff and orphans raced about, juggling various tasks.

Bits and bobs of Halloween costumes lay scattered here and there, like the aftermath of a raging party in Frankenstein's castle. Mr. Dobasch dashed back and forth between computer and costume duty, prepping for two missions. Meanwhile, Victor Vazquez, Wyatt, and several girls were trying to hack deeper into RookTech and Hercules's computer systems, learning all they could before the go-team headed into the lions' den.

As for Max, he was immersing himself in the life and

times of Addison Rook, the sixteen-year-old boy genius he'd be impersonating. Luckily for Max, his subject possessed an ego so vast it made the Pacific Ocean look like a Li'l Squirt baby wading pool. The Internet simply overflowed with Rook's exploits. Regretfully, Max put aside his own personal projects—little things like sorting out why LOTUS wanted him and how they were bugging Merry Sunshine—in favor of the mission.

But whatever their task, whatever their frustrations, all of the orphanage's inhabitants were keenly aware of one thing: time was running short.

They had just over thirty-six hours to suss out RookTech's security, work up a plan, break in, and steal the mind-control device—all before LOTUS managed to beat them to the punch. Tempers frayed. Polite niceties flew out the window.

And in the midst of all this chaos, someone buzzed at the front door.

"Go see who's there," ordered Hantai Annie to the room at large. She was working at one of the library's computers with Vespa and Rashid.

"You mean me?" asked Vespa.

"I'll go," said Max, rising from another computer station. He stretched, scrubbed at his eyes with the heels of his hands, and padded out into the entryway to peer at the security monitor.

The face of a Chinese Johnny Depp gazed up at the

camera lens, backed by two hefty bodyguards. All were frowning.

"It's Mr. Elbow," Max called out.

"*Souka?*" Hantai Annie muttered to herself in Japanese. "*Chotto mate.* I coming." And in moments she stood beside Max, pressing the intercom button. "Yes, Elbow-*san*? How can I help?"

"You can let Mr. Elbow in, of course," said Mr. Elbow. "It's bloody cold out here, and he wants his progress report."

Hantai Annie released the intercom button, sighed, and unlocked both sets of locks to let their client in. When she opened the outer door and revealed the trio on the porch, Max saw another surprise waiting in the wings: Mr. Krinkle. The marshmallow man strode up the walk behind them, waving a hand.

"This can't be good," Max murmured.

The director ushered her client and his bodyguards into the holding corridor. For a second, she hesitated with a hand on the outer door, as if contemplating slamming it in the government inspector's face.

"I say!" called Mr. Krinkle. "Hold that door!"

Hantai Annie's reluctance showed in the set of her shoulders, but she did as the man asked. Max shared her concern. This chance meeting between client and inspector carried more potential for disaster than juggling nitroglycerine while clog dancing on a burning boat. One wrong word from Mr. Elbow, one mention of a school for spies, and the inspector would close down Merry Sunshine faster than a chop from a butcher's cleaver.

And then?

Bye-bye, orphanage. Hello, foster home.

The little group tromped through the narrow corridor between inner and outer doors, with the ponytailed body-guard taking the lead. Max's nerves quivered like a too-tight guitar string.

"You . . ." Ponytail Man squinted suspiciously at Max, one hand reaching for his underarm holster. "What are you doing?"

"Um, holding the door?" said Max.

"Oh." The man slipped inside and scanned the entryway. Finding it empty, he reached over to grip the door's edge. "That's my job."

Max stepped back to make room for the rest of the visitors, keeping a careful watch to see that they didn't try to plant any bugs. He noticed that Hantai Annie had seized Mr. Krinkle's arm and was attempting to steer him directly into the dining room.

"So, how goes the mission?" asked Mr. Elbow loudly.

Krinkle's head slewed around. "Mission? What mission?"

"Um." Max stepped between them. "He means Merry Sunshine's mission of rescuing orphans and giving them a better life, of course." He winced. Even to his ears, this sounded hopelessly cheesy.

Mr. Krinkle nodded in approval, but Mr. Elbow looked

like someone had stirred his cappuccino with a rat's tail. "That is most certainly not—"

"Elbow-*san*," Hantai Annie interrupted. "You and your men please wait in my office. I'll come soon."

The billionaire pursed his lips and tugged on a pair of surgical gloves. "Mr. Elbow doesn't like to wait," he said. "Tick-tock, time is money." But, having made his point, he and his bodyguards drifted toward the office door.

"Not *the* Mr. Elbow," said Henry Krinkle. He planted his pudgy self in the hall and resisted Annie's efforts to guide him away. "Not Reginald Demetrius Elbow?"

"Is there more than one?" said Mr. Elbow. "Mr. Elbow doesn't think so."

An awed look spread like melted butter across the government inspector's doughy face. Breaking away from Hantai Annie, he lunged toward the billionaire with hand extended. "It's such an honor, sir."

"Mr. Elbow don't shake," said Ponytail Man, brushing his hand aside and blocking his way.

"On account of the G-word," said Mustache Man.

Mr. Krinkle frowned. "Goiters?"

"Naw," said Ponytail Man

"Gout?"

"Naw, naw. You know—*germs*."

Hearing it spoken, the billionaire blanched and glanced about nervously. "Mr. Elbow needs Purell," he said.

"Told you never to mention the G-word," Mustache Man

muttered to his partner. With an efficiency born of much practice, he produced the hand-sanitizer bottle and squirted it into his boss's gloved palms.

"But why is Mr. Elbow visiting—" Krinkle began.

"Elbow-*san* is client." Hantai Annie caught his arm and began dragging him off once more. "Clients need privacy."

Max thought that would shut Mr. Krinkle up. But no. At the dining room door, the puffy man pulled away from Hantai Annie one last time.

"You're doing a beautiful, beautiful thing," said the inspector, chin trembling with emotion. "You'll make some orphan very happy."

Puzzlement darkened Mr. Elbow's chocolate-drop eyes. Before he could speak, Max jumped in.

"Oh yes," he said. "All us orphans are thrilled to pieces with what he's doing. Absolutely chuffed."

"Absolutely," said Vespa, beaming an innocent smile from the library doorway.

With that, Elbow and bodyguards disappeared into the office while Hantai Annie finally managed to shove Krinkle into the dining room. Vespa nodded after the inspector.

"What does he want?" she asked.

"To give me a heart attack," said Max.

Somehow, the S.P.I.E.S. staff managed to keep Mr. Krinkle busy and away from Mr. Elbow until the billionaire had left the premises. But that was only part of the problem. The government inspector insisted on roaming about observing the orphans' activities, so they shunted him from work group to work group, each pretending to study something academic while he was in the room. But all were aware that time was running short.

When their ruse grew old, Miss Moorthy took the man for an extended tour of the orphanage's outer reaches (leaving out the spy in the cellar). Meanwhile, Victor Vazquez yielded to Wyatt's repeated requests and convened an impromptu class in spy gadgetry—seeing as how a device or two might come in handy on the upcoming missions.

Max, Wyatt, Vespa, Nikki, and a few others gathered in the garage for the lesson. Chilly, damp, and smelling faintly of paraffin oil, the space was not a luxury suite at the Ritz by any stretch. But it was practical. Stepping inside, Max couldn't help but recall poor dead Roger Stones, as this had been his Surveillance Training classroom.

He grimaced. Memories lurked everywhere.

"You ever think about Mr. Stones?" he asked Wyatt as they were settling onto the metal folding chairs.

"All the time, mate," said Wyatt. "The way he went . . ." The blond boy shivered. "I see it in nightmares sometimes."

"Do you ever wonder . . . ?" Max began.

"What?"

Max caught Vespa looking their way and shook his head. "Never mind." He'd almost asked if Wyatt thought a spy's spirit could haunt the place where he used to work, but he didn't want to seem like a complete nutter in front of the new girl.

Victor Vazquez lugged a couple of boxes into the room, set them on a workbench, and began removing tins of chemicals. When he'd lined them all up, he brought out a six-pack of Coke.

"Now we're talking," said Wyatt. "Refreshments and gadgets. Totally bonzer class!"

Mr. Vazquez allowed himself a wry smile. "In this case, the refreshments *are* the gadgets. My friends, today we will turn something that rots your teeth into something that can, if only temporarily, blind you."

"Huh?" said Jensen.

"Flash grenades from Coke cans," said the teacher. "Shan, Vespa, will you assist?"

Jumping to their feet, the girls rushed to help Mr. Vazquez empty the soft drinks into a pitcher and carefully saw off the tops of the cans. While they dried the cans' insides with a hair dryer, the teacher continued his explanation over its whirring.

"The flash grenade, or flashbang, is not designed to kill your enemy, just disorient him," he said. "When you mix aluminum and an oxidizer, and then ignite it? Flash! Bang!"

"Hence the name," said Max.

Wyatt grinned. "I bet that thing goes off like Chinese New Year's!"

Nikki shot them both a dirty look—her crush on the teacher was fiercer than a bagful of wolverines.

"Precisely," said Mr. Vazquez. "Now, it would be irresponsible for us to give you younger students guns—"

"Aw," whined Jensen.

"—but you might encounter a situation where a brief distraction could save your hide," the teacher continued. "That's where these come in. Everyone gather 'round and watch closely."

He passed out safety glasses and demonstrated the process of reinforcing the cans, adding the chemicals, and setting the ignition trigger.

"Be particularly careful with this step," Mr. Vazquez warned them.

"Why's that?" asked Shan.

Vespa smirked and caught Max's gaze. "Because it's hot stuff," she purred.

Max laughed nervously, feeling a flutter in his chest and a wide smile on his face. Shan narrowed her eyes at him, and he looked away guiltily—even though he hadn't done anything.

Girls were truly confusing.

"Now, I'll need someone with a delicate touch to help me with this last part," said Mr. Vazquez.

"Me," said Shan.

"No, me," said Vespa, stepping forward.

"*I'll* do it," Nikki growled, elbowing the other girls aside. Vespa shoved back, hard.

A voice came from the doorway: "I say, what class is this one?"

Victor Vazquez turned to answer Mr. Krinkle, and Max saw it all unfold in an instant without being able to lift a finger.

"It's . . ." Mr. Vazquez began.

Nikki stumbled back, off balance from Vespa's push. Her elbow grazed the Coke can.

It toppled, setting off the trigger.

Then: *Flash!*—an explosion of blinding light; and

BANG!—a deafening clap of sound.

". . . chemistry class," Mr. Vazquez said. But nobody in the room could hear him.

CHAPTER 15

TEENS AND CHEMICALS DON'T MIX

IN A BLINK, Max's whole world had turned to white light. No shadows, no shapes. Just white. His ears rang like Big Ben at midnight, and his head felt like the inside of an industrial clothes dryer—spinning so fast he couldn't tell which way was up.

He tried to take a step, and found himself toppling sideways, cannoning off a hard chair. After he hit the floor, he lay with his cheek on the cool concrete, waiting for his wits to return. Had he been brutally maimed? Had his eyes and ears been blown off?

No clue. Tentatively, Max ran a hand over his features.

Eyes? Check. Nose and mouth? Functioning. Ears? Still attached. Nothing was missing.

His eyes streamed with tears. After ages of vigorous blinking, Max found he was beginning to make out dim shapes around him, like actors doing a play behind heavy gauze curtains. Slowly, slowly, the world came back into focus.

The other orphans were scattered about the garage, some sprawled on the floor, some leaning on a worktable for support. Max pushed up to a sitting position and rested his back against a chair.

The ringing in his ears was subsiding, bit by bit, but now it was replaced by a sort of shooshing sound, like someone spraying an enormous can of whipped cream. Turning his head, he made out Victor Vazquez shooting a fire extinguisher at gouts of flame dancing along the workbench. The fire was doused in seconds.

The next sound he heard held fewer pleasant associations. In fact, absolutely none at all.

"Completely unacceptable!" Mr. Krinkle yelled from somewhere near the door. His voice reached Max as if through layers of blankets. "You're putting orphans at risk, and I will not tolerate it."

Levering himself up to standing, Max noticed that Mr. Vazquez was ignoring the government inspector. Instead, the teacher made the rounds of his students, checking each one for injuries.

From the floor beside Max came a rusty chuckle.

"Wowzer!" said Wyatt. "So that's living on the Coke side of life." The blond boy's smile shone porcelain white in his soot-stained face. He seemed unhurt.

"Do you hear me?" roared Mr. Krinkle, who was leaning against the door frame for support. "I have half a mind to shut this place down this instant."

"He's right," Max said in Wyatt's ear.

"About what?"

"He does have half a mind."

Max wobbled his way over to Vespa, who lay on the floor, just beginning to stir. Her face was stained even blacker than Wyatt's, and her lavender blouse had gone mostly charcoal gray. Max's heartbeat stuttered. Was she . . . ? He knelt and gingerly touched her shoulder.

"Are you okay?" he asked.

She rose onto an elbow, offering a tentative smile. "Told you it was hot stuff."

Max helped her sit up. Vespa assured him that she was completely undamaged, "except for my hairdo," which as far as Max could tell, was the same tousled mass of blond curls it had been before, with a few singed bits.

Mr. Krinkle stomped to the center of the room. "You're not treating this with sufficient gravity," he scolded Mr. Vazquez. "You just broke several pages' worth of regulations, and I, for one—"

Something in Max snapped. His own personal flashbang

detonated in his chest, and the heat surged up into his face. He rocketed to his feet.

"If you didn't care more about your bleeding regulations than about human beings," he cried, "you'd see that Mr. Vazquez *is* treating this seriously. He's making sure we're all right."

"Now see here—" the inspector began. But Max wasn't finished.

"And if you had half the sense God gave a lemur, you'd shut your gob and help him."

Wyatt hooted. "Too right, mate!"

Mr. Krinkle's mouth gaped like a salmon marooned in the Sahara. "Well," he huffed, "well, I never . . ."

Max gave a wordless growl and spun away to help Mr. Vazquez with Nikki. They each took an arm. The beefy girl sat up slowly, glassy-eyed. Her flyaway red hair looked even wilder than usual, and scorch marks covered her T-shirt.

"Whuzza?" she mumbled, shaking her head groggily.

"Don't move," said Mr. Vazquez, holding her hand. "You were closest to the blast. Are you injured?"

Her gaze focused on him and a soft expression crept over her usually belligerent features. Then Nikki noticed Max clasping her other arm and backhanded him away.

"Clear off," she growled. "I'm weak." Her eyes returned to Victor Vazquez's chiseled features.

Max snorted. "She'll be all right."

As it turned out, Nikki had sustained the most serious damage of anyone in the room—some powder burns on her arm that required salve and a bandage. But from the way she gazed at Mr. Vazquez as he tended her, it was clear she was feeling no pain.

The same could not be said for Hantai Annie Wong.

When Mr. Krinkle took Vazquez, Max, Wyatt, and Nikki to her office to report what had happened, the director unleashed a string of what Max assumed were very dirty words in Japanese (or one of her six other languages).

Stopping for breath at last, she steadied herself and asked Mr. Vazquez, *"Hontou ka?* Nikki is only one hurt?"

"Yes, Director," said Victor Vazquez. "The rest were a bit shaken up, but there are no other injuries."

"Good."

"Humph!" Mr. Krinkle planted his fists on his hips, giving him the appearance of a giant sweet potato with handles. "Injuries are the least of your problems. You, sir, are a dreadful chemistry teacher. On behalf of the orphans, I shall have you banned from this facility and from the teaching profession."

Max bristled. "Why not ask us orphans what *we* want?"

"Yeah," said Nikki. "Mr. V is the best teacher here, and that explosion was totally my fault."

"That's true," said Wyatt. "I saw it."

"He's incompetent," huffed Mr. Krinkle.

Hantai Annie's eyes narrowed. "He has master's degrees from Stanford *and* MIT."

"He's careless," said Mr. Krinkle.

"The only reason this happened is because *you* interrupted him," said Max.

Mr. Vazquez stepped forward and raised a calming hand. "It's true that I was temporarily distracted," he said, "but I accept full responsibility. The children were under my supervision."

Hantai Annie clasped her hands behind her back. Her frown looked carved into her face. "Teens and chemicals," she said. *"Abunai.* Dangerous mix. We very, very lucky nothing worse happened, Victor-*san.*"

"Lucky?!" Pop-eyed, Mr. Krinkle goggled at them in disbelief. "You are anything *but* lucky. Mrs. Wong, you are running a decidedly peculiar operation here, and I'll have you know that as of this moment, it's hanging by a thread."

"That's not fair!" Nikki cried, her cheeks flushed. "After all those ratbag foster families I had, this place is like a . . . a sanctuary. It's the best thing that ever happened to me."

Max gaped. In all his weeks at the orphanage, this was the first time he'd heard Nikki express any honest emotion other than contempt.

Even Mr. Krinkle was affected. His tone softened. "Yes, well, orphans don't always know what's best. That's why the government keeps an eye on things."

"*We* know what is best," said Hantai Annie. Her quiet voice rang with intensity. "I hire good people—Victor-*san* is good people. We all have orphans' best interests at heart."

Mr. Krinkle pursed his lips. "This place is like no orphanage I've ever seen."

"That doesn't make it bad," said Max. "That just makes it different."

The inspector eyed him briefly, then returned his attention to Hantai Annie. "I have a few more interviews to conduct. You will have my decision tomorrow."

"Give us a hint?" asked Wyatt.

"I wouldn't be signing any long-term leases," said Mr. Krinkle. "Good day to you all." And with that, he waddled from the room, closing the door behind him.

Gloom hung heavier than London fog in January. For a long stretch, no one spoke.

"He wouldn't really close us down," Wyatt said in a small voice. "Would he?"

Hantai Annie cleared her throat. "That is tomorrow's problem. This is today."

Clapping his hands, Victor Vazquez said, "Back to work, my friends. No matter what happens, we have two missions to prepare for." He led the way out of the office, trailed by Nikki and Wyatt. But as Max reached the threshold, Hantai Annie bade him to stay.

"Why?" he asked suspiciously.

"*Suware*," she said. "Sit."

Max perched on the edge of the visitor's chair beside her desk. The director got straight to the point.

"Why do you go see prisoner?" she asked.

"How did you—" Max began. "Was it Nikki?"

Hantai Annie tented her fingers and watched him. "You forget where you are, Max-*kun*. I knew already. Why?"

"To help stop LOTUS," said Max.

"He is dangerous man," she said. "A top agent. It's not safe for you."

"But it's safe to keep him in our cellar like a sack of potatoes?" said Max. He tried to put his reasoning into words. "I thought maybe . . ."

"What?"

"Maybe I could turn him—or at least learn some intel that'd help us."

A corner of the director's lip twitched, in what might have been the ghost of a smile. "Madame Chiffre, tough interrogator, cannot get him to crack. And you think he talks to you?"

Max ducked his head. When she put it that way, his move sounded as daft as a kindergartner expecting to fly a jumbo jet.

"I wanted to find out more about LOTUS, uncover their plans," said Max. "You never tell us anything." He hated that he sounded like a resentful little kid.

"We protecting you," said Hantai Annie.

"Maybe I don't need protection," Max blurted. "Maybe you need *my* help. Somehow, LOTUS is getting information about us, and I think—"

The office phone jangled loudly, making Max jump. Hantai Annie raised a finger, said, *"Chotto shizuka ni,"* and answered.

Upon hearing the voice on the other end, she grew as still as a panther waiting to pounce, all coiled energy. Her face revealed nothing.

"Yes, I know who you are," she said. "Yes . . . he is."

Max looked a question at her, but the director's full attention was riveted on the phone call. Something she heard brought her up short.

"Uso daro!" she said. "What you mean?" Hantai Annie's eyes widened, and she rose to her feet. "Where? When?" She scribbled something on a piece of notepaper. *"Wakatta.* Understood."

"What?" said Max, standing now and desperately curious.

The director's face and tone turned severe. "See you then. And no funny business." She hung up the receiver.

"Well?" said Max. "Do you tell me, or do I burst a blood vessel guessing?"

Her ebony eyes glittered. "Hostage swap. With LOTUS, tonight, in capital."

Max frowned. "A swap? Did they just capture someone?" A sudden thought chilled him. "It's not my dad, is it?"

"No."

"Then who?" asked Max.

"Roger Stones."

For a moment, Max thought his hearing had been damaged in the flashbang blast after all. "Sorry? For a second, I thought you said—"

"Roger Stones," Hantai Annie repeated. "He's alive."

CHAPTER 16

ENTERING
THE DRAGON

CINNABAR JONES was not a happy camper. Not only would she have to share a costume with Nikki Knucks and her grubby little mate Dermot, but Cinnabar's sister, Jazz, wasn't even coming along on the Hercules Security mission. Jazz's expression when she learned that the sisters were being separated yet again?

Heartbreaking.

"Cinn, what do you mean I'm not going?" Jazz's brown eyes were wide and haunted.

"They need you here."

"But—"

Cinnabar brushed a curl back from her older sister's forehead. "We won't be long," she said. "You'll hardly notice I'm gone."

"No, I know," said Jazz. But her hands gripped Cinnabar's

like a drowning woman's. "It's just . . ." Her voice trailed off, and Cinn knew the rest of that sentence was *I don't know if I'll ever see you again.*

Cinnabar suppressed a sigh. It was excruciating to leave, with Jazz's condition still so delicate.

And the cherry on top? Max and the other team were going to the hostage swap with that bottle blonde, Vespa da Costa. The girl wasn't even trained, for crying out loud, except maybe in heavy-handed flirting.

It bothered Cinnabar. And it bothered her that it bothered her.

Max wasn't her boyfriend, after all. Even though they'd been through a lot together, she had no claim on him. And honestly, he'd been a bit of a jerk lately about Cinnabar's need to spend time with her sister. He didn't seem to get how fragile Jazz was since being rescued from LOTUS, how much she needed her sister's presence.

But still, that was no reason for him to get all goo-goo-eyed over a tart who probably learned that fake Brazilian accent from a rerun of *Girls Gone Wild: Rio Edition.*

Since the hostage-swap team was headed into the capital, they had to leave promptly in one of the school's two Range Rovers. Cinnabar nearly collided with Max as he was clattering down the stairs to join his group.

"Oh, hi," she said.

"Hi," he answered, pulling to a halt.

Max immediately buried his hands in his jeans pockets, hunched his shoulders, and examined the stairwell carpeting.

"So . . . Mr. Stones is alive?" she said after a pause that seemed to stretch the length of a bad foreign movie. "That's brilliant."

"Yeah," said Max, nodding vigorously. "Brilliant."

Another longish pause. He glanced up at her with a searching look, like he wanted to ask something important. But all he said was, "They're probably waiting for me. Good luck on your mission."

"Yeah," she said. "You, too."

He wheeled and clomped off down the stairs.

You, too? she thought. That was the best you could come up with? Cinnabar shook her head, disgusted with herself, and went on upstairs to help her group prepare.

Maybe after this whole thing is over, she thought, maybe then I'll have the nerve to sit down and really talk with Max about feelings and stuff.

Or maybe I'll just chicken out again.

Three hours later, night had fallen and it was Halloween proper. A gibbous moon leered down on small knots of costumed revelers and the crisp air smelled of wood smoke and petrol. Cinnabar's team had ducked into an alleyway a half block down from the Hercules Security building, one of those sleek chrome-and-smoked-glass structures that looked as though it should contain wizards of high finance.

Mr. Vazquez and Stanislav Dobasch gathered their team into a huddle and passed out their bags of tricks. Tremaine, Cinn had to admit, was looking pretty fine as a dreadlocked pirate, while Catarina was rocking her Goth angel outfit. The rest of the students, however—Wyatt, Cinnabar, Nikki, and Dermot—were dressed in simple cat-burglar black, ready to don their ridiculous costume over the top of it.

"Do we have to?" Nikki whined. "I'd make a much better ninja."

Ninja? thought Cinnabar. Try troll.

Mr. V looked like he wanted to roll his eyes, but his voice remained mild. "We've been over this. Only those tall enough to pass for adults will wear their own costumes. As for the rest of you . . ." He and Mr. Dobasch unrolled a bundle of red, yellow, and gold fabric done up in a scaly pattern.

"Type-two blue blub," said Mr. Dobasch. At least that's what Cinn thought he said—the massive beard of his Evil Dictator costume swallowed so many of his words. (On reflection, he might have been saying, "Time to suit up.") By contrast, Mr. V's Zorro costume was far more practical and attractive.

With a great deal of grumbling, the four orphans donned their red-and-gold matching leggings.

"Who goes in front, then?" asked Dermot peevishly. "I don't want to be breathing nobody's fumes under there, if you get my drift."

"Nikki first, as she's the tallest," said Mr. V. "Then Cinnabar, Dermot, and Wyatt."

"Why do I have to bring up the rear?" said Wyatt.

"If the shoe fits . . ." Nikki sneered.

Wyatt made a face at her but didn't say anything. Then they all lined up in order, holding the waist of the person in front as if their trousers were radioactive, while the teachers draped the Chinese dragon costume over them. The fabric covered the orphans to midthigh.

"Cut that out," said Nikki as she writhed under Cinnabar's touch.

"Ooh," said Cinn. "Ticklish, are we?"

"Not a bit of it," growled the redheaded girl. "You pinched me, that's all."

Lastly, Mr. Dobasch attached the papier-mâché dragon head, and Nikki gripped its support poles in her hands. Hunched over and half blinded by the costume, Cinnabar could see nothing but Nikki's legs and a strip of the gritty brick alleyway beneath them.

She heard Tremaine laugh. "Nice mug, Nikki Knucks," he said. "It's actually an improvement."

Nikki snarled and clacked the dragon's jaws at him.

Cinnabar noticed that Dermot's grip on her waist had migrated southward. She reached back and slapped one of his hands. "Keep 'em higher, ferret-face!" she snapped.

Dermot snickered, but he obeyed. "Sorry. Your bum's so skinny, I didn't notice. Ow! Stop pinching me!"

"I'm not—" Cinnabar began.

"I am," said Wyatt. "Hands off of Cinn."

Dermot's voice took on a mocking tone. "Ooh, is she your girlfriend, then? Ow! Cut it out!"

Cinnabar gritted her teeth. If that slimy Dermot tried any more funny stuff, he'd learn just how painful a well-placed back kick could be.

"How long must we wear this thing?" Cinnabar demanded.

"Just until we get through the party and into a quiet room," said Mr. V. "You know the plan. Com links on, every-one. Here we go!"

Cinnabar saw his shiny black boots tromp past, leading the way. She slipped the communications device into her ear and felt Dermot take a hand off her waist to do the same.

"Come on, you lot," growled Nikki. "Let's get this dragon on the road."

Clumsily at first, they set off. Dermot trod on Cinnabar's heels a couple of times, and they all collided with Nikki when she stopped short at a street crossing, but the orphans soon got the hang of it. Before long, the concrete sidewalk gave way to granite steps, and they stood outside the Hercules Security building.

Mr. V's voice whispered through the com link in her ear, and a shiver danced down Cinnabar's spine. "This is the trickiest part. I don't know how much security they'll have up front, so stay sharp."

Tremaine held the door for them (Cinn spotted his pirate

boots as they passed), and the dragon followed Mr. V into the lobby.

"May I help you?" said a brusque female voice.

That was their cue. "Trick or treat!" chorused the students.

"This isn't a residence, sir," said the guard. Her voice was frostier than an icicle farm.

Mr. V chuckled. "And a Happy Halloween to you," he purred. "Arnie in accounting said it would be all right to bring the kids to the party for a little while."

"Arnie . . . ?"

"Armom Bipnip," said Mr. Dobasch, in his beard-muffled voice.

"Arnold Dudnik," Mr. V translated.

Cinnabar could hear a muffled bass thumping somewhere nearby. Apparently, Halloween at Hercules was in full swing—getting into the spirit like the rest of the city.

"Mr. Dudnik?" The female guard sounded doubtful. "I'll have to call him first."

"Don't bother," said Mr. V. "He'll be at the party. Second floor, right?" He began walking off.

"Sir!"

"Yes?" said Mr. V, with a hint of steel in his voice.

"I don't even know your name," said the female guard.

"Robert Garcia from RookTech." Cinn could hear the threat in his tone. "One of your biggest clients and an invited guest."

The guard spluttered. "Well, but I—"

"Ah, let 'em through," said a quiet male voice. Another guard, Cinnabar surmised. "We don't want trouble with Mrs. Helling—that's her account."

"Excellent," said Mr. V. "Come along, children!" Heels clicking on the marble floor, he strode past the security desk.

Ahead of them, a loud ding sounded. Then laughter and voices, as if people were exiting an elevator.

"Ooh, scary dragon!" said a man teasingly.

An uncomfortable pause yawned.

"Trick or treat!" Cinnabar cried. She slapped Nikki's back twice. "Trick or treat!" Nikki echoed, clacking the dragon's jaws. The teasing man chortled, and several pairs of fancy dress shoes strolled past, just visible from under the costume.

They entered the elevator, and the doors whisked closed.

"Don't you *ever* hit me like that," Nikki rasped.

"Then pick up your cues faster," Cinnabar retorted.

As they rode upward, Mr. Vazquez's murmur came over the com link. "Careful. The lift may be monitored. Stay in character."

The chime sounded again, the doors opened, and the music hit them like a fist to the solar plexus. *Boom, boom, boom!* The relentless beat of the electro-house—or maybe progressive-house music? Cinn wasn't sure—throbbed, vibrating down to her bones. People laughed and shouted, straining to be heard above it.

Cinnabar began bobbing in place. She shook Nikki. "Come on, dance! We're meant to be partygoers."

With a grumble, Nikki Knucks began swaying. From the corner of an eye, Cinn saw Dermot kicking his feet out awkwardly. Who knew what Wyatt was doing back at the tail end. He'd never been much for dancing.

The dragon wove its way into the mob of employees and guests. Cinnabar spotted Roman sandals, Spider-Man boots, spike heels, bare feet, and once, cloven hooves, passing through her field of vision against the boring charcoal-gray carpet. Many times, people jostled them or petted the dragon's back and guffawed.

"Niiice lizard!" slurred a woman in fur-covered boots. When Nikki snapped the dragon jaws at her, the boots quickly backed away.

"Corduroy under light," came Mr. Dobasch's voice over the com link.

"Huh?" said Cinnabar and Wyatt together.

Some beard-scrapy sounds, then more clearly, "Corridor on the right."

"Let's take it," said Mr. V.

It was hotter than a busload of boy bands under the fabric. Sweat trickled down Cinnabar's face, and she hoped they'd be able to ditch the wretched costume soon.

At last the dragon turned into a less crowded hall, and the music eased up its pressure. "Stairwell ahead," murmured

Mr. Vazquez, his voice on the com link sultry enough for a late-night DJ. "We'll head up to the fourth-floor offices and—"

"Jolly good costume," a deep, posh voice interrupted. A pair of expensive leather shoes stopped off to one side. "Who's under the flap, then?"

"My kids," said Mr. V. "Arnie said I could bring them for a little bit."

"Oh, really?" said the man. "You must have just missed him—he's in the other room."

"What a shame," said Mr. Vazquez. "But I'm sure we'll see him later."

The leather shoes shifted. "Oh, he'll go simply mad over this. I'll fetch him; don't move a muscle." And the shoes retreated toward the party room.

Cinnabar's heart climbed into her throat. Would Arnie unmask them?

Then Mr. V said, "Make for the stairs. Hurry!"

CHAPTER 17

HACKER BOY AND EVIL JESTER

THE DRAGON TRIED to hustle along, but Cinnabar's feet tangled with Nikki's, and they stumbled, nearly falling.

"Watch it, git!" Nikki snapped.

"Pick up your feet, cow!" Cinnabar shot back.

"Girls, girls," said Mr. V. "Run now, fight afterward."

Somehow, they managed to clomp down the hall and into the stairwell. The instant they reached the other side of the door, Cinnabar flung the costume off her shoulders. Nikki stood before her, glowering. It was a toss-up which face looked more horrific—Nikki's, or that of the dragon head in her hands.

"Later," said the redheaded girl.

"Count on it," Cinnabar replied.

The four orphans rolled up the costume fabric and stuffed it inside the head. Up the stairs they pounded, following Tremaine and the adults.

"Did we lose Catarina?" asked Wyatt.

A Greek-accented voice floated over the com link. "I'm searching the third floor. Sweet of you to worry."

Wyatt blushed. Of course, he blushed at the sight of a girl's shadow, thought Cinnabar.

"Be careful, Catarina," said Mr. Vazquez. "And stay in contact."

"Roger that, Mr. V," she replied.

The group paused on the fourth-floor landing and stashed the dragon costume behind a rubbish can. "Let's break you into teams of two," said Mr. Vazquez. "Work fast . . . who knows how long we've got."

Cinnabar stood beside Wyatt, and Dermot joined Nikki. "Think I'll go single-o, mon," said Tremaine.

Mr. Vazquez nodded. "Fair enough. I'll take Helling's office. The rest of you spread out and search for the plans. Start with accounting and customer service."

"Dibs on accounting," said Nikki.

"You can keep it," said Cinnabar.

Mr. V regarded them all with a sober expression. "And if you get caught, remember . . ."

Wyatt held up his bag. "Use the tricks, not the treats."

"*Udachi*, everyone," said Mr. Dobasch from behind his pile of whiskers.

"'Blue budgie'?" said Dermot, frowning in puzzlement. "I swear I can't understand him."

The Gravlaki spy pulled the fake beard away from his face. "It's Russian. Means good luck. If we are all killed, it's been a pleasure working with you."

Cinnabar and Wyatt swapped an uneasy glance.

Dobasch shook his head, smiling wolfishly. "This sure beats playing nursemaid for that son-of-a-Cossack Baghirov."

Replacing his beard and turning the door handle, the Gravlaki led the way onto the fourth floor. They entered a symphony in beige. Beige carpet, beige cubicles, beige walls—everything the color of sand and shortbread.

Wyatt caught Cinnabar's eye. "Because nothing says security like beige, eh?"

They followed the others down the passage leading between a row of offices and the maze of worker-bee cubicles that filled most of the floor. Nikki and Dermot peeled off almost immediately and began picking the lock of an office door labeled BRADLEY STOAT—VP ACCOUNTING.

Tremaine and Mr. Dobasch each chose other offices, and Mr. V made for the corner suite, which turned out to belong to Mrs. Helling. When Cinn stopped at the office next door, Wyatt took her arm.

"Come on," he said.

"Where are we going?" she asked.

He nodded at the cubicles. "Out where the people who do the *real* work sit."

"And how do you know that?"

Wyatt smirked. "One of my foster mums was a cubicle worker."

She shrugged. "Lead on."

He threaded into the maze, reading nameplates on the partitions, until he reached a wall whose plaque read NATHALIE PYGG-GWYNNE, PROJECT LEADER. Wyatt hooked a thumb at her desk. "The ridgy-didge," he said.

"The which?" said Cinnabar.

"Genuine article," said Wyatt, stepping into the cramped little cubicle. "Guaranteed, this sheila's working harder than a sheep tick on a kangaroo buck."

"Sheila?" She quirked an eyebrow. "Her name's Nathalie."

"A sheila's a woman," said Wyatt.

"Not around me, it's not," said Cinn. "Get to work, Hacker Boy."

Wyatt plugged a flash drive into the machine and dropped into a faux-leather chair while the computer booted up.

Drawing her lock-picking kit from a pocket, Cinnabar selected a couple of the tools. She cocked her head and frowned at the filing cabinet. Just on the off chance, she tried one of the drawers before picking the lock. It slid open.

"Because nothing says security like unlocked file drawers, eh?" she said.

Wyatt chuckled. His fingers danced over the keyboard.

She began systematically flipping through the folders, looking for any mention of RookTech. Employee records, expense reports, and gobs of interoffice memos were all she found.

Cinnabar closed the top drawer and pawed through the second. More forms, more blah-blah-blah. But no client job records. She blew out a sigh. If they didn't find the RookTech security layout tonight, tomorrow's mission stood a very high chance of going pear-shaped, landing the go-team in prison or worse.

A picture rose unbidden to her mind, of Max in a gray prison tracksuit. Cinnabar bit her lip. He might be a total prat sometimes, but she didn't want to see him behind bars. Still, if only he could be a bit more sensitive . . .

"Well, stone the crows!" said Wyatt.

Cinnabar looked up from inspecting the bottom drawer. "Found something?"

He cackled. "I'm as flash as a rat with a gold tooth!"

"And that means . . . ?"

"I'm in," said Wyatt. "For a security project leader, her password is pretty weak."

Finishing up with the third drawer and finding nothing, Cinn came to stand behind the blond boy. A door closed somewhere nearby, telling her that one of the others had completed their office exploration.

"Let's see," said Wyatt, searching the computer files. "RookTech bids . . . RookTech correspondence . . . ah!"

"What is it?"

"There's something poky in her chair." Wyatt shifted to one side and prodded the seat cushion beneath him. "How does this woman sit here?"

"Wyatt . . ." said Cinnabar in a warning tone.

He held up a hand. "Right, right. Back to the grindstone." Wyatt hit some more keys and scrolled down the page. "That's the stuff: RookTech job specs. Now I'll just copy the—"

"Here, now!" A sharp voice behind them made Cinnabar jump. "What are you lot doing in this office?"

A tall, pale man with bushy eyebrows stood blocking the cubicle entrance. His scowl contrasted sharply with his floppy jester's cap, black-and-white harlequin outfit, and mock scepter topped with a tiny jester head.

Wyatt stood, fascination trumping his fear. "What are *you* meant to be?"

"An evil jester."

Wyatt stifled a laugh. The man grimaced. "Nobody gets it," he said, half to himself. Then his voice sharpened. "Answer my question! This place is off-limits." Goofy though he might look, the jester was bigger and stronger than both Wyatt and Cinnabar, and a serious threat.

Cinnabar tried for a weary tone. "We got bored at the party, so we thought we'd see if anyone had video games on their computer." She sent a quick glance at Wyatt, prodding him to play along.

"Uh, yeah," said Wyatt. "But not Tetris. Tetris is lame."

The man glanced past them at the screen and his eyes narrowed. "How did you log on? All our computers are password-protected."

Wyatt cut his eyes over at Cinn. "Someone, uh, gave it to us?"

"Miss Pygg-Gwynne is an old friend of my father's," Cinnabar said. "She told us it'd be all right."

"*Mrs.* Pygg-Gwynne is the meanest crosspatch I've ever known," said the evil jester. "She has no friends. Her husband died to get away from her—even her cats don't like her."

Cinnabar's smile froze. "My father has really, really low standards in friends?"

Wyatt edged closer to the computer.

"You're coming with me," the man said, reaching for her right arm. "We're going straight to security."

She slumped in defeat. "All right, just let me get my bag. . . ."

Evil Jester's fingers closed around her biceps. "Hang on. How do I know that's *your* bag?" The mock scepter suddenly seemed like a club in his other fist.

Cinn kept her cool. "Because," she said, "it says 'trick or treat' on the side. See?" She held up the sack.

The man's eyebrows rose. "So it does. Come along now, both of you."

Where was the rest of their team? Cinnabar wondered. This would be a particularly handy time for them to appear. She dragged her feet, stalling.

Surreptitiously, Wyatt tried to remove his flash drive from the computer.

"Get away from there, you," said Evil Jester.

"Who, me?" said Wyatt innocently, his blue eyes wide.

Taking advantage of the distraction, Cinn shifted her bag to the arm Evil Jester still gripped, plunged her hand inside, and plucked out an egg.

The man's attention returned to her. "What's that, little missy?" he said with heavy sarcasm. "Planning on giving me a treat?"

"You?" said Cinnabar, stomping down as hard as she could on his instep. Evil Jester released her and hopped back, one-legged. "You deserve a trick."

And with that, she flung the egg into his face. As it broke, white powder coated his features, and a noxious puff of smoke engulfed his head.

"Aagh!" cried Evil Jester, pawing at his eyes and coughing.

Cinnabar planted her foot, wound up, and kicked him in the stomach full force. He staggered back into the opposite partition wall with a thud.

"Come on!" she cried.

Wyatt snatched the flash drive. Together, they darted past the distracted joker. Racing toward the offices, Cinn heard Evil Jester roar behind them, "You little beggars can't escape! I'll get you!"

They reached the hall that bordered the cubicles, and the

gaunt Mr. Dobasch loomed up beside them. "Trouble?" he asked.

"A bit," Cinn admitted.

A twinkle showed behind his deadpan expression. "Just like the old days. Don't worry, I'll neutralize him."

Before Cinnabar could ask exactly what that entailed, the Gravlaki spy had vanished into the maze of cubicles.

"Aagh, my bleeding eyes!" bellowed Evil Jester. "What's in this bloody powder? I'm calling security right now, see if I don't. You filthy—"

A soft grunt, and his rant stopped abruptly, as if someone had pulled the plug on an annoying TV program.

Drawn by the commotion, Mr. V and the rest of the team had joined Cinnabar and Wyatt in the corridor. "Someone caught you spying?" asked Mr. Vazquez, his eyes wide behind the Zorro mask.

"Yes, but Mr. Dobasch handled it," said Cinnabar.

Nikki sneered. "Getting sloppy, Cinn-Cinn?"

Wyatt bristled at her comment. "The bloke came out of nowhere. It could've happened to any of us."

Before a full-fledged confrontation could erupt, Mr. Dobasch appeared at Cinnabar's side. "He'll be out for a while, but we should—"

"Yes," said Mr. V. "Did anyone find what we need?"

Wyatt held up the flash drive. "Got it."

"Then I suggest we make our exit." Mr. Vazquez led the

group back down the corridor and into the stairwell, where they retrieved the dragon costume.

"Aw, this again?" whined Dermot.

"Unless you fancy a night in jail," said Mr. V.

Dermot rolled his eyes, but he followed the rest of them downstairs. When they reached the second-floor landing, Cinnabar was about to continue down to ground level, but Mr. Dobasch caught her arm.

"The street door is alarmed," he said. "Better to exit through the party."

Worry gnawed at her like a rat at loose wiring. "But what if that man brings Arnie Whosie-Whatsit to—"

Mr. V interrupted. "If we keep moving, we'll be fine." He held out the red, yellow, and gold fabric. "Now let's bring this dragon back to life, shall we?"

Despite her concerns, Cinnabar slipped under the costume with the other orphans. They'd been lucky so far; perhaps their luck would hold?

On second thought, she doubted it. Orphans are not, as a rule, terribly lucky.

Nikki donned the dragon head, Mr. V told Catarina to meet them at the elevators, and the team stepped through the door back into the party. As before, the music pulsed, and the people chattered. Someone in oversize green monster feet stumbled and plowed into them, nearly toppling the dragon.

"Sorry, sorry!" called a muffled male voice. "Can't see a blasted thing in this."

"Plonker," Nikki growled under her breath.

They forged onward through the crowd, enduring still more dragon petting and foolish comments. Honestly, were all office workers such gits? Cinnabar wondered.

Over the music she caught the chime of the elevator, so it must be close at hand. Just a few steps more, she thought.

Then a familiar posh voice carried over the din. *"There you are!"* It was the man in the fancy shoes, which Cinn could now see, off to one side. "I thought we'd lost you. Arnie! Here's your mate and his children."

Uh-oh. Cinnabar's nerves went as taut as a supermodel's tummy.

Their luck had run out.

A pair of elf shoes with turned-up toes joined Fancy Shoes. "And who is this, then?" said a high, scratchy voice.

"Your friend," said Fancy Shoes. "You know, erm . . . I'm sorry, old chap, what was the name again?"

Mr. Dobasch's beard-free whisper came over the com link. "Into the lift. Now."

The dragon ambled forward, maddeningly slowly, while Mr. V said, *"Arnie?* No, you must have misheard." He forced a chuckle. "I said *Barney*—Barney, er, Rubble, that's who invited me."

"But . . ." Elf Shoes sounded confused. "We don't have any Barney Rubble here."

"Well then, my mistake," said Mr. Vazquez. "Sorry to trouble you."

"Half a mo'," said Fancy Shoes. "Isn't Barney Rubble a cartoon character?"

Cinnabar stepped off the gray carpet and onto the tiled elevator floor, but collided with Nikki, who had stopped short. The dragon was stuck—half in, half out.

"Move it!" Cinn hissed, pushing Nikki Knucks.

"I *said*," Nikki whispered back, "don't ever push—"

Fancy Shoes shouted, "Wait! Who are you people? How did you get in here?"

Losing patience, Cinn body-slammed Nikki, sending them both onto the floor, and dragging Dermot and Wyatt on top of them. There they sprawled, in a tangle of colorful fabric and smashed dragon head. As Cinn struggled to free herself from the costume, she heard Elf Shoes say, "Should we call security?"

Ding . . . the doors closed.

"Now you've done it," said Cinnabar.

"Me?" snarled Nikki, shoving the ruined costume head to one side. "You're the one who caused a scene, you manky twit."

Strong hands reached down and yanked away the fabric. The worried faces of Tremaine, Catarina, Mr. Dobasch, and Mr. V stared down at them.

"Can I crush her now, Mr. V?" asked Nikki.

"No," said Mr. Vazquez. "Now we flee."

197

The orphans scrambled to their feet. "But how do we get past the guards?" asked Wyatt, his eyes as round as croquet balls.

"Everyone have their bags?" asked Mr. V. The team members nodded. "Then it's time to revive an old-timey British tradition."

"What's that?" asked Catarina.

"Why, Mischief Night, of course," said Mr. Vazquez. His white-white smile under the black Zorro mask shone as bright as a beach in the moonlight. "At my signal, not before."

When the motley group burst through the elevator doors, the curly-haired female guard was just answering her phone. Her eyes widened as she tracked the team hustling toward the exit.

"Oi! No running!" shouted her partner, a burly man with a long face.

"Stop!" called Miss Curly.

The orphans drew even with her security desk.

"Now!" cried Mr. V.

A fusillade of eggs bombarded the two guards, spattering them with powder, smoke, and various bright liquids. The foul cloud that nearly obscured them from view stank of rotten eggs, sulfur, and skunk.

Wyatt whooped. "Cowabunga, cobbers! Bull's-eye!"

The guards tumbled back behind their desk, hacking, coughing, and gagging, while the costumed spies raced across the lobby. A thrill of elation danced through Cinnabar.

At the street door, she pivoted and sketched a mocking salute.

"And if you think that's fun, you should see our treats!" she cried. "Happy Halloween!"

CHAPTER 18

MAKING NICE-NICE AT A HOSTAGE SWAP

EARLIER THAT SAME Halloween evening, Max found himself sitting beside the Death Ape and wishing the S.P.I.E.S. team had thought to provide their prisoner with deodorant. Preferably the industrial-strength stuff. After two weeks in the basement holding cell, Mr. Ebelskeever (a.k.a., the Death Ape) was riper than the monkey cage at the zoo.

Max couldn't wait to swap him for Mr. Stones.

It wasn't that their handcuffed prisoner had put up a fight. In fact, he hadn't struggled a bit, once he understood that he was about to be traded for a captured S.P.I.E.S. agent. But his boastful, insulting monologue had grown so tiresome that Hantai Annie had stopped the silver Range Rover to gag him, less than half an hour into their journey.

Now, just past dinnertime, they were pulling up to the park where the swap would take place. A high, white wall separated the green space from the tree-lined street of Victorian town houses. The light from scattered streetlamps struggled to penetrate the murky evening, and the low-hanging clouds were stained as yellow as a smoker's teeth by the city lights.

All the lovers, all the dog walkers, all the families with children had gone home. The park lay dark and deserted behind the fancy curlicues of a locked iron gate.

"And it's supposed to be safer to meet in a public place?" Max muttered. He scowled at the shadowy mass of trees beyond the wall. "You could hide an army in there."

Ebelskeever chuckled behind his gag, coffee-bean eyes alight with merriment.

"That's why we arrived so early—for reconnaissance," said Miss Moorthy. She stepped out of the car and buttoned her midnight-blue trench coat against the chill. "Rashid, with me."

The solemn-faced teen joined her in picking the lock on the gate. In deference to the cold, he had tossed a peacoat over his usual tracksuit.

"Rest of you," said Hantai Annie, with a broad circular gesture, "make *shuui*."

"Make shoe-y?" Jensen frowned at his feet.

The director blew out a sigh. "A . . . how-you-say, permitter?"

Vespa wrinkled her nose. "I'm not sure that's a word."

"Perimeter," called Miss Moorthy, before heading out with Rashid.

"English." Hantai Annie snorted. "Crazy language." She swung out of the front seat, barking orders. "Jensen, inside by benches. Vespa, down street. Max, back of car."

With one hand on the door handle and the other on her boomerang (the junior spies had nonlethal weapons), Vespa flashed Max a tight smile. "Here goes nothing, Max Segredo. Wish me luck."

An answering smile sprang to his lips. "You'll be brilliant. You're much readier than I was for my first mission."

"That's so sweet," she said, tucking a stray blond lock behind an ear.

Max blushed. The Death Ape rolled his eyes and groaned.

The hearty thunks of closing car doors broke the stillness of the evening. Ebelskeever hunched in the backseat, a massive dark shape. Somewhere nearby, a siren swelled and dwindled as the orphans took their posts.

Max lifted his voice. "You know, of course, they'll try to double-cross us."

"Mochiron da." Hantai Annie stood on the sidewalk in front of the Range Rover, her eyes taking in the surroundings. "Of course, they try. So we prepare—a good spy is always prepared. How many escape routes you count?"

Surveying the quiet road and the park, Max said, "This entrance and the other entrance—that's two." He called to mind the map of the park he'd studied earlier. "Plus, four pathways through the hedges, so . . . six altogether."

"Seven."

"Seven?"

Hantai Annie nodded. "Manhole cover near meeting site."

Max made a face. "Let's hope it doesn't come to that."

They fell silent. Thirty yards away, Vespa paced and watched the night, her breath making frosty puffs in the chilly air. Max tucked his hands into his armpits. A forest-green Volvo rolled past. Inside, two adults and a teen girl chatted animatedly, bright-eyed and laughing.

So that's what families look like, thought Max. *Some* families anyway, he amended, with a glance at his team.

"You know," said Hantai Annie, "I never want to bring you along on this mission."

Max bristled. "Why? After all I've been through, you think I can't handle it?"

She shook her head. "Not that. Is *abunai*—dangerous. No place for young orphans. I would leave you, Vespa, Jensen at home if I could. But we shorthanded."

Max released a bitter chuckle.

"What?" asked the director.

"Like an orphan's whole *life* isn't dangerous," said Max.

She grunted, conceding the point.

"Besides," said Max, "I'd be bored stiff back at home. This spy stuff is fun. I'm not half bad at it, and it lets me make—I don't know . . ." He looked off down the road. "A contribution."

Hantai Annie kept still for few heartbeats, watching him. "You good boy, Max-*kun*," she said quietly.

He shrugged, uncomfortable with the compliment.

Another long stretch passed with nothing much happening. The park was tranquil, the team kept watch. Max checked his pepper spray and Taser for the tenth time, but he found his thoughts turning to his father, Simon. Where was he tonight? Lying in a pine coffin? Or had he managed to escape LOTUS yesterday?

"What will happen to my father?" Max asked the director.

"Simon Segredo is very tough agent," said Hantai Annie. "One of the best."

"So why did you turn down his help?" asked Max, genuinely curious. "I mean, he's on our side. I think."

Her mouth turned down in an expression of distaste. "We on same side, yes. But he is *reikoku*, too extreme. If I do what he says, we become what we want to destroy—evil."

Max struggled to understand. "But maybe that's what it takes to stop LOTUS."

"No." Hantai Annie shook her head emphatically. "There is another way."

But before Max could ask what way that might be, Miss Moorthy and Rashid emerged from the shadows beyond the gate. They joined the director, and she whistled for Vespa, Max, and Jensen to approach.

"Well?" said Hantai Annie. "What you learn?"

"They're parked on the other side, and their scouts are in place," said Miss Moorthy. "We spotted five agents hiding in the trees, and five more with Stones at the cars."

The director gave a humorless smile. "So, they cheating already. Agreement was six agents each side."

Vespa's eyes widened and she gripped her boomerang tightly. "Do you think they'll attack?"

"Of course." Rashid glanced back into the park. "The only question is, when?"

Regarding each of them in turn, Hantai Annie nodded to herself. "We ready. You know plans. Be prepared and stay alert. Time to rescue one of our own."

Despite the almost tangible presence of danger, a bubble of happiness swelled in Max's chest. He hadn't gotten Mr. Stones killed after all. And with a bit of luck, the sarcastic Surveillance Techniques teacher would be back home that very night.

Rashid stayed behind to guard their escape route. The rest of the team eased Mr. Ebelskeever out of the car and surrounded him, keeping their distance as if transporting a rabid wolf, which wasn't too far off the mark.

Hantai Annie placed a call on her phone. "Is me," she said. "You ready, we ready, so why pretend? *Ikuzo*—let's make trade."

The person on the other end must have agreed, because the director hung up. "We go," she said.

"Mm-mffm," said Ebelskeever. When Annie glanced around, he jerked his chin at her, then looked downward at his gag.

"You want gag off?" asked the director.

The Death Ape cocked his head with attitude, as if saying, *What do you think?*

Hantai Annie smiled. "Maybe your boss will do that." She turned her back on his glower and stalked down the paved trail into the park, flashlight beam slicing through the gloom.

Cautiously but steadily, the group made its way past the shrubs and greensward at the park's edge and into the dimness beyond. Trees closed about them like muggers around an easy mark. Leaves crunched underfoot, and the breeze keened in the treetops. All was dark, cold, and still. The night waited.

As they passed a stately elm, an owl hooted and launched itself from a branch, gliding over their heads and into the darkness. Max started, but then recovered quickly. When you're facing a ruthless band of enemy spies, it doesn't pay to let them see you get spooked by a bird.

Miss Moorthy fell in beside the director, just ahead of Max. In the flashlights' glow, he saw her jerk her head to the left, muttering, "Three of them are waiting in the trees over there; two more on the right."

"They try cut off our return," said Hantai Annie.

"Or sneak up behind us while we make the trade."

Spies? Doing a double cross? thought Max. Will wonders never cease?

Before long, the trees fell away as the path opened into a wide, grassy expanse. On the far side of it huddled a small complex of brick buildings, lit by two yellow security lights. A cluster of dark figures waited at the far edge of the lawn, and one of them waved a flashlight back and forth as a signal.

"Yeah, we reckoned it was you," Max muttered. "Who else would it be? Goldilocks and the Three Bears?"

Vespa chuckled nervously. Miss Moorthy sent a disapproving glance over her shoulder, while the director ignored the comment.

Is it just me, thought Max, or do most spies have no detectable sense of humor?

Hantai Annie brought her group to a halt about fifteen paces away from the LOTUS agents. Their flashlights illuminated a familiar, bald-headed black man, Mr. Stones, dwarfed by two bronzed blokes who looked like mixed-martial-arts champions. Stones carried one arm in a sling. He looked hollow-cheeked, grouchy, and tired, but he was most definitely alive.

Max let out a long, slow breath.

Arranged around Stones and his muscular minders were a slightly less menacing white man, Dijon the evil supermodel, and a pale, grandmotherly woman in a pixie haircut. Oddly

enough, the grandmother was probably the most dangerous of the whole lot: Mrs. Frost, head of LOTUS.

"Well, as I live and breathe," she said. "Hantai Annie Wong." Mrs. Frost's voice was as perfectly modulated as an anchorman's, her tone as upper-crusty as the queen's croissant. "How many years has it been? Ten, twelve? Time has been kind to you."

Max disliked the woman on sight.

"Enough nice-nice," said Hantai Annie. "Let's trade."

"Ah, but don't you want to inspect the merchandise?" asked Mrs. Frost, letting her flashlight beam play over the handcuffed Mr. Stones, who blinked owlishly in its glare. "Engage in some witty spy-versus-spy banter, perhaps?"

"Doushite da?" The director eyed her coolly. "What for? You hate me and what I do; and I dedicate my life to stopping LOTUS. What we talk about, the weather?"

Mrs. Frost gave a phony little chortle. "There, you see? Was that so difficult? We must not allow the harshness of our work to degrade civility and common courtesy. Manners are what sets us apart from the apes, don't you agree?"

Yack-yack-yack. What was her game? Max wondered.

He glanced behind them to see if the other LOTUS agents were trying to sneak up as she talked. But all he observed was the grassy lawn, and beyond it the shadowy bank of trees.

Miss Moorthy also scanned the surroundings, one hand hovering near her concealed holster.

"*Baka yarou,*" Hantai Annie said, mostly under her breath. She shone the flashlight beam up and down Ebelskeever. "See? He is unharmed, he is ready."

"But he's gagged," said Mrs. Frost. "Was my Ronnie a bad, bad boy?"

"Not particularly," said Max. "But just like you, he wouldn't shut up."

The two martial-arts monsters guarding Mr. Stones actually flinched. The rest of the LOTUS team showed Max their best hard-eyed look. But their boss released a peal of laughter.

"Max Segredo," said Mrs. Frost. "Still playing for the wrong team? When are you going to come and work for me?"

Everyone's eyes turned to Max.

"Depends." He cocked his head. "When are you going to stop this whole taking-over-the-world bit?"

LOTUS's leader let slip a tut-tut, like a gently chiding teacher. Max wasn't fooled. He checked the edges of the open space again. Was that a dark shape lurking behind one of the trees?

"My dear Max," said Mrs. Frost, "it is best not to make decisions when you're not in possession of all the facts. You have the wrong notion about LOTUS."

"Oh, you mean you're *not* an evil organization bent on world domination?" Max asked.

"Poor deluded boy, loyal for all the wrong reasons." She shook her head. "I could help you change your way of thinking."

Max thought of the mind-control device that LOTUS so dearly wanted to possess. If he had anything to say about it, by tomorrow night they would face a disappointment on that score.

"Enough talk," said Hantai Annie. "You want this guy or not?"

Mrs. Frost pursed her lips. "We do. Send two of your people forward with him. We shall do the same with your man."

The director nodded. "Max, Moorthy-*san*, you go."

The two muscle-heads gripped Mr. Stones's arms and led him onto the lawn. Miss Moorthy and Max did the same with Ebelskeever, and they met halfway between the two groups. On high alert, Max flicked his gaze from Mrs. Frost, to the woods, to the trio in front of him.

If my nerves were stretched any tighter, he thought, you could pluck me like a banjo.

"All right, then, sunshine?" said Mr. Stones.

"Never better," said Max. "You?"

The teacher glanced up at the two guards looming over him. "Haven't been keeping the best company lately, but otherwise I'm tip-top."

"I couldn't help noticing," said Max, "you're not dead."

"Kevlar." Stones thumped a cuffed hand against his chest. "Bloody marvelous stuff."

Muscle-head No. 1 scowled. "We gonna do this, or just chat?"

Miss Moorthy held up a small key. "Let's trade."

"Right, then," said Muscle-head No. 2. He swapped the key to Mr. Stones's handcuffs for the captured LOTUS agent's key.

"Now the hostages," said Miss Moorthy. Watching to make sure that the LOTUS guards were following suit, she and Max released their captive's arms and stepped back.

Stones and Ebelskeever circled each other like wary Dobermans, eyes locked and shoulders stiff.

"Mm-fmm mmgh," said Ebelskeever through his gag.

"Right back at ya, peaches," said Mr. Stones. As he reached Max and held out his wrists for the cuffs to be unlocked, the teacher muttered, "They're planning to spring a trap."

"Tell me something I *don't* know," Max said, turning the key.

"Very well," said Stones. "They're springing it right now."

FRESH OUT OF BANG-BANG

ONLY LATER was Max able to sort out the sequence of events at the park. In the heat of the moment, all was chaos and confusion.

A woman barked, "Now!" The LOTUS group faded back, making for the cover of a row of potted saplings behind them.

"Plan B." Hantai Annie's voice was as calm and cool as a glacier.

The S.P.I.E.S. crew dashed across the lawn—not back the way they'd come, but toward the shelter of the nearest trees and the path that led to the side exit. Gunfire erupted from the woods behind them.

"*Danado!*" cried Vespa, slipping into Portuguese. "They're shooting at us!"

"Idiots!" Mrs. Frost roared, sounding not-so-genteel now. "Wait till I'm under cover."

"Sorry, guv'nor!" called a male voice from the tree line.

The firing stopped. Vespa spun and whipped her throwing arm, and her boomerang clipped the shadowy figure in the head. The 'rang returned to her hand even before the man collapsed to the ground. Max and his team dove into the bushes.

"Nice shot," Max said.

She grinned. "You should see me with a blowgun."

Then the gunfire resumed with a vengeance, spraying from all three groups of enemy spies. Bullets thudded into the sheltering beech tree and whistled through the leaves.

"Lights off!" hissed Hantai Annie. "You make target."

The team members doused their flashlights. Faint moonglow painted the lawn, but the woods and shrubbery lay drenched in shadow. The bombardment slowed.

"Everyone all right?" whispered Miss Moorthy.

Max could barely distinguish the dim forms of his comrades crouching among the shrubs, but all confirmed that they were unhurt.

"We create distraction, then *kodomotachi* can go," said the director.

"Eh?" said Jensen.

"Children."

Mr. Stones piped up from a bush beside Max. "Got a spare *pistola* for your old teacher?"

"Sorry," said Max. "They still don't trust me with real guns."

"And rightly so." Miss Moorthy pressed a weapon into Stones's free hand. "Here. It's got beanbag rounds, to incapacitate."

"Ta, love," said the burly teacher, teeth gleaming in a splash of moonlight. "I've got some scores to settle."

Bullets pocked into the tree trunk above them. The enemy's chatter continued, but Max couldn't make out what the LOTUS agents were saying.

"Moorthy-*san*," said Hantai Annie. "At my signal, take Max, Vespa, and Jensen to exit."

"No!" Max blurted. "I'm staying."

"Max-*kun* . . ." The director's voice held a warning.

Mr. Stones worked his way up behind the trunk. "Let him stay, Director," he said. "He's earned it."

Hantai Annie grumbled and shook her head, but in the end relented. "*Jya*, okay, okay. Get ready. . . ."

Then she popped around the trunk, low, and hurled a tear-gas canister at the LOTUS agents behind the potted shrubs. Simultaneously, Stones fired at the spies in the woods to their right. Surprised cries greeted their attack.

"Go!" whispered the director.

Miss Moorthy duckwalked into the bushes, Jensen right behind her. Vespa paused just long enough to kiss Max's cheek and whisper, "Be safe," then she, too, was gone, leaving behind the scent of jasmine.

The spot where her lips had touched tingled.

Gunfire shredding the greenery brought Max out of his reverie. Now he found himself wondering why, without a long-distance weapon in hand, he'd been so eager to stay. "Um, how can I help?" he asked.

"Don't get shot," said Mr. Stones. "It hurts."

Hantai Annie reached into a pocket of her overcoat and fished out a chunky little pistol. "Flare gun," she said. "Only one cartridge, so spend it wisely."

Max took the piece, feeling oddly comforted by its weight. While Stones and Hantai Annie continued to fire rubber and beanbag rounds at the LOTUS agents, Max figured he'd watch their back. Creeping to the edge of his clump of bushes, he looked off after Miss Moorthy's crew.

A faint, shielded light wobbled along the side path. They were getting away.

But then he noticed another light making its way through the woods from the left. The second group of enemy spies was trying to slip around and cut off Max's crew. His gut clenched. Max thought about firing his flare, but he decided it would do as much harm as good.

Instead, he edged back through the bushes, tapped the director's shoulder, and indicated the light. "Don't look now, but the trap is closing."

Hantai Annie grunted. "*Ikuzo*. Stones-*san*, we go."

"Aw," the bullet-headed man complained. "Just when it was getting lively."

Still, he joined them in slipping away through the under-growth. They chose a route that angled toward the path to the exit, hoping to reach it ahead of the LOTUS agents. Soggy branches slapped Max's face and briars tore at his clothes.

Max pictured the park map in his mind. It wasn't far from side to side; Miss Moorthy and the others must have reached the gate by now. But with a sinking heart, he saw three dark shapes emerge from the trees onto the path ahead of his team.

They were cut off, trapped between two forces of enemy agents. Their odds looked worse than the southbound end of a northbound camel.

"Got a Plan C?" Max whispered.

"Mochiron da," Hantai Annie replied. "A good spy has many plans."

She crouched in the bushes at the edge of the path and slid fresh rounds into her weapon. Ahead, the three agents crept along the path, searching for them. Behind, Mrs. Frost and her crew were still dealing with the effects of the tear gas, but they wouldn't stay out of the action for long—heads were already poking out around the potted shrubs.

"Care to *share* that plan anytime soon?" said Max.

Hantai Annie snorted. "You funny boy, Max-*kun*."

"But looks aren't everything, eh, cupcake?" said Mr. Stones, nudging Max. He checked his gun. "Got some more beanbag rounds, Director?"

She shook her head.

"Then I'm fresh out of bang-bang," said Stones.

"Wonderful," said Max. "This night just keeps getting better."

Hantai Annie felt along the ground with one hand. "For young person, you very cynical. You worry too much."

"It's the easy life I've led," said Max. "After all, foster care is such a breeze."

"Watch and learn," she said, picking something up. "Sometimes simple plans are best." And with that, Hantai Annie cocked her arm and slung a rock far into the woods.

At the sound, the LOTUS agents ahead of them tensed. Spreading out, they began stalking back through the trees toward where the stone had landed.

Hantai Annie glanced both ways, then motioned to Max and Mr. Stones to follow her onto the path. Max left the bushes, feeling as exposed as a cockroach on a kitchen floor. Any second now, someone would spot them, and that would be that: three spies down.

So he could scarcely believe it when the director led them not down the path after Miss Moorthy, but directly across it toward the buildings.

Max couldn't contain himself. "The exit's that way," he whispered. "Where are we going?" Along to their right, he could see Mrs. Frost's group emerging from their cover, coughing and wiping their eyes.

"Down," said Hantai Annie. She stopped in a patch of shadow, pulled a short length of metal from her overcoat, and passed the pistol to Stones. "Hold this," she said.

The burly teacher covered her as she crouched in the center of the cement path and plunged the tool into the ground, where it rasped against something metallic. Hantai Annie pushed down hard. The sound of grating metal grew louder.

"Help me," she whispered to Max, effort making her voice tight.

With a glance toward Mrs. Frost's group, Max fumbled in the shadows where the director labored. His fingers found the edge of a heavy metal disk.

A manhole cover.

"Oh no," said Max.

"Oh yes," said Hantai Annie. "Pull!"

Max took a firm grip on the curved iron surface, and with a concerted effort, he and the director muscled the cover over to one side. He winced as metal scraped on cement.

"Over there!" came a cry from Mrs. Frost's team. "I hear them!"

Mr. Stones cursed and fired off a couple of rubber bullets at the enemy spies. The agents dodged back under cover.

"Give me gun," said Hantai Annie. "You go first."

Stones began to argue, but then seemed to recall his injury. He swung his legs down into the hole, fumbled for the ladder, and began descending one-handed.

Bullets sprayed off the cement near Max's feet. He pivoted. The second enemy group was emerging from the woods again.

"Behind us!" he cried.

Hantai Annie knelt and held her weapon in a two-handed grip. *Bam! Bam! Bam!* She squeezed off three deliberate shots. Voices cried out, and a heavy weight crunched back into the undergrowth.

"Go now," she told Max.

Everything in Max was screaming at him to dive down the shaft. But somehow it felt wrong to leave a woman behind to cover him, even if she *was* an ace spymaster.

He turned to Hantai Annie, then froze. Past her shoulder, Ebelskeever had stepped out of concealment and was bringing up his pistol. Yellow security light glinted off the gun barrel.

Without thinking, Max leveled his flare gun and fired.

Tchooom!

A comet of pure fire streaked toward the enemy agent. Ebelskeever's eyes went wide. He dodged, but too slowly.

The cartridge struck him squarely in the shoulder, setting his tracksuit top aflame. The two muscle-heads rushed to his aid.

"Ikuzo!" barked Hantai Annie.

This time, Max didn't argue. He hit the dirt, swung his legs into the hole, and groped with his feet for the ladder rungs. Then he slipped and scrambled downward into darkness, until he splashed knee-deep into ice-cold water.

The rank odor of the tunnel made his whole face pucker. It wasn't just a foul stench. No, it was the kind of foul stench that follows you home, breaks into your house, and slaps your friends around while defacing your comic-book collection. It was mean, it was aggressive, it was eye-wateringly noxious.

Max took a step and instantly lost his footing on the slippery tunnel surface. His feet flew out from under him, and he smacked down onto his bottom with another splash.

"Eeugh!" burst through his lips.

He was sitting up to his armpits in a river of poo.

"Gracefully done," said Stones, shining the flashlight on him.

Max struggled to his feet. "Next stop, *Dancing with the Stars.*" He flung his hands back and forth to shake off the water, then fished his own flashlight from a sodden pocket. His soaked clothes clung to his body like a second, incredibly stenchy skin.

"When they tell you how glamorous spy work is," said Max, "they never mention this bit."

"'Course not." Mr. Stones snorted. "Then everybody'd want to join."

In the beam of his light, Hantai Annie clambered down the ladder. Max had time to notice the graceful curve of the old brick tunnel and the greenish-brown flow of the water.

"Kusai!" she spat. "This stinks."

"You picked the escape route," said Max.

The director splashed down and instantly whipped out her pistol to cover their escape. A head peeked over the rim of the hole, and she popped off a round. In the close tunnel, the boom reverberated like cannon fire.

The head ducked out of sight.

"We go," said Hantai Annie.

"No argument here," said Max.

They waded carefully downstream, with Mr. Stones in the lead. Short though he was, the curved brick ceiling hung less than a foot above his bald head. Tall Simon Segredo would really have trouble down here, Max mused, and the thought of his father gave him a twinge.

The trio sloshed onward through the sewer. Several times they stopped to listen, but they heard no sounds of pursuit. At the first branching, Hantai Annie chose the right fork, which led to the nearest manhole.

"So, what's new at S.P.I.E.S., sunshine?" Mr. Stones asked over his shoulder, as if they were chatting at a coffee shop, without a care in the world.

"Oh, you know," said Max, "the usual. We're trying to steal a mind-control device from a highly guarded location, we've got a wicked security leak, and Nikki is being a right pain."

The burly man chuckled. "I knew it. You silly buggers are going right down the drain without me."

Max glanced around at the sewer walls. "And *with* you, apparently."

"No one likes a cheeky monkey, cupcake," Stones rumbled. But Max could hear a smile in his voice.

When at last Mr. Stones's flashlight beam picked out their escape ladder, Hantai Annie spoke.

"Max-*kun*," she said, "promise me something."

He glanced back over his shoulder at her. "Never to come down here again? Done."

Hantai Annie grunted. "This is serious promise."

"Okay . . ." said Max.

"Promise, if LOTUS ever captures you, you won't resist."

Max frowned. "I don't understand."

"What, I speaking Swahili? Next time, if they corner or capture you, don't fight."

"Okay, then," Max said. "What do you want me to do?"

"Join them."

Max stopped dead, utterly gobsmacked. He wheeled around to face her. "Join the outfit that's trying to kill my dad? That's trying to destroy S.P.I.E.S.?" He felt like he couldn't possibly have heard right.

"Yes," said Hantai Annie, her face grim.

"Have you gone completely mental?" Max blurted.

"Max." Mr. Stones's voice held a warning.

The director's eyes burned, but not at Max's cheekiness. "Is the only way to stop LOTUS—from inside."

"But—" Max began.

"They want you; who knows why," said Hantai Annie. "So you join them. Then you work with us to bring them down. Promise me."

Max felt like an old dry brick had lodged in his gullet. "I—I can't," he choked out at last. "Anything but that."

The director searched his face for a long moment. The tunnel was quiet—only the burble of the water and the distant rumble of traffic on the street above penetrated their hiding place.

At last, Hantai Annie nodded once. "Maybe, if situation changes, you reconsider?"

"Maybe," said Max. But what he really meant was, *Never in a month of Sundays.*

THE BEST
WORST PLAN

EVEN AFTER two showers, much skin-peeling scrubbing, and a spritz of Jensen's sandalwood aftershave, Max still smelled of *eau de sewer*. And he could tell it wasn't just his imagination either, since nobody at the orphanage's midnight meeting would sit beside him—not even Wyatt. As they took their seats at the dining room table, he left an empty chair between himself and Max.

"No offense, mate, but you stink like a Tassie dunny at high noon," said the blond boy.

Max rolled his eyes. "None taken," he grumped. "'Cause I have no idea what you just said."

Cinnabar's team seemed thrilled with the success of their operation, but Cinnabar herself remained deep in conversation with Jazz at the other end of the table. Max couldn't even catch her eye. Vespa, on the other hand, kept chattering about the excitement of her first mission and sending warm glances Max's way.

Every time she looked at him, Max felt a fizzy, sparkly feeling inside.

Hantai Annie marched into the dining room with the great dog Pinkerton at her heels. Planting her fists on her hips, she nodded at Mr. Stones.

"Oi, you mouth breathers!" he growled. "Shut your pie holes, and listen up!" As the room fell quiet, he grinned at the director. "You don't know how I've missed doing that."

The corner of her lip twitched in what might have been a smile. "*Yoku yatta*, everyone. Good job. Two successful missions: Stones-*san* is back with us"—here the group broke into cheers while the teacher offered a royal wave—"*and* we have intel on RookTech security system."

"We rock!" cried Wyatt, to a chorus of hoots and upraised fists.

Hantai Annie lifted a palm. "But job is not over yet. Hardest part is still to come. Victor-*san*? Tell them."

Wyatt glanced Max's way, mumbling, "Way to kill a buzz."

Max covered a smirk.

Since Victor Vazquez was still wearing most of his Zorro costume, the laptop computer he carried made him look rather like a swashbuckling nerd, Max thought. The teacher flipped open the computer, tapped a few keys, and then turned the screen toward the rest of the group.

"The street door of RookTech we already know about," he said. "Face recognition and key card."

Cinnabar raised a hand. "I know we've got disguises so Max and Mr. Dobasch can fool the face recognition, but how do we get a key card?"

Mr. Vazquez smiled. "We've been working on that. Addison Rook—"

"The little wazzock who looks like Maxie?" said Nikki.

"Er, yes," said the teacher. "He's got a key card, and a date with Vespa tomorrow afternoon."

"He does?" said Vespa, her toffee-brown eyes wide.

Tremaine gave a piercing wolf whistle, and Jazz tossed a biscuit at him.

"And that's when we'll steal the key card," said Mr. Dobasch, from his seat far down the table.

"Why Vespa?" sneered Nikki. "Why not a more experienced girl?"

Mr. Vazquez gazed at her with a mix of exasperation and kindness. "Because," he said, "Addison likes blondes."

At this, Max's fizzy feeling suddenly went flat.

"Oh." Nikki shut up.

Mr. Dobasch leaned onto his elbows, cupping a fist. "He has other plans for tomorrow night, so we know he won't need his card while we're at the building."

Arms crossed, Hantai Annie nodded her approval.

"Right," said Max. "That gets us in, but then where do they keep the whatsit?"

With a few more keystrokes, Mr. Vazquez pulled up a different document, a floor layout.

"Our best guess?" he said, pointing at the screen. "Right here."

Max craned his neck to see. "And where's that?"

"The most secure room at RookTech."

The computer teacher's eyes danced at the high-tech wonder of it all, but Max felt the pit of his stomach drop like a solid-steel kite. Mr. V continued, half chuckling in admiration, "Note the pressure-pad alarms under the hallway carpet outside—one wrong step and you set them off. Devilishly clever."

"Brilliant," Max muttered.

"So Maxi-Pad will have to play Spider-Man," Nikki sneered, her natural spitefulness reviving.

Mr. Vazquez ignored her. "Once you're past that, Max, you've got the door security to contend with."

"Biometrics?" asked Cinnabar.

"The best," said the teacher. "Key card, thumbprint reader, *and* iris scanner."

"What's that, then?" asked Dermot.

"It scans your eyeball, peaches," said Mr. Stones. He ruffled the teen's hair, and Dermot ducked away, grimacing.

Max frowned at Mr. Vazquez. "So how do we beat that?"

"Hack it," said Wyatt with confidence. "We hacked the front-door system; we can hack this one."

The teacher shook his head. "It's closed—no external wires or input ports."

Wyatt whistled. "Blimey. That's a piece of work."

"Right, then we pop out this Addison's eyeballs?" said Nikki.

"Charming notion," said Mr. V. His smile seemed a little queasy around the edges. "But the scanner only accepts living eyes. And I haven't even mentioned the motion detector *inside* the secured room."

"So . . ." said Mr. Dobasch.

"So," said Max. "I repeat, how do we beat it?"

The Gravlaki raised his eyebrows and gave a sly smile. "I've got three ideas."

He told them to the group. When he finished, the orphans looked about at each other, incredulous.

"No offense," said Nikki. "But those plans are wretched, ridiculous, and total rubbish."

Mr. Dobasch shrugged. "Perhaps. But they're the best rubbishy plans we've got."

"Then those," said Hantai Annie, "are the plans we use."

The S.P.I.E.S. team toiled on into the early morning hours, working against the clock to prep everything for the big mission. One by one, the orphans succumbed to exhaustion and staggered to bed. Even Max found himself nodding off at one of the library's computers, so at last he, too, pushed back from the table, said good night to Wyatt, and left the room.

Engrossed in his hacking, Wyatt barely noticed.

As Max was crossing the entryway, voices reached him from Hantai Annie's office. One sounded like Nikki's. Noticing that the door was ajar, Max drifted closer to listen in.

". . . took me ages," Nikki was saying. Through the crack, Max could see her sitting in the visitor's chair before Hantai Annie's desk, talking with the director. "But nobody spent extra time with him, outside of their interviews."

Hantai Annie nodded, her face partly visible past Nikki's wild red hair. *"Mochiron da,"* she said. "Complaint was anonymous, so person who complained would never confess to Krinkle. Or they must prove their lie is true."

Mr. Krinkle. With all the activity, Max had temporarily forgotten about the man threatening to close down the orphanage. Had Nikki been trying to identify the rat for Hantai Annie? Was that the big assignment she'd boasted of?

Max eased closer. A faint incense smell drifted from the office.

Nikki leaned forward in her seat. "That's what I thought, too. Then I realized something. Whoever told that lie wants to sabotage us, so I should just look for whoever acts the most like a traitor. And that's when I found him."

"Who is it?" asked Hantai Annie, her expression harder than the stone heads on Easter Island.

Max's eye was right up against the crack now. He couldn't

imagine who had betrayed the orphanage. Was it Dermot, or even Rashid . . . ?

"It's Max Segredo," said Nikki. Her tone was smug and satisfied.

"*Hontou ka?*" said Hantai Annie.

A snarl of outrage bubbled up in Max's throat, but he choked it off.

"What was that?" asked Nikki, half turning in her chair. The director frowned and peered at the doorway as Max ducked back out of sight.

"*Nandemonai,*" said Hantai Annie after a pause. "Nothing there. This very serious accusation, Nikki. You have proof?"

"Proof? He's too slippery for that," said Nikki. "But look at the facts: he was passing information to LOTUS."

"Before he learned lesson," said the director. "Max is with us now, one hundred percent."

"Is he? Then why was he talking to that LOTUS prisoner? I caught him, not once, but twice."

Hantai Annie's voice held a hint of doubt. "He told me he tried to learn about our enemy, find something to help us."

Nikki's chuckle was as cruel as a year's worth of Januaries. "He would say that. But Max Segredo has been selling us out since the beginning."

Max's fists knotted. He wanted to burst into that room and punch Nikki bang on her spotty nose, but something held him back. What was her game, exactly? Could *she* be the real traitor, using him to cover her tracks? And how could he find the evidence to prove it? He forced himself to listen for clues.

"I don't believe it," said Hantai Annie. "Why would he want Health Ministry to close us down? He would lose his home."

"Maybe Maxi-Pad's got another home already lined up," said Nikki. "With his old man, at LOTUS headquarters."

Jaw clenched, Max risked another peek through the door crack.

Hantai Annie was scowling. "LOTUS tried to kill Simon Segredo. I saw them."

Nikki leaned back in her chair and spread her hands. "Maybe. But it'd sure put Max and his dad back in their good graces if they helped close down S.P.I.E.S., wouldn't it?"

Hantai Annie said nothing, but her expression was thoughtful.

At this, a sharp sadness knifed through Max's chest. Could the director really be taking Nikki's accusation seriously?

With a wrench, Max tore himself away from the door and shambled toward the staircase. Here he was, risking his life to keep the orphanage together, but given what he'd just overheard, he had to ask himself one important question:

Why?

The next day dawned chilly and overcast, the clouds packed into a dismal gray layer, as if someone had pulled a filthy sheepskin rug over the city. Not a speck of blue sky showed through. The mood at the orphanage was tense and muted. A lot was riding on this day, from the results of Mr. Krinkle's audit to the mission that would make or break S.P.I.E.S.

By day's end, the orphans would either be celebrating or heading back into the foster-care system, cursing their luck.

A morning check of the RookTech surveillance footage showed that LOTUS had cased the building but still hadn't broken in to steal the mind-control device. Max's mission—dubbed "Operation Brainwave" by Wyatt—was all-systems-go.

Given the heavy focus on the operation, the morning's class schedule was light. After the usual warm-ups with Hantai Annie, they had just one session, taught by Mr. Dobasch: Lying 101.

"Why must we take this wretched class?" whined Dermot as he took his seat with the other orphans. He'd been miffed to learn that he wouldn't be part of either team tackling the RookTech job, and now everything he said came out sounding like a complaint.

So what else was new? Max thought. He wondered if Dermot was collaborating in Nikki's deception.

"We take this class," said Cinnabar tartly, "because not only must a spy be able to lie convincingly, but we also must know when someone else is lying to us."

Max smiled. Could this be a way to learn the truth about Nikki?

"Couldn't have put it better myself," said Mr. Dobasch, appearing suddenly at the front of the classroom.

Max flinched. That man had some serious sneaking skills.

The Gravlaki spy rested his fingertips on the desktop and leaned forward, sweeping the room with his ice-blue eyes until the last of the chatter died out.

"Everyone lies," he said quietly. "In ways large or small, we lie every day."

"Not—" Shan began.

"*Every*one," said Dobasch. Shan flushed and looked down at her desk. "Once you accept that," he continued, "the issue becomes, how can you tell when they're lying, and how do you hide your own lies?"

The orphans watched him, fascinated. Every one of them, Max knew, had lied to foster parents or caseworkers and been caught in the act. Every one of them had been lied to. Dobasch was offering a real survival skill.

"What do we look for, then?" asked Rashid.

The corners of Dobasch's mouth turned down in what might have been a dour smile. "For that, I need a volunteer." From the raised hands, he chose Vespa's. "Stand up here and face the class, Comrade da Costa."

The blond girl joined him at the front of the room, smoothing the front of her flowery blouse and favoring Max with a quick smile. Max returned it, then glanced away, uncomfortable, when he noticed Cinnabar's frown.

Mr. Dobasch counted off three points on his fingers. "We begin by observing face, voice tone, and body language."

Tremaine grinned and started to make a comment, but Jazz swatted him before it could even leave his mouth.

"First," said the teacher, "establish the baseline. Observe behavior when you know the subject is telling the truth. For example, what is your name, my dear?"

"Vespa da Costa," said Vespa, standing straight and tall.

"True," said Mr. Dobasch, watching her closely. "How old are you?"

"Almost fifteen," said the girl.

"Also true." The Gravlaki indicated Vespa. "Notice her relaxed posture, normal vocal pitch, no big changes in eye contact. One more: are you an orphan?"

"I, er, yes," said Vespa.

Dobasch's eyebrows lifted. "An increase in ums and ers often signals a lie. Are you truly an orphan?"

Vespa folded her arms across her chest. "I . . . um, well, almost. I have an aunt, but we don't get along."

The teacher gestured at her crossed arms. "True, but notice the defensive posture. She doesn't want to talk about it, so perhaps we shouldn't push.

"Now—"

"*I've* got a question," Nikki cut in, eyes glittering with malice. "Are you a lousy, rotten spy?"

"Yes," said Vespa. "I am."

CHAPTER 21

HOW TO FOOL
A BOY GENIUS

BEHIND MAX, someone gasped. Max's mouth dropped open. Could *Vespa* be the mole? For a moment, Nikki looked gobsmacked, and then she sneered in triumph.

Vespa smiled, opening her hands. "I mean, aren't we all?"

Chuckles bubbled through the room like unattended stew in a soup kitchen. Max relaxed. Nikki's sour expression would've made a lemon pucker.

Mr. Dobasch gestured for quiet. "Now, Comrade da Costa, tell us an obvious lie."

"I adore Nikki Knucks!" Vespa gushed with a wicked grin. "She's my BFF."

Big laughs from the class. Bigger scowl from Nikki.

"Notice the change in pitch, how her voice went higher than usual?" said the teacher. "Another sign of lying. Thank you, my dear. You may sit down."

Vespa beamed at Max and took her seat.

"Max Segredo," said Dobasch.

"Hmm?" said Max, distracted.

"You're the point man on today's mission. Let's give you some practice."

Let's not, thought Max. But he levered himself up from his desk, trudged to the front of the room, and faced the class. He didn't much fancy the avid look in Nikki's eyes.

"Let's make this more interesting," said the teacher. "I need an interrogator."

To Nikki's disgust, Mr. Dobasch chose Cinnabar. She sauntered up to join Max, and he relaxed slightly.

"Start with easy, true answers," the teacher directed.

"What's your name?" asked Cinnabar, her smile open, her golden eyes soft.

"Max Segredo," said Max.

"Where do you live?"

"Merry Sunshine Orphanage." He breathed more easily. This wasn't so bad.

Mr. Dobasch perched on the edge of his desk. "Now step it up a little, Comrade Jones."

"Very well." Cinnabar's eyes narrowed. "Do you have a crush on Vespa da Costa?"

"I, uh . . ." Max's face blazed with heat as the students giggled. He avoided Cinnabar's gaze and appealed to the teacher. "Don't we have more important things to talk about?"

237

"Answer the question," said Dobasch evenly.

"Um, no," Max told Cinnabar. "Not that it's any of your business."

The Gravlaki indicated Max. "Textbook case! Notice the ums and uhs, the change in eye contact, the crossed arms, and the higher vocal tone."

"Our boy Maxwell has a crush!" crowed Tremaine.

Cinnabar's face clenched like an angry fist. Her cheeks went red and her eyes grew moist. Max didn't need to be an expert face reader to recognize her hurt and disapproval.

But what did she expect? First she ignores him, and then she blames him for spending time with Vespa.

Girls were complicated. And speaking of girls . . .

"My turn," said Nikki. She eyed Max like a pit bull at a gopher hole. "Did you make that fake complaint to the Ministry of Health so Krinkle would shut us down?"

Like a flipped switch, the mood in the room instantly turned serious. Heads swiveled toward Max.

His jaw tightened. "No, I did not," Max said deliberately. "Did you?"

With a growl, Nikki surged to her feet. "How dare you!"

"Answer the question," snarled Max. "You're so quick to accuse everyone else, especially me. Did *you* file that bogus report?"

Her face had gone a really interesting shade—somewhere past red and approaching puce. "I . . . did . . . not," she rumbled, "but someone did. And my money's on you, dimwat."

"As far as I can tell, your money's in the wrong place," said Mr. Dobasch. "Both of you appear to be telling the truth."

"About *some* things, maybe," huffed Cinnabar. She stormed past Max and dropped into a seat in the back of the room.

Max sighed. Heading for his own chair, he cast an eye over his fellow orphans. The room seethed with suspicion— suspicion of him, suspicion of Nikki, suspicion of each other. He massaged his temples, which throbbed with a growing headache. If LOTUS and Mr. Krinkle didn't manage to bring down the orphanage, there was an excellent chance that the orphans themselves would.

After an early lunch, two teams gathered by the Range Rovers for the trip to the capital. Cinnabar still wasn't talking to Max, but her pointed glances spoke volumes. She, Tremaine, and Wyatt piled into one car. They would accompany Mr. Vazquez and Miss Moorthy to the safe house, where they would establish a base of operations and monitor the RookTech building.

Mr. Stones approached Hantai Annie as she was supervising departure preparations. "Come on, Director," he said in low, urgent tones. "You need me there to watch your back."

"*Tondemonai,*" she said, her gaze flicking to his sling-wrapped arm. "I need you here more. Someone must protect school."

Stones's grimace said that he wasn't buying her reasoning, but he thumped the Range Rover's roof and told the team, "You plonkers try not to have too much fun without me."

Max, Vespa, Nikki, and Rashid climbed into the second car with Hantai Annie and Mr. Dobasch. Theirs was the Addison Rook operation—lifting fingerprints and key card from the boy genius.

Throughout the long drive to the capital, conversation was limited. All felt the pressure, all knew the price of failure. Occasionally, Vespa in the front seat would find an excuse to turn around and look at Max in the back. Max felt all muddled up. He craved her attention, sure, but it made him feel disloyal somehow.

At long last, they topped a hill and the sprawl of the great city filled the horizon. A haze shrouded the skyscrapers, but here and there rays of sunshine poked through the clouds, shining a spotlight onto this or that district.

Mr. Dobasch found a car park in a hip neighborhood of art galleries, highly specialized clothing stores, and restaurants with names like Fishcoteque, Ciao Mein, Kebab 'n' Suds, and Hard Wok Cafe. The pedestrians all seemed to dress in black, and most wore sunglasses, despite the day's gloom.

In the car park, the team activated their communications devices as Hantai Annie Wong issued last-minute instructions.

"Remember, Vespa-*kun* is alone on date," she said. "Nobody talks to her."

"No worries," said Nikki. "That's the last thing I want to do."

She and Vespa traded insincere smiles whose meaning was, *Hate you so much!*

"Shop owner owes me favor," the director continued, ignoring the interruption. "So Nikki Knucks will pretend to be server."

"Why not me?" asked Rashid. "I'm older; it's more believable."

Hantai Annie shook her head. "Because you are best pickpocket."

"I do have mad skills," Rashid allowed, with a rare smile.

"If Vespa cannot get key card, you must steal wallet. *Wakatta?*"

"Got it, Chief," said Rashid.

The director nestled her com device into her ear and brushed her hair down to hide it. "We go in three groups. First, Nikki and Rashid; then Max, Dobasch, and me; last of all, Vespa."

The blond girl bit her lip.

"Everything all right, little fish?" Mr. Dobasch asked her.

Vespa pasted on a sunny smile and glanced around at her team members. "Peachy keen, sports fans. Ready when you are."

But Max could sense the nervousness behind her brave front.

"Jya, ikkou!" grunted Hantai Annie. "Rashid, Nikki?"

The two teens slipped out of the car, zipped up their coats against the November chill, and headed off. A few minutes later, Hantai Annie nudged Mr. Dobasch, saying, "We go."

Max flashed a thumbs-up to Vespa. "Go get 'em, Mata Hari." He gripped the seat back and began to swing his legs out. But before he could leave, she rested a hand on his.

"Max," she said.

"Um, yeah?" His throat went suddenly dry.

"I know that must have been really awkward for you, in Lying class."

"Oh, that." Max looked down. "I, uh, that is . . ."

A finger reached out and tilted up his chin so Max's eyes met hers. "And I just wanted you to know," she said, dimples deepening, "I have a little crush on you, too."

Max felt his jaw drop and his ears go warm.

"Max-*kun!*" barked Hantai Annie from outside the car.

He cleared his throat. "I should, uh . . ."

"Yes," said Vespa, gazing at him steadily. "You should."

Max chuckled nervously. Why did everything she say sound like it had two meanings?

Simultaneously relieved and confused, he slipped out of the Range Rover and joined the adults.

The coffee shop proved to be a narrow but surprisingly deep space, with exposed-brick walls, café tables, and a scattering of love seats and comfy armchairs. Soft jazz purred through hidden speakers, and impossibly hip lettering on the plate-glass window spelled out CAFFIEND in devilish crimson.

Emanating from the shop like a genie escaping from a bottle was the rich, earthy aroma of brewing coffee. Max wondered, not for the first time, how something that smelled so good could taste so bitter.

This time of the day, the shop was barely half full. Hantai Annie steered them toward a table with a commanding view of the other patrons while Stanislav Dobasch ordered their drinks from the barista at the brushed-steel counter. Over in a corner, Rashid sipped coffee while texting on his smartphone, just like any random prep school student. Nikki lurked behind the counter, wearing a red-on-white Caffiend T-shirt, a black apron, and a glower.

Lucky thing she's not working for tips, thought Max.

Before long, a bell chimed on the street door, and in sauntered Addison Rook. Max would've recognized him even without having studied the teen's photo. Addison reeked of entitlement. He'd clearly spent a ridiculous amount of time on his black hair, which was spiky and artfully mussed. His soft leather jacket cost more than a good-quality used car, and his torn, faded blue jeans screamed, *I'm so rich I can get away with wearing rags.* Addison's expression was set to Permanent Smirk.

Max wanted to shove a strudel right into that smirk. *This is the guy I'm supposed to look like?* he thought.

Addison surveyed the room as if it were his personal kingdom, adjusted his cool-nerd glasses to the correct angle, and strolled toward a love seat three tables away from Max. Sinking into it, he began tap-tapping away on his phone.

"Don't watch him so closely," Mr. Dobasch muttered.

"Why not?" came Nikki's voice over the com link. "He's kind of cute, for a total wanker."

Max forced his gaze back to the door, where a muscular Asian man with close-cropped hair and a cold, lizardlike gaze had entered. The man strode directly to Addison's seat.

"Incoming," Rashid murmured over the com link.

The beefy man spoke in low, emphatic tones to Addison. Max couldn't make out what he was saying, but his tone was clearly disapproving.

"Rook has babysitter," said Hantai Annie.

"Great," muttered Max. "Because this job was already too easy."

Addison's voice rose. "And what I do with my free time is my business," he said. "So fetch me a cappuccino, go sit by the door, and stay out of my personal life, hmm?"

Lizard Eyes said something else unintelligible.

"Toddle on now," said Addison. "Or I'll tell Papa on you." Max noticed that the teen had stressed the second syllable of "Papa." *Pretentious twit.*

Addison's minder bit back a comment, nodded curtly, and stalked up to the counter. Score one for the spoiled brat, thought Max.

The door opened again, and in sashayed Vespa, her eyes sparkling, her cheeks flushed from the cold. She hung her overcoat on the rack and shook out her thick blond mane like a slo-mo model in a shampoo ad.

Max had to admit she knew how to make an entrance.

Addison did a double take, hopping to his feet and momentarily losing his aura of practiced cool. Then he remembered himself and ambled over to meet her. Vespa shook his hand and gave him the two-cheek kiss, taking time, Max noticed, to frisk his jacket pocket for the key card. Her hand came out empty.

The button microphone on Vespa's blouse relayed their small talk as Addison ordered her a café au lait at the counter while ignoring his minder, who was just finishing up. Lizard Eyes sent Vespa a watch-yourself-my-girl stare, then retreated to a table to wait for his own drink.

"What's his problem?" Vespa asked, jerking a thumb at the bodyguard.

"Jealousy," said Addison. "He wishes he was young enough to date someone as pretty as you."

She swatted his arm playfully. Out of their line of view, Nikki Knucks pretended to stick a finger down her throat.

For once, Max found himself agreeing with her.

Back at the love seat, Addison and Vespa settled into getting-to-know-you conversation. Max noticed how Addison kept clumsily flirting—resting a hand on her arm, telling her how brilliant her smile was. He also noticed how quickly the spiky-haired boy managed to let drop that his IQ was 177 and that he played an indispensible role at his parents' company.

Through it all, Vespa smiled and nodded and flirted right back.

Disgusting.

When their order was ready, Nikki clomped over to the love seat in her combat boots and banged her tray onto their table. The drinks sloshed as she set them down.

"Watch it," said Vespa.

Nikki fished a grimy rag from her apron pocket and smeared it around the tabletop, missing most of the spilled coffee as she glared at Vespa.

"What's *her* problem?" asked Addison after the redhead had stomped off.

"She's jealous that I'm with someone as handsome as you," said Vespa.

Addison's smirk deepened. "Hmm, yes, we *are* a hot couple," he said, and they laughed together uproariously.

Max thought he might hork up his croissant.

When Vespa insisted on taking a self-photo of the "hot couple" with her phone, Max had to remind himself that it was only for the purposes of capturing an image of Addison's irises.

Heading back to her station, Nikki passed another table of customers. An older woman asked, "Miss, could we please have some more hot milk?"

"Sure," said Nikki. "If you get it yourself." She stomped behind the counter, folded her arms, and glowered at the room.

For what seemed the length of the Paleozoic Era plus a Roman Empire or two, Vespa and Addison chatted, flirted, and sipped their drinks. After five minutes, Max felt he'd seen enough of the boy genius to last him a lifetime. After ten minutes, he looked down to discover that he'd shredded his napkin into tiny bits.

"Steady now," muttered Mr. Dobasch. "Your girlfriend can handle herself."

Max rolled his eyes. "She's *not* my girlfriend," he said between gritted teeth.

The Gravlaki just smiled.

At long last, Addison Rook stood and went to use the loo upstairs. Once the boy genius was out of sight, Vespa reached for his leather coat, which he'd left draped over the love seat.

"*Chotto mate.*" Hantai Annie spoke into the com link. "Vespa, wait. The babysitter is watching."

"No worries," said Rashid. He rose, pretending to text on his phone, and ambled along until he blocked the bodyguard's view of Vespa. "Okay," he mumbled, gaze still riveted on his phone.

Vespa rifled the inside jacket pockets. Lizard Eyes leaned one way, trying to see her, but Rashid shifted and blocked him again. Quickly, the bodyguard canted back the other direction, just as Vespa withdrew her hand from the last pocket.

"Nothing," she whispered. "The key must be on him. He carries his wallet in the left hip pocket."

"How'd you suss that out?" Nikki's sneer carried over the com link. "Checking out his bum?"

A chair scraped, and before Max knew it, Lizard Eyes had risen to his feet and slipped around Rashid. In several quick strides, he loomed over the love seat.

Vespa shrank back.

"What are you up to, my girl?" the bodyguard growled.

OPERATION BRAINWAVE

CHAPTER 22

"SORRY?" Vespa played it innocent, toffee-brown eyes wide and lips parted.

"I saw you rummaging in his jacket," said Lizard Eyes. "You're not the first gold digger I've run off."

Vespa stood, switching to outrage now. "I beg your pardon?" she said frostily. "And who exactly are you?"

A nasty smile oozed across the bodyguard's face as he gripped her arm. "The man responsible for taking out the rubbish."

Max had pushed back his chair before he knew it, but Hantai Annie gripped his wrist. "Wait." At his own table, Rashid covertly watched the drama, ready to step in. But Vespa was cooler than a moonbeam shining on an ice floe.

"If you don't take your hand off me," she said, "I'll tell Addison how his rubbish man's been treating—"

In the midst of the confrontation, Addison appeared.

"What's going on?" he demanded, eyes flashing between his bodyguard and his date.

"This man—" Vespa began.

"She was rifling through your jacket," said Lizard Eyes. "I told you Internet dating was risky."

Addison turned a reproachful face toward the girl. "Vespa?"

"I wasn't searching it," she said, adopting a pouty tone. "It's so *soft*. I was just feeling the leather." Max was agog at how quickly she could switch expressions.

"She's lying," snapped Lizard Eyes.

The boy genius looked back and forth, emotions warring in his face. Clearly he didn't want to believe that this pretty blonde was interested in him for anything other than his charming self. But on the other hand, the annoying minder *was* charged with protecting him. . . .

Hantai Annie Wong must have sensed the situation slipping away from them.

"Nikki," she said, "get his cup. Fingerprints. Also, we need that wallet."

"Rashid," said Max, "I'll bump, you grab." The director nodded her approval.

"On it," said Rashid.

Max shot to his feet, glaring at the director and Dobasch. "You're ruining my life!" he cried, in full hissy-fit mode. "You never let me have any fun!"

Inwardly, he smiled—Vespa wasn't the only actor on their team. Head down, Max stormed toward the love seat, arriving simultaneously with Nikki Knucks.

"Anything else?" she asked Addison in a sullen tone. As Nikki collected the cups, Max charged around her, bumping the boy genius's chest, as if by accident, with his shoulder. At the same instant, Rashid passed behind, snagging the teen's wallet from his hip pocket.

"You there!" said Addison to Max. "Watch where you're going!"

Max had struck the boy a bit harder than was strictly necessary, which was satisfying. But this was no time for a confrontation.

"Sorry, mate," he said, patting Addison's arm as he moved onward. "All right?"

Feeling his macho-ness called into question, Addison huffed, "'Course I'm all right. But that was unforgivably rude."

"Said I was sorry."

Max took a step for the door and found his path blocked by Lizard Eyes. Up close, the man radiated quiet menace and garlic fumes. Past his shoulder, Vespa looked worried.

"Hang on." Lizard Eyes' callused paw clamped onto Max's shoulder like a vise. His other hand began patting Max down.

"Easy there, sailor," said Max. "At least buy a guy flowers first."

"How do I know you're not a pickpocket?" growled Lizard Eyes.

"How do I know you're not a perv?" said Max, trying to break free.

A figure materialized at Max's side. *"Omae dareda?"* growled Hantai Annie. She got up in Lizard Eyes' face like a mama Rottweiler protecting her pups. "What you doing to my son?"

Her ferocity took the bodyguard aback. Lizard Eyes released Max and held up his palms. "Honest mistake. I thought he'd picked my employer's pocket."

Unaccountably, Max felt a warm glow at Hantai Annie calling him her son.

"No, he would never do that," she said. "He's a good boy." She shot Max a narrow look. "Headstrong, but good. You apologize, mister."

"Sorry, son," said Lizard Eyes. Max had to bite the inside of his lip to keep from smiling at how quickly Hantai Annie had cowed the man. "No hard feelings."

Max nodded.

Addison had been patting his pockets, and now he turned to the bodyguard with an aggrieved expression. "Well, he may not have done it, but someone nicked my wallet!"

Lizard Eyes squinted dangerously.

"Oh, look," said Vespa, pointing to the love seat. "Is that it?"

A cognac-colored billfold rested on the black leather. Rashid, passing behind the bodyguard, gave Max a subtle sign.

"Now, how did that get there?" Addison's brow furrowed.

"I don't know, and I don't care," said Vespa. She turned her back on them and stalked toward the coatrack.

"But, where are you going?" asked Addison plaintively.

She glared back at him, all furious beauty. "Do I look like the kind of girl who lets her date accuse her of theft and be grabbed by a . . . a—whatever you are?" This last was aimed at Lizard Eyes.

"Um, no?" said Addison.

"That's the first smart thing you've said all day, boy genius." Her sarcasm was sharp enough to slice a pear. Without another word, Vespa shrugged into her coat and pushed her way outside.

Hantai Annie put a hand on Max's back. "Good, good," she said. "Wallet found, everybody happy. We go." And with a haughty glance at Lizard Eyes, she steered Max toward the door. Rashid finished his coffee and got up to leave. At the coatrack, Mr. Dobasch held the director's jacket for her.

"Nicely done," he muttered. "Your orphans make a good team."

Hantai Annie scowled. "Not bad," she said. "Not bad at all."

A smile tugged at the corners of Max's lips. For the gruff director, that was the equivalent of saying *the best*.

At precisely nine o'clock that night, Max's team left the safe house headed for RookTech. The night was as cold and crisp as a McIntosh apple straight from the fridge. Traffic was light, for the capital, and the Range Rover reached its target with no delay.

The latex half mask itched around Max's eyes and nose, his hair contained the better part of a bottle of mousse, and the cool-nerd glasses cut into his field of vision. To top it off, he kept forgetting he wore greasepaint to adjust his skin tone, and he'd rub his face, smearing it about.

Disguise work: not nearly as cool as the movies pretend.

Wyatt had appointed himself Max's disguise consultant, repairing the occasional smears and reminding his friend not to touch the latex.

"Easy, mate." For the fifteenth time, he caught Max's hand on its way to scratch his nose. "You mess that stuff up now, and we can't fix it. Then you can't get into the building."

"Yeah, yeah," Max agreed, bouncing his foot. He'd been antsy all evening.

A lot was riding on this mission, and Max felt the responsibility weighing heavily on his narrow shoulders.

"Should've been *me* going in there," Nikki griped. "There's gotta be someone at this crummy company who looks enough like me."

"Nobody's that unlucky," said Tremaine with a wicked grin.

Nikki merely scowled at him.

Just around the corner from the RookTech building, Hantai Annie pulled the car to the curb. She, Wyatt, Nikki, and Tremaine would stay there as backup while Max and Mr. Dobasch conducted the heist. Clever Wyatt had worked out a way to monitor RookTech's security cameras on his laptop computer so at least they wouldn't be traveling blind.

"Remember, always keep com system on," said Hantai Annie, half turning in her seat to look at Max. "If something goes wrong, we make distraction."

What she didn't mention, he noticed, was that they wouldn't actually be able to come to the rescue, if one were needed. Once inside, Max and Mr. Dobasch were on their own.

Max gnawed his thumbnail.

The Gravlaki angled the rearview mirror to check his appearance and made a final adjustment to his dark blond wig. He blinked twice, ensuring that his hazel-brown contact lenses were well placed. Then he turned to the director.

"Thank you, Madame Wong," said Dobasch.

"For what?" she asked.

"More fun than I've had since Comrade Gorbachev was running things. I've missed the great game."

She inclined her head. *"Nandemonai,"* she said. "You're welcome."

The Gravlaki sketched a salute. "Don't wear sandals, try to avoid the scandals."

"Pump don't work 'cause vandals took the handles," Hantai Annie replied solemnly.

Max leaned forward between the seats. "All right, that's the second time you've done that sign-countersign thing. What gives?"

The adult agents traded a glance. Hantai Annie lifted an eyebrow and the lean Gravlaki answered with a nod.

"A few of us spies, both East and West, have a little . . . secret society," said Mr. Dobasch.

"What, a social club?" said Wyatt.

"Like a club," the spy allowed, "but with danger and guns."

"Maybe someday you will be asked to join," Hantai Annie said.

"But for now . . ." Dobasch opened his door. "Showtime, Mr. Rook." He flashed a wolfish grin at Max.

"Let's roll, Mr. Medved," said Max. He turned to Wyatt. "How do I look?"

The blond boy cocked his head. "Seven kinds of freaky, but enough like Addison to fool the face recognition. I hope."

"Your confidence is such a comfort," said Max.

Wyatt gave him a double thumbs-up. "Operation Brainwave begins!"

"*Gambare*," said Hantai Annie. "Everyone, good luck!"

Max joined Mr. Dobasch on the sidewalk, and they strolled around the corner, just two RookTech employees coming in for a late-night work session. It was cold enough for Max to see his breath, and he was grateful for his leather jacket, a cheap knockoff of the one Addison had worn earlier that day.

Their footsteps echoed, loud on the quiet street. Most of the businesses that lined it were dark, but RookTech's illuminated windows provided a beacon, throwing rectangles of light across the pavement.

Two doors short of their goal, a shadowy form stepped from hiding.

With the hand that held his briefcase, Dobasch swept Max back, reaching for his concealed weapon with the other.

"Wait!" said the figure. "I'm Max's father."

Simon Segredo wore the shabby clothes of a homeless man, but his eyes burned with urgency. A familiar rush of mixed feelings pulsed through Max.

"Um, not the best time for a visit," he said, motioning Dobasch to stand down. "We're kind of busy." Max scanned the street for RookTech security guards, but they were alone for the moment.

"Max, I—" For the first time, Simon seemed to register his son's disguise. "What's wrong with your face?"

Max pushed down his impatience. "I'm on a job. Can't this wait?"

Simon took his son's arm and pulled him aside. "I'm afraid it can't. LOTUS is planning some kind of strike at S.P.I.E.S."

"What will they do?" asked Mr. Dobasch, butting into the conversation.

"I don't know." The elder Segredo shot him an irritated glance. "I only know it's big." He drew his son out of the Gravlaki's earshot. "Look, Max, I want you to come away with me."

"Er, sorry?" said Max, thrown by the change of subject.

Simon's fingers dug into his arm like talons. "Run away with me, and we'll make a fresh start in another country."

It felt like a giant fist had punched its way into Max's chest and squeezed all the air from his lungs. He gaped, he stammered, and finally he choked out, "No."

"No?"

"You . . . you . . ." said Max, groping for words. "You pop up . . . try to run my life. How . . . how do you even know where I am?"

His father had the good grace to look shamefaced. "The picture I gave you? It's got a tracker."

Fresh outrage blazed through Max like a hungry brushfire. Unconsciously, his fingers sought the photo in his jacket pocket.

"You bugged your own son?!" he burst out.

"Well, I—" Simon began.

"What kind of ratbag are you?"

Hurt registered on his father's face. "I had to know where you were," said Simon. "I failed your mother; I couldn't bear it if anything happened to you."

"You—" Max's tongue came untied with a vengeance.

"You couldn't bear it if something happened to me? How about all those years of foster care? Eh? You didn't seem to mind something happening to me then."

Max's father rubbed a hand over his long jaw. His eyes were haunted pools. "That almost killed me. I can't lose you again. Please?"

Part of Max wanted nothing more than to be with his father, to have a normal family, a normal life. But he'd already made his choice—they both had.

That road was closed.

Mutely, Max shook his head. He pulled away from his father and stumbled down the sidewalk toward RookTech, Mr. Dobasch falling into step beside him.

It took everything Max had not to look back.

Just out of range of the security cameras, he and Dobasch activated their com devices, then they stepped into the entranceway where Max had conducted surveillance only two days before. It seemed like a lifetime ago. Inside the lobby, a male and female guard sat behind a reception counter. Another pair stood by the elevators, watching.

Max took a deep breath to calm his nerves, drew the key card from his pocket, and fed it through the scanner, turning his face up to the wall-mounted box that held the camera. He tried to maintain a bored smirk, as Addison did. He felt sure that the camera's merciless eye would pick up the faint seam where the latex met flesh, the subtle difference in skin tone.

For a long moment, nothing happened.

"Steady," muttered Mr. Dobasch.

Despite the cold, sweat prickled at Max's scalp. He cast a nervous glance at the security force. Were they even now preparing to rush out and apprehend him?

The intercom on the wall crackled. "Master Rook?" A stiff-sounding male voice. "Didn't expect to see you tonight." Through the glass, Max could make out the chubby, gray-haired guard on the receiver.

Max tried to deepen his voice, aiming for Addison's drawl. "Big day tomorrow," he said. "Just wanted to make a final check."

"Ah," said the guard. "Of course. Can't be too careful, eh?"

"One can *never* be too careful," said Max. "Now, if you don't mind . . . ?" He waved a hand at the door.

"Certainly," said Gray Guard. "Just remove your glasses and try it again, young master. You know how fussy the scanner can be."

"Oh, right," said Max, with a forced chuckle. "Silly of me." He carefully removed his spectacles, swiped the key card once more, and looked up at the camera, holding his breath.

This time, the lock released with a click.

Max blew out a small sigh, replaced his cool-nerd glasses, and opened the door.

They were inside.

THE AMAZING SPIDER-MAX

CHAPTER 23

IT WAS LONGER than the Great Wall of China, longer than Magellan's voyage, longer than a trip to the moon on a mini-scooter. The walk from the front door to the elevators felt like the longest of Max's life. All four guards stared flinty-eyed as he and Mr. Dobasch paced across acres of pearl-and-rose-veined marble floor.

Max felt sure the alarm would wail at any moment.

"Not so fast," murmured the Gravlaki.

Catching himself, Max slowed to Addison's arrogant saunter. He reminded himself again, I am the world's biggest spoiled brat, and all these people work for my parents. Still, his breathing remained shallow and tight.

"Who's that with you, Master Rook?" Gray Guard called out.

"Um." Max's brain froze, instantly forgetting which

employee Dobasch was impersonating. "Some . . . peon," he said after a pause. "Tell them your name, peon."

"Ivan Medved," said Dobasch in a bored singsong. He waved a fake ID badge, which wouldn't hold up to close scrutiny.

Gray Guard squinted at it from fifteen feet away.

Don't ask to see it, don't ask to see it, Max thought furiously.

The guard looked down at his computer monitor and tapped a few keys. "Medved . . . from publicity?" he said. "What brings you here?"

"Um, we're . . ." Max began. Then he remembered who he was supposed to be and assumed an expression snottier than a roomful of rug rats in flu season. "That's above your pay grade, mister. . . ."

"Leatherby," the guard said. "But I—"

Max pulled out his phone. "Are you going to let us through, or shall I ring Papa and wake him? Hmm?"

Flustered, Leatherby stammered, "I, er, that is—your father's in the building, Master Rook."

Max gulped. This was not joyous news.

The gray-haired guard misread his frown. "But no—no, please don't trouble him. They told us to be thorough, that's all."

Slipping the phone back into his jacket, Max said, "All right, then, Leatherby. I suppose I'll let it slide this time. Come along, Medved."

He sauntered on toward the elevators, drawing nearer and nearer to two terribly tall, terribly grim-looking male guards, whom Max pretended to ignore. He prayed that the disguise would hold up to close examination.

They passed between the guards, took two steps, then—

"Mr. Rook?" said the younger of the pair.

Max's heart quivered and jumped in his chest like a ferret in a trap. Turning slowly, he offered the man a bored expression. "Mmm?"

Light glinted off a piratical-looking gold ring in the guard's ear. Max sent that ring all his attention, hoping Pirate Guard wouldn't notice his nervousness.

"Good luck tomorrow," said the guard.

With a smirk and a lordly wave, Max swaggered over to the call buttons and pressed UP. Beads of sweat trickled from his hairline, seeping down under the half mask.

Max tensed. Would the moisture weaken the adhesive and make the latex come loose?

At the elevator's sudden chime, he started.

Pirate Guard covered a smile. "Guess we're all a bit nervy, eh, Mr. R?"

Forcing a chuckle, Max said, "I really must lay off the espresso."

The young guard sent him a curious look, but Max and Mr. Dobasch stepped into the car, and the doors closed before the man could comment further.

"Whew," said Max, reaching up to blot the sweat. "That—"

Mr. Dobasch cut him off. "Hope we don't go too late tonight, sir." Under cover of scratching his nose, he whispered, "Don't forget, they're watching."

"Oh. Right," said Max. "Not *too* late. I've got to . . ."—he searched for some activity Addison would probably engage in—"er, rebuild my computer."

"Ah," said Dobasch.

The com link in Max's ear gave a faint hiss. "Rebuild my computer?" said Wyatt's voice.

"You try making this stuff up," Max whispered. "See how you like it."

Hantai Annie's voice spoke: "*Oi, omae.* Stay quiet, stay focused."

The elevator stopped at the seventh floor, but the doors wouldn't open, even after Max repeatedly punched the door-open button.

"Forget your key card?" Dobasch-as-Medved asked, inclining his head toward the elevator controls.

Duh.

This was a special floor with limited access. Belatedly, Max noticed the card reader and thumbprint screen above the bank of buttons.

"I'm so distracted lately," he said, for the benefit of any microphones in the elevator. "I'm really not myself."

He slipped a hand into his jacket pocket, inserting his thumb into the thimblelike cap they'd created with Addison's thumbprint. Then he swiped his card and pressed the bogus print to the scanner.

Whoosh—the elevator doors slid open.

Max and Dobasch proceeded to a conference room right around the corner from the secured chamber that—they hoped—held the mind-control device. Fortunately, the seventh floor seemed deserted. Addison Rook's father was nowhere in sight.

So far, so good.

After ensuring that the room was free of security cameras, Mr. Dobasch sat at the long table and opened his briefcase. Instead of the usual papers and such, it contained Max's climbing gear, a laser pointer, a small rucksack, and a black box with a suction cup on one side and two wires extending from the other.

"What's that?" asked Max.

"Your cover," Dobasch replied. "Evading the floor sensors won't help much if they can watch you climbing the walls."

"Good point."

The Gravlaki helped rig Max's gear around his torso: a length of lightweight rope, belaying harness, and climbing hooks. Max hoped his brief practice session in the safe house would prove sufficient.

Snagging the empty rucksack, he followed Mr. Dobasch into the corridor. The Gravlaki stopped just shy of the corner, pointing to a camera mounted high on the wall.

"And here it begins," he said.

They stayed carefully out of camera range as he attached the black box to the wall and connected its wires to the back of the camera.

"Now for a little rock and roll," said Mr. Dobasch, flicking the box's switch.

"I'm more of a hip-hop guy myself," said Max.

The spy quirked an eyebrow. "Rock and roll is when we sample a video feed of the empty corridor and keep repeating it over and over, so the guards think nothing's happening."

"I knew that," said Max.

Dobasch offered him a boost, and Max stretched to push aside a ceiling tile. Clutching the metal bar the tile had rested on, he hauled himself up until he could wriggle his way into the space above the drop ceiling.

The flat smell of dust and warm, stale air filled his nostrils. Max sneezed explosively.

"Everything all right?" asked Mr. Dobasch.

Through the gap in the ceiling, Max could see only a bit of the spy's blond wig. He scootched forward to meet his gaze.

"Peachy," said Max.

"Now remember, when you're working on the door, don't touch the floor, no matter what."

"Got it."

"I'll be here waiting," said Mr. Dobasch.

"And if a guard shows up?" Max asked.

The Gravlaki drew a finger across his throat and made a

kzztch sound. "That, or I'll hide like a little girl. Depends on how tough he is."

"Right," said Max.

"*Udachi,*" said Dobasch. "Good luck."

Wyatt's voice crackled in Max's ear. "Luck, mate."

Everyone was wishing him luck. Max figured that meant he really needed it.

He slid the tile back into place, switched on his flashlight, and played it about the cramped space. A small forest of thick wires held up the metal grid that supported the drop ceiling. Through that enclosed space snaked cables and air ducts. At a glance, Max could see why he, rather than the Gravlaki, had been elected to make this journey.

It was a tight squeeze, even for a teen.

Gingerly, Max crawled along the grid work, making sure to keep his hands and knees off of the flimsy tiles. It was stifling in the subceiling, and hotter than the devil's rec room. Max began sweating profusely.

In a few short minutes, he'd reached the far end of the hallway. Removing another tile and hooking his climbing rope to the metal bar, Max swung his legs down into space. With one hand on his belaying device, he took a deep breath. He said a quick prayer to the god of spies, whoever that might be.

Then he pushed off.

Instantly, he plummeted six feet.

Purely on reflex, Max's hand squeezed the device,

arresting the free fall with a teeth-jarring jerk—his bum only eight inches from the floor. He clutched the rope above him with both hands, straining to keep his legs up.

"Forgot to lock your device first?" Dobasch asked.

"What . . . makes you . . . think that?" Max grunted, wobbling like a demented top.

His stomach and leg muscles screamed. Max swore if he ever made it out of there, he'd do a hundred sit-ups a day. Well, at least fifty.

First one foot then the other nearly touched the floor. He was only a wiggle and a bump away from triggering the pressure sensors.

"No worries." Wyatt's voice in his ear was cheerful. "Just press the up button, mate."

"Ha, and ha," said Max through gritted teeth.

Mr. Dobasch's tone was soothing. "Max, first you must brace your legs against the door to stabilize."

Max did as directed. He felt movement against his hip and glanced down to see the cell phone slipping from his pocket.

Yikes.

One-handed, Max snatched it just before it hit the carpet. He blew out a long breath. Ever so carefully, he stowed the phone in a jacket pocket and zipped it closed.

"Then," said the Gravlaki, "pull as hard as you can to create slack, and slide the device up."

"Sure," Max muttered. "A piece of cake." But with his

feet resting against the door, he found he could indeed haul himself up far enough to create the necessary slack and slide the belaying device up six inches.

"And again," said Mr. Dobasch.

Max repeated the maneuver over and over, until his biceps burned and his legs trembled. But at last he found himself in position before the door lock.

"Good," said the Gravlaki. "We may make a spy of you yet."

Hantai Annie, silent until now, spoke up over the com link. "Max-*kun*. Guards are making random patrols. They on sixth floor now. If you can hurry, this is good thing."

"Gee, thanks," said Max. "No pressure there."

Groping in his pocket, he located the high-res photo of Addison Rook's eyeballs, their centers cut out so Max's own pupils would show. With this in one hand, he took out the key card and slid it through the scanner. Before leaning into the iris reader, he paused.

"This *will* work, right?" he asked.

"Theoretically," said Mr. Dobasch.

Max held the photo up to his eyes and brought his face close to the device.

"And if it doesn't?"

The machine emitted a grating buzz, like the noise a wrong answer earns on a TV game show. Two beats later, red lights flashed in the hallway, and a deafening Klaxon blared.

"Time for Plan B!" cried the Gravlaki.

CHAPTER 24

TO BREACH THE UNBREACHABLE DOOR

ADRENALINE PUMPED through Max's veins as pandemonium broke loose in that quiet corridor. His ears rang with the noise; the strobing lights assaulted his eyes.

"Up, up!" yelled Mr. Dobasch. "Back into the ceiling!"

"Brilliant tip," said Max. "And here I'd been thinking of waiting for the guards."

He ignored his fancy belaying gear. Hand over hand, Max heaved himself up the rope, feet scrabbling against the door. At the other end of the hallway, Mr. Dobasch was presumably running for cover.

"Doushite da?" Hantai Annie asked over the link. "What's happening?"

"Kind of . . . busy now," Max grunted.

"He set off the alarm," said Dobasch. "Now we hide."

Wyatt's voice cut in, sharp with worry. "The guards are running up the stairs. Might want to hide soon-ish."

Max still hung a good two feet below his escape hatch. "How . . . soon?"

"Maybe twenty seconds," said Wyatt. "Maybe—"

Ba-BAM! The unmistakable sound of a body hitting a door and an open door hitting a wall.

The guards were just around the corner.

Arm muscles burning, Max put on a burst of speed. If I survive this, he thought, I swear I'll also start doing a hundred press-ups a day. He hooked his elbows over the edge of the grid, twisted and jerked like a marlin on a line, and swung his legs up into the hole.

Rolling onto his side, he slid the ceiling tile back into place. He didn't bother being quiet; no one could hear him over the alarm's howl. Max lay there, heart thudding, trying to slow his panting breath.

Two voices—a male and female—barked terse commands in the hallway.

Max noticed that the tile he'd replaced sat askew, revealing a sliver of the corridor below. He pushed it down, but it wouldn't fit. Fingers fumbling along the edges, he discovered that a loop of the rope was dangling through the crack.

Careless! He berated himself.

Max managed to tug most of the line back inside, but before he could reclaim the last bit, two figures clad in blue-gray appeared.

He froze.

If he pulled the rest of the line through, they'd see the

movement. On the other hand, if he did nothing, they only had to look up to spot the intruder.

EEE-ooh, EEE-ooh, yowled the alarm.

"I *hate* that bloody noise," bellowed the male guard, in a bullfroggy voice. "It's like bloody fingernails on a blackboard."

"Then turn it off," a woman's voice shouted.

The emergency Klaxon stopped in midwail.

Max held his breath.

"The lock's intact," said the female guard, sounding like a perky aerobics instructor at the local fitness center. "Doesn't look like anyone's gotten inside."

"'Course, if they *have,*" croaked Bullfrog Guard, "how could we tell? We're *out*side."

Perky Guard cocked her head. From his lookout, Max could see the dark roots of her blond hair. "Fair point," she said. "Let's have a look, shall we?"

Max heard the *snick* of a card being swiped and the *bip-bip-bip* of numbers punched into a keypad. Bullfrog Guard put his face to the iris scanner, and the door opened. As they stepped inside, the motion-detector alarm began to keen.

"Not again," moaned Bullfrog Guard. "Turn that bleeding thing off."

Max thought quickly. For their heist to work, he had to sneak inside and hide while the security was disarmed. . . .

Time to see whether Dobasch's Plan B was a boon or a bust.

Max eased his rope out of the crack and fit the ceiling panel back into place. His flashlight illuminated the wall separating his section of the subceiling from the part that lay above the secured room. He pressed a hand to the barrier. The "wall" was flimsy plastic, like the ceiling panels.

Max grinned. The room was accessible from above.

While the motion detector still wailed, he punched the wall panel as hard as he could. It fell back into the space beyond.

The alarm cut off like a throttled chicken.

Max recalled Mr. Dobasch explaining that motion detectors responded to heat, not movement. That meant that if you were standing in the room when the device was armed, it would accept your presence without a peep. Then you could move about at will, as long as you didn't get too hot.

Was it possible? Could he drop into the room during those few seconds between the guards' closing the door and the motion detector's rearming?

Clamping the flashlight between his teeth, Max crawled, as slowly as glacier melt, over the fallen barrier and above the secured room.

Down below, he could hear the guards checking the chamber.

A burst of walkie-talkie static. "What's going on up there?" a metallic voice demanded. "Report? Over."

"All quiet," said Bullfrog Guard, confusion evident in his voice. "Nothing missing, no one here. Over."

"Roger that," said Walkie-Talkie Guy. "Lock up and carry on. Over and out."

Bullfrog Guard signed off.

"It's a system glitch, most likely," said Perky Guard. "Rearm the blasted thing and let's go. I need maximum coffee."

Max maneuvered himself into position, to be ready to drop down as soon as they left. But unfortunately, his shoe bumped a support wire.

"What was that?" said Perky Guard.

"What?"

Max held stock-still.

"Sounded like something up above," she said. "We should check."

No, thought Max, you really shouldn't.

"When you say 'we,' you mean 'me,' don't you?" groused Bullfrog Guard.

"Well, you *are* the tall one," said his partner.

The man mumbled something Max couldn't make out. A grunt and the scuff of a shoe later, a tile near him bumped upward. Light shone through the crack.

Max's heart thumped so loudly he was sure the man could hear it. He glanced about for something to use as a weapon— something other than an empty rucksack and a length of rope. But there was nothing.

He clenched his fists and gathered his strength.

The tile tilted up more sharply. Max couldn't see the

man's head because the gap lay on the side facing away from him. Bullfrog Guard's flashlight beam wandered about the space, coming closer, closer.

Max hesitated. Should he bop the man through the tile, or wait until his face was exposed and go for the eyes? Which would be more effective?

"I don't see any . . ." Bullfrog Guard began. The shaft of light froze, its edge only a foot away from Max. "There!"

Max stiffened. This was it—time to act. He doubled his fists and raised them high.

"What is it?" asked Perky Guard.

"A big, fat rat."

Max froze, midstrike. A rat? His eyes traced the beam's path and spotted the rodent at the far corner, waddling along with a length of copper wire clamped in its jaws. It chittered, less than thrilled with the interruption.

"Eeeugh," said Bullfrog Guard. "I hate rats."

"Well, I think they're cute," said Perky Guard. "But it's not our problem. Leave it for maintenance, and let's get a move on."

The light vanished, the tile clattered back into place, and Max heard the man clambering down from the desk or chair or whatever he'd stood on.

"Remember, this thing rearms in thirty seconds, so no dawdling," said Perky Guard.

"Who's the dawdler?" said Bullfrog. "Not me, I can tell you that."

Another *bip-bip-bip* on the keypad below, followed by swift footsteps brushing carpet and the door clicking shut.

Hastened along by thoughts of rats, Max sprang into action.

He lifted the nearest tile out and set it to one side as the guards' voices receded down the hall. In a flash, he hooked his rope to the metal grid, swung his legs into the hole, and dropped down into the room.

This time, he *wanted* the free fall. The floor rushed up to meet him, and Max clamped the belaying device just in time. He stopped with a jolt, his backside a foot above the carpet.

Lowering his legs to the floor, Max whipped his head around, scanning for the control panel. As he spotted it, the warning light turned from green to red.

The alarm was activated.

It wasn't that Max didn't trust Mr. Dobasch's vast store of spy knowledge, but he stayed perfectly still, eyes glued to that little red light. It held steady. The motion detector seemed to have accepted him.

Slower than the class airhead reaching for his homework, Max waved, testing the device. Nothing.

Wyatt's voice in his earpiece made him jump. "Well, mate? How ya goin'?"

"I'm having a heart attack," whispered Max.

"No, really," said Wyatt.

Max's eyes swept the room, a posh-looking office with a

cherrywood desk, ultramod chairs, burgundy carpeting, a bookshelf, and all the usual office-y furnishings.

"I'm in," he said.

"Bonzer!" the blond boy crowed over the com link.

Max winced. Wyatt had many talents; volume control wasn't one of them.

"I'm starting the search now," said Max. "Send up a signal flare if someone's coming."

"Too right," said Wyatt.

"Just one question," said Max.

"What's that?"

"What's this mind-control gizmo look like?"

Wyatt fell silent. Hantai Annie cleared her throat. "All we know: it fits in small rucksack."

"So does a Chihuahua," Max heard himself saying. He caught himself. "Sorry, that was rude."

"Find it, Max-*kun*," said Hantai Annie.

Moving like one of those tai chi blokes in the park, Max stepped around the desk. Atop it rested a telephone, an in-box full of papers, and a pen and pencil cup that said WORLD'S BEST DESPOT on the side. Methodically, he searched every drawer, using his picks to break into the locked ones. He found nothing that could be used for mind control, unless one counted back issues of the employee newsletter.

The workstation beside the desk yielded nothing but a pricey Mac computer and another stack of reports.

Even in this high-tech company, office work seemed to be all about the paper.

He prowled onward, rifling through the filing cabinet and a matching cherrywood credenza. Neither held anything remotely promising. Temporarily stymied, Max rested his hands on his hips and let his gaze wander about the room.

"*Nanika attaka?*" Hantai Annie's voice buzzed in his ear. "Anything yet?"

"Not a sausage," said Max.

"Look for a safe," came Mr. Dobasch's voice over the com link.

A surge of relief swept through Max. "The guards didn't find you."

"Heh. Mere guards never visit the executive toilet," said the Gravlaki. "Check behind paintings, or under furniture. It's got to be somewhere."

Keeping a wary eye on the motion detector's warning light, Max stepped up his search. He lifted paintings, flipped over rugs, shifted aside pillows. No luck. If the room held a safe, it was hidden somewhere beyond his powers of detection.

"Nothing," said Max. "Bugger all."

"Search harder," said Hantai Annie. "It *must* be there."

Max interlaced his fingers on top of his head and thought hard: If I were a thingamabob that could manipulate minds, where would I be? He revolved slowly, scrutinizing every inch of the room as if it were the first time he'd seen it.

Mini–conference table and chairs? No. Leather sofa? No. Desk and office chair? Not there either. Bookshelf?

Max stopped turning.

In four strides, he stood before it. Five shelves of leather-bound volumes and random knickknacks stared back at him. Max worked from the bottom up, running his hands over the objects and occasionally lifting one to check it.

A golf trophy. A photo of a pale, dark-haired man and woman with a bratty-looking kid that must have been a younger Addison Rook. An ancient personal computer, chunky and square as a cinder block. More photos of the man and woman, including one with eccentric billionaire Reginald Elbow.

Interesting, but irrelevant.

Max continued, pulling out larger books to check if something had been hidden inside them, picking up wooden statues from Africa and India, even examining the back wall of the bookshelf for signs of a hidden safe.

Nothing.

A sense of mounting panic rose in his chest.

The device *had* to be there. It had to. The entire future of the orphanage depended on it, depended on Max's finding it. Why else would this grotesque office have such ridiculous security if the invention wasn't somewhere inside?

Max gritted his teeth. *Think*, Segredo, he commanded himself.

Once more, he scanned the room, and this time his eyes lingered on the sleek computer beside the desk. His gaze flicked over to the ancient PC and back to the new one.

Two computers? Who needed two computers?

He reached for the blocky old machine, and discovered that its beige plastic casing was loose. Max lifted, and the entire shell of the computer came away in his hands. Underneath it sat a gleaming cobalt cube not much bigger than a high-end toaster. One surface was covered with a bank of buttons, dials, and switches, and atop the cube rested a blue-and-silver C-shaped strip of metal that looked like a headband for a hippie from Alpha Centauri.

The mind-control device.

He had found it at last.

THE THINGAMABOB THIEF

CHAPTER 25

MAX OPENED his mouth to tell his team the good news, but the words died on his tongue like daisies in December snow. A sudden realization staggered him.

This invention—*this* was what LOTUS wanted above all things.

And right now it was *his*—not the orphanage's, not Hantai Annie's. It was Max's, to do with as he wished.

This device was leverage. With this in his hands, he could bargain with LOTUS; he could get anything he wanted. He could make them leave S.P.I.E.S. alone; he could have more money than Gates, Trump, and the guy who built the Taj Mahal put together.

He could even make them take his father off the hit list.

For an eternal instant, Max stood rooted, possibilities shooting off like sparklers in his mind. The invention was his for the taking. All he had to do was lie to Hantai Annie, lie to his friends, and . . .

Max's stomach dropped, like he was teetering on the edge of a high cliff.

"Well?" came Wyatt's voice in his earpiece. "Anything yet?"

"I . . . I found it," Max choked out.

"Strike me pink!" Wyatt cried. "Good on ya, mate!"

Hantai Annie and Dobasch added their congratulations to Wyatt's, which Max accepted in a daze.

"Take it and go," said Mr. Dobasch. "We're a long way from home free."

With shaking hands, Max placed the device and the headband thingummy (a headset, perhaps?) into his rucksack. He restored the room to the way he'd found it, and then, with one eye on the motion detector, began his slow ascent up the rope.

Twice, he froze when the red light began blinking. Twice, he waited until it returned to normal.

"Will someone tell me how I'm meant to climb a rope and not heat up?" Max muttered.

"Tremaine says, 'Chill, Winston,'" said Wyatt. "Whatever that means."

"Easy, Max-*kun*," said Hantai Annie.

After what felt like a short forever, Max finally rested his elbows on the ceiling's grid work. Though he longed to jerk his legs through the hole and scurry off, he deliberately brought himself up, a little at a time. His arms and shoulder muscles burned with the effort.

But at last, he lay along the metal beam, panting and slick with sweat. *My disguise must look a regular dog's breakfast,* he thought. But no time for worrying now. Max replaced the tile and crawled back along the subceiling to the place where he'd first entered.

Dust tickled his nose. The rucksack snagged briefly on a support cable.

"Talk to me," he said, wriggling free. "Where are the guards?"

"Your two?" said Wyatt. "Coffee break. And the rest are at their posts on the ground floor."

In another minute, Max reached the end of the corridor and lifted a ceiling tile. The gaunt face of Stanislav Dobasch gazed up at him.

"Good start," said the Gravlaki.

"Start?" said Max.

"Of course," said Dobasch. "We still have to escape in one piece."

"Oh," said Max. "Is that all?"

He clambered down and stowed his climbing equipment in the briefcase. Dobasch tsk-tsked when he saw the state of Max's latex mask.

"Sweat isn't good for the adhesive," he said, smoothing

down the edges of the disguise. "Let's hope no one comes close enough to notice."

They hurried down the hall, making for the elevators. On the digital display above the doors, Max noted that one car was already headed up toward them.

"Wyatt, who's in the lift?" he asked.

"Hang on," said Wyatt. "Running a face check . . . looks like . . . some office-worker type, and . . ."

"I know that man," said Hantai Annie. "It's Montgomery Rook, Addison's father!"

Max stopped dead, adrenaline flooding his already over-loaded system.

"Go, take the stairs!" the director snapped. *"Isoge!"*

Max and Mr. Dobasch whirled. The stairwell exit lay at the far end of a long cross-corridor, in full view of the elevator. They bolted down the corridor, but just before they reached the door, the elevator pinged behind them.

Dobasch gripped Max's arm, slowing him to a walk. It wouldn't do for RookTech's big boss to see two people running into a stairwell. Not tonight.

Max grasped the doorknob as voices sounded behind them. Two more steps and they'd be free.

"Addison!" a man called.

Max froze.

"Answer him," Mr. Dobasch whispered, edging around Max to open the stairwell door.

Pasting an Addison-like smirk onto his face, Max turned.

"Ah, Da—um, Pa*pa*," he said, emphasizing the second syllable.

"What are you doing here?" It was the dark-haired man Max had seen in the office photos, accompanied by a stressed-looking Indian woman. They stood at the intersection with the main corridor. "I thought you had a date."

"I, er," Max began. Quick, what would Addison say? "She bored me, Papa." Max tried to match the older boy's drawl. "I came in to check on things."

The elder Rook chuckled, taking a couple steps nearer. "None of the girls is bright enough for my boy. Is that it?"

Not too close, thought Max in alarm. He felt movement on his temple and pressed a hand to the edge of the mask, angling away so Mr. Rook wouldn't see.

"Isn't it always?" said Max.

"Join us." Montgomery Rook gestured to the hallway that led to the office Max had just burgled.

Max faked a chuckle. "Coffee first," he said, pointing to the stairwell.

A brief frown crossed Mr. Rook's face, but all he did was lift a hand. "Very well. See you shortly." He nodded at Mr. Dobasch. "Medved."

"Sir," said the Gravlaki.

"Everything ready for tomorrow?"

Max was in an agony to leave—it felt like fire ants were eating him from the inside. But he forced himself to hold his smirk in place while Dobasch answered.

"Ready as can be, sir," said Mr. Dobasch.

"Carry on, then." With a shooing gesture, Mr. Rook and his companion turned into the side corridor.

Max and Dobasch slipped through the door and dashed downstairs.

"You've got to get out of there," said Wyatt over the com link.

"Brilliant advice, Captain Obvious," said Max.

"If he checks his thingo before you get clear, they'll lock the place down."

Max's feet flew down the steps. "Oh, do you reckon?"

Two floors. Three floors. Now they were pounding down from the third floor to the second, nearly there.

"Wait!" Alarm colored Wyatt's tone. "Someone's entered the stairwell below."

Max could hear it now, the hollow, echoing clomp of footsteps. He glanced at Mr. Dobasch, who hooked a thumb toward the second-floor exit door, still half a flight beneath them. Max nodded.

As quietly as possible, they descended the last few steps onto the landing. This time Max was able to get the door open before a man's deep voice called out.

"Oi! Where you going?"

Max resumed his Addison impression and turned a jaded face on their interrogator. "Coffee break, if it's all the same to you," he said.

When he saw who was coming up the stairs, his eyes widened.

It couldn't be.

But it was: bald, burly Zigfrid Plotz, Mr. Dobasch's old boss from the Gravlaki Embassy.

Plotz stepped onto the landing and pulled up short with a snort of surprise.

"Dobasch?" he said. "Your hair . . ."

"Plotznik," said Dobasch, his tone light but his body coiled with readiness.

"What are you doing here?" Plotz's uni-brow crinkled in the middle with puzzlement. One hand drifted down to his side, where a pistol hung in a holster.

"He's with me," Max drawled. He tried for a confident attitude, but his voice wobbled a bit, and it felt like a corner of his mask had come loose again.

Plotz sent Max a suspicious glance and then returned his stare to his former employee. "Well?"

Mr. Dobasch shrugged, drifting closer to the beefy officer. "A man has to eat. If the Gravlakis will not pay my salary, I work for whoever will. But enough about me; why are *you* here?"

Plotz's frown deepened into a scowl. "Baghirov fired me, no thanks to you."

"Pity," said Dobasch. But his eyes twinkled.

"I recently signed on with RookTech security—but I don't recall seeing *your* name on the employee list." Plotz lifted an electronic tablet, punched a button, and began scrolling through a menu.

Max's fists clenched involuntarily.

"That's because," said Dobasch, taking another step nearer, "I'm not on it."

"Eh?" Plotz's broad face wore a confused expression that looked right at home on it. "But you just said—"

"I lied."

Mr. Dobasch's hand lanced out, stiff-fingered, directly into Plotz's throat. The brawny man choked and folded forward.

"Not only do you have the brainpower of lukewarm borscht . . ." Dobasch delivered a knee strike that seemed to come all the way from the basement. ". . . But you, Plotz, are a terrible security officer."

A devastating right cross, and RookTech's newest employee tumbled to the concrete.

Dobasch shook his hand, wincing. "You don't know how long I've waited to say that."

Plotz made no reply, being completely unconscious.

After a quick survey of the second floor, Max discovered an unlocked office. He helped Dobasch drag the motionless guard inside, handcuff him to a desk, and duct-tape his mouth closed.

"That won't keep for long, once he wakes up," said Mr. Dobasch. "Plotz may not win any medals for intelligence, but he is strong like bull."

"Then we should . . ." Max jerked his head toward the door.

"Yes," said Dobasch. *"Arrivederci,* Plotznik!"

After a brief debate, they decided to take the elevator—less suspicious that way. When its doors opened on the ground floor, Max had to restrain an impulse to sprint for the entrance like a cheetah on hot concrete.

Instead, he slipped back into the Addison Rook saunter, as if he had all the time in the world and all the money to spend. He nodded to the two tall guards beside the elevators.

"Hullo, Mr. R," said Pirate Guard. "Everything okay?"

Max offered a condescending boy-genius smile. *"Now* it is," he said. "I don't know what Pa*pa* would do without me."

"Too right, sir," said the guard.

Leading the way, Max strolled across the acre of marble floor as if he were walking the red carpet at a Hollywood premiere. It was the best performance of his life so far.

From the corner of an eye, he monitored chubby, gray-haired Mr. Leatherby, who sat at the long reception desk chatting with a younger female guard. When the man noticed them, he opened his mouth as though to call out a greeting, but the telephone's muted buzz claimed his attention.

Max's eyes lasered in on the entrance.

Only twenty steps away. It felt like twenty miles.

Leatherby answered the phone and spoke with the caller. A frown. He said something that sounded like "Are you sure?" and shot to his feet.

It was torture for Max to keep up his plodding pace,

wondering all the while whether that phone call came from Montgomery Rook. Dobasch, seeming to sense his apprehension, muttered, "Steady."

The guard's voice rose, radiating tension and concern.

Only ten steps away now.

Max examined the door. At least it had no fancy biometric lock on this side; it was designed to keep people out, not in.

"Master Rook!" Leatherby called.

The rucksack on Max's back felt heavier than the right hand of death.

It took all of his control not to bolt right then and there. Instead, he swiveled his head as he kept moving forward, saying only, "Mmm?"

Pretending to straighten his tie, Mr. Dobasch dropped behind Max. His hand edged closer to his concealed shoulder holster.

"It's your father, sir," said the gray-haired guard.

Max made a brushing-off gesture. "Tell him I'll ring him later."

He lifted a palm to the glass door, preparing to push through to freedom.

"There's been a break-in," said Leatherby, his voice shaken. "Someone's stolen the device." His gaze flicked from the rucksack on Max's shoulder, back up to Max's face. His brow furrowed in bafflement.

Max raised a hand to his forehead and discovered a corner of the latex mask drooping like a slice of stray lunch meat.

His eyes met Leatherby's. Time seemed to slow. He shrugged.

"Cheap stickum," said Max.

Before the words "Stop them!" could fully issue from the guard's lips, Mr. Dobasch whipped out his pistol and fired beanbag rounds. Leatherby and his coworker dove behind the desk.

Two more shots sent the elevator guards scurrying for cover. But since Dobasch's gun wasn't firing real bullets, they wouldn't stay hidden for long.

Max's shoulder slammed into the door. He and Dobasch spilled out into the chilly night air as an alarm siren began shrieking like a maddened banshee.

"Director Wong!" the Gravlaki barked into his com link. "They're on to us. Where's that diversion?"

No answer. The com link was silent.

CHAPTER 26

DANGEROUS DOINGS AT THE SAFE HOUSE

DOWN THE SIDEWALK they pounded, making for the rendezvous. But when Max and Dobasch turned the corner, no Range Rover awaited them.

The street was empty.

"Wyatt?" Max called into his com link. "Director?"

Absolutely brilliant, he thought. By all means, let's play hide-and-seek with the getaway car.

At last, a voice crackled in his ear. "Sorry, mate," said Wyatt. "Cops made us move the car, and I had to go off-line. We miss anything?"

Shouts echoed behind them. Mr. Dobasch peeked around the corner and squeezed off a couple of shots at their pursuers.

"Oh, not much," said Max. "Where in blazes are you?"

"Trot down to the next corner," said Wyatt. "We're coming 'round the block."

Max and Mr. Dobasch took off at a dead run. Police sirens wailed, echoing off the office buildings, drawing closer. Gunfire popped behind them, and something whistled through the leaves of a spindly tree that sprouted from the sidewalk.

If the car didn't show soon, Max and Dobasch were in the soup, for certain.

Panting, they rounded the next corner and scanned the sparse traffic. There! A silver Range Rover screeched to a halt and its curbside doors flew open.

"In!" cried Hantai Annie. *"Haire!"*

Max and Mr. Dobasch dove into the car, which squealed away before the doors had closed. Bullets pinged off the side panels.

Tremaine whooped. "Yesss, Maxwell! Swaggerific!"

Max hauled his legs inside the car and found that his head was resting on Nikki's lap.

"Move it or lose it," she growled, roughly shoving him off. But Max caught the traces of a grin on her face. The excitement of the heist was contagious, even for Nikki Knucks.

"You have device?" asked Hantai Annie, swerving around a slow-moving car.

Max sat up. "In my rucksack."

"Beauty!" Wyatt crowed. "Can't wait to check it out." He sank back into the seat and waved his hand in a lordly manner. "To the safe house, Jeeves, and step on it!"

It was a mark of Hantai Annie's delight in their success that she didn't even scold, but only smiled.

Their destination was less a safe house and more a safe luxury town house. Vaulted ceilings, immaculate ivory-colored sofa and chairs, and a massive stone fireplace with room enough to roast a family of boars were the first things Max registered. Then the support team surrounded him, thumping his back and piling on questions and congratulations.

"How did you beat the lock on the secure room?" asked Miss Moorthy.

"When did they tumble to you?" asked Rashid.

Vespa pushed through to his side. "We were so worried." She laid a hand on Max's arm and indicated the laptop computer on the table, still showing the RookTech building's entrance. "When you and Mr. Dobasch came running out with the guards right behind you, we thought you were in for it."

Cinnabar elbowed her aside. "*I* wasn't worried for a second," she said, firing a sharp glance at the blond girl. "Anyone who's been on a mission with you knows you always pull through in the end. Well done, Max." She took his other arm.

Max began to feel uncomfortably warm.

"*Anyone who's been on a mission with you* cares about your safety," said Vespa in a dangerous purr.

The two girls traded glares. Max longed for the peace and

quiet of dodging bullets while fleeing from a well-guarded office building.

He welcomed the distraction when Miss Moorthy handed him a cell phone, saying, "Someone wants to speak with you."

"Hello?"

A familiar chuckle tickled his ear. "So, peaches, it seems you didn't entirely bungle the job after all," rumbled Mr. Stones.

Max tried for nonchalant. "I did all right."

"Top marks, lad," said the teacher. "We just might make a spy of you yet."

Max hung up with a wide smile. At Mr. Vazquez's request, he removed the mind-control device from his rucksack and set it on the dining table beneath the crystal chandelier. When Wyatt reached out for it, Hantai Annie ordered him back.

"*Abunai*," she said. "Don't touch. Elbow-*san* is coming soon, and he won't pay for broken invention."

"But I only wanted to—" Wyatt began.

An electronic warble sounded.

"*Chotto mate.*" The director cut him off with a raised hand as she drew her phone from a pocket. "This may be him." But when she heard the voice on the line, she scowled and spoke another name: "Mr. Krinkle?"

Like a bucket of ice water dumped on a lit birthday cake, the mention of that name extinguished all the joy in the room. It was funny—not ha-ha funny, but the other kind—in the midst of all the excitement, Max had forgotten all about the inspector from the Ministry of Health.

His spirits plummeted.

Could they have pulled off the mission and rescued Merry Sunshine from the brink of bankruptcy only to be shut down by a marshmallow man?

All eyes in the room tracked Hantai Annie Wong as she paced, talking on the phone. "Wait," she said to the man on the other end. "No matter if news is good or bad, everyone should hear together. They deserve that much." She instructed Mr. Vazquez to transfer the call to the laptop computer.

After a quick bit of high-tech wizardry, Henry Krinkle's puffy white face appeared on-screen. "I say," said the inspector, peering at their surroundings, "rather posh digs you have there. Where exactly are you?"

"Um," said Max, too tired to make up a story.

"Another field trip," Hantai Annie lied.

Krinkle's eyebrows lifted. "At night?"

"Cultural enrichment is our middle name," Cinnabar responded with counterfeit enthusiasm.

"You're certain it's not Trump?" Mr. Krinkle chortled at his little joke. The team was too tense to join him, even if the remark had been actually funny.

"Merry Sunshine Orphanage has powerful friends," said Hantai Annie. Her lips set in a tight line. "So, what is your news, Krinkle-*san*?"

The room became as still as a seaside resort moments before a storm. Everyone waited, nobody breathed. Krinkle cleared his throat.

"It's bad news, isn't it?" said Wyatt. "Stone the crows! I knew it."

Cinnabar shushed him.

"First, I must apologize for calling so late," Mr. Krinkle began. "I was off-site all day—just returned."

Yeah, yeah, yeah, thought Max miserably. Get it over with.

"I want to tell you," Krinkle continued, "that after inspecting the premises and talking with all of you, I have reached the conclusion that Merry Sunshine is a very strange orphanage—"

Nikki's jaw thrust out. "I'll give you strange, you poxy blubberball," she muttered. Hantai Annie glared at her warningly.

"Eh, what's that?" said the inspector.

"She says it's true; we *are* strange, overall," said Miss Moorthy.

"Er, yes," said Mr. Krinkle. "Quite. I observed unconventional teaching methods, highly questionable off-site activities, and"—here he looked pointedly at Max—"disrespectful behavior in the children."

"Hey—" Max started to protest, before a look from Hantai Annie cut him off.

"But, as Mrs. Wong just stated, your strange orphanage does indeed have powerful friends. For instance, it is obvious that Mr. Elbow has taken a special interest in the children."

Hantai Annie's lips clamped together briefly, as if reining in some strong emotion.

"I ultimately decided that, if a quality person such as himself, who cares deeply about orphans, supports Merry Sunshine, then"—Krinkle inserted a dramatic pause—"it should continue to shine. The orphanage stays open."

Relief flooded Max.

A cheer rose from the group. Cinnabar brushed away a tear, and even Nikki looked misty-eyed.

Hantai Annie displayed no expression as she thanked Krinkle and clicked off the Skype call. But a grin spread over her face when Mr. Vazquez led them all in singing "For She's a Jolly Good Fellow." Cinnabar couldn't help pointing out that, being a woman, Hantai Annie wasn't exactly a "fellow."

"This calls for drinks!" cried Max. At Mr. Dobasch's raised eyebrow, he said, "Of the nonalcoholic type, of course." Max spotted a Coke can beside some gear on the table and reached for it.

"Not that one!" cried Rashid, catching his arm.

"Warm, is it?" said Max.

The older teen shook his head. "That's one of Wyatt's flashbangs."

"You might say it's got a wee bit of a kick," Wyatt added, grinning.

Mr. Vazquez headed for the kitchen to round up some cold drinks. Tremaine cranked the music, grabbed Vespa, and began dancing, but although she grooved along with him, Max noticed a sad expression flit across her face.

A few minutes later, the adults had settled into examining the mind-control device, and the teens were chatting in twos and threes, hashing over the week's events. Max found Vespa by the garden door, her face curtained by blond hair, gazing out into the night.

"Hey," he said. "What's wrong?"

"Wrong?" She tossed her mane back and sent him an incredulous glance.

"Yeah. You look kind of . . . sad or something."

Vespa glanced back out the window. "No. It's just that . . ." She shook her head. "You won't understand."

"I will," said Max. He leaned his back against the door, the better to see her lovely face. And then he couldn't help noticing Cinnabar standing with Rashid across the room, frowning at him. "Try me."

Vespa cocked her head, considering. "Every instant of happiness," she said, picking her words carefully, "carries the seeds of sadness inside it."

She was right; he didn't understand. "So happiness makes you sad?"

"Melancholy, maybe. This instant, this feeling . . ." Her gesture took in the room and its occupants, aglow with success and camaraderie. "It cannot last. And so I feel a little *saudade*."

Max raised an eyebrow at the unfamiliar word.

Vespa shrugged. "It's Portuguese. I don't know how to say it in English."

The moment stretched.

Max wanted to say something to comfort her, but as drawn to her as he was, he still felt a little tongue-tied. Besides, he suspected she might have hit upon some truth. Most of his life as a foster kid, he'd found himself longing, even in the brighter moments, for something . . . else. Happiness was fleeting. He opened his mouth to say something profound, philosophical, and borderline pretentious, and was rescued by Wyatt.

"All right then, mates?" said the blond boy, munching crisps from a bowl of party snacks.

"Superduper," said Max.

Wyatt chuckled. "Quite a caper, eh? But we pulled it off, slicker than a greased-up wombat through a drainpipe. Snackies?" He offered the bowl to Max, but just then, the doorbell chimed.

"Our client at last," said Hantai Annie. "Victor-*san*, please?"

Mr. Vazquez peeked out the peephole and unlocked the door. In shuffled their client, Reginald Demetrius Elbow, wearing a thousand-dollar fedora, a five-thousand-dollar suit, and a deeply unhappy expression. His ponytailed bodyguard followed, hands clasped behind his back.

"Mr. Elbow," Hantai Annie greeted him.

"Mrs. Wong." From the billionaire's expression, you would've thought that S.P.I.E.S. was plundering his bank account rather than delivering the object of his desire.

The director's eyes narrowed. "We have device. Is something the matter?"

"Mr. Elbow doesn't much fancy being held hostage," said Mr. Elbow.

"But we not holding you hostage," said Hantai Annie.

"No," came a familiar posh voice from the doorway. "But I'm afraid *I* am."

Max whirled. Instead of the second bodyguard, the doorway held Mrs. Frost, the head of LOTUS.

Dobasch and Annie both reached for their weapons.

"Ah-ah-ah," said Mrs. Frost. "I wouldn't do that if I were you."

The door swung wider to reveal Ebelskeever and a half-dozen LOTUS agents, all carrying semiautomatic rifles trained on the S.P.I.E.S. team. Ebelskeever's grin looked as wicked as a witch's wardrobe.

"Take out your weapons—slowly—then put them on the floor and kick them over here," said the gorilla-like spy.

Reluctantly, Annie, Dobasch, and Moorthy complied.

"Now then," said Mrs. Frost. "What shall we talk about?"

CHAPTER 27

FROST
BITES

MAX FELT LIKE his stomach had been stomped on with hobnail boots. He raised his hands along with the rest of his team, still in shock. The LOTUS agents swaggered into the room, patted everyone down, and collected their weapons. Then they returned to flank their leader.

"How rich," said Mrs. Frost.

She looked like a cat that had cornered the last budgie left in the birdcage. Her storm-gray eyes roamed the room, taking in the sullen orphans, the disgruntled billionaire, and the cobalt-blue cube on the tabletop.

She chuckled.

"We let you steal the device for us, and we didn't even need to lift a finger. Now, *that* is why LOTUS is on top, and your little ragtag band"—she waved a dismissive hand at Hantai Annie—"is destined for the ash heap of history."

"But how did you know our plans?" Wyatt spluttered, his eyes round as twin full moons.

"Isn't it obvious?" said Nikki. "Segredo told them."

"Simon?" said Wyatt.

"Max," growled Nikki.

Anger bubbled in Max's chest like bile. "That's a lie," he snarled. "I would never help them."

"Oh, really?" said Nikki. "Then who was it feeding them our secrets only a few weeks ago? I swear he looked so much like you."

Max clenched his jaw. He couldn't argue with that one.

Folding her arms, Mrs. Frost arched an amused eyebrow. "Young Max is right; he didn't help us this time."

"Then, how . . . ?" asked Victor Vazquez.

"Trade secret," said Mrs. Frost. "Suffice to say, that's what separates the big dogs from the little ones. Ronnie dear, fetch the invention, if you please."

The burly Ebelskeever stalked over to the table and collected the blue cube and headset. Mr. Elbow's eyes followed with a wistful hunger as the agent carried it back to his boss.

"That's Mr. Elbow's device," muttered the billionaire.

"You may as well say it is RookTech's, or even Mrs. Wong's," the LOTUS chief drawled. "It belongs to whoever has the power to possess it."

Mr. Elbow's mouth turned down in a pout. "But the Rooks developed most of that technology while employed at

Elbow Industries. It is Mr. Elbow's by right." He straightened and took a tentative step toward the invention.

Ebelskeever shook his head. "Don't make me laugh, Pops." His look radiated the relaxed menace of a jumbo alligator. The billionaire hesitated.

Mrs. Frost instructed one of her agents to remove the handcuffs from the ponytailed bodyguard.

"You and your incompetent guardian are free to go," she told Elbow.

"Imagine Mr. Elbow's gratitude." The billionaire's manner was anything but grateful. He raised a warning finger. "Know this: Mr. Elbow will never rest until that device is his once more."

"Is that so?" said Mrs. Frost. "In that case, Mr. Elbow, you have a choice: the invention, or your life?"

Elbow's brow furrowed. "How's that?"

With a gentleness as false as Max's Addison Rook disguise, LOTUS's leader explained. "Mine is an immensely powerful, worldwide organization. Should you, or anyone in your employ, attempt to take what is ours, your life is forfeit."

"Now see here!" the billionaire blustered.

"Forfeit," Mrs. Frost repeated. "And you may die now"—at her gesture, Ebelskeever raised his pistol—"or later. Entirely your choice."

At the sight of the weapon, Elbow seemed to visibly shrink in his expensive suit, as if all the air had been suddenly let out of him. This was a fate not even all his money could thwart. "Keep it," he mumbled. "It's yours."

"I told you that you should have hired us for the job," said Mrs. Frost, in the tone of a disappointed teacher.

"Would you have given Mr. Elbow the invention?" His eyes held hope.

She smirked. "Goodness no," she said. "But still."

Defeated and dispirited, the billionaire shuffled toward the door.

"By the by," Mrs. Frost said, "I recommend that you withhold payment from S.P.I.E.S., seeing as how they failed so abysmally to deliver you the invention."

The stringy-haired billionaire glared at Hantai Annie. "Don't you worry. Not another shilling." With a glower at his chastened employee, he trudged through the doorway. Ponytail Man trailed behind like a whipped pup.

Max's heart sank. He knew too well that without Mr. Elbow's payment, Merry Sunshine was out of business. All that work, all that sacrifice, for nothing. A bitter taste filled his mouth.

"Pity about your financial troubles," Mrs. Frost told Hantai Annie with barely concealed glee. "However shall you manage?"

The director had remained silent and impassive since surrendering her weapon. Now she turned her gaze to LOTUS's chief.

"Never you mind," said Hantai Annie. "No matter what, we *gambaru*."

Mrs. Frost sniffed. "Yes, I'm certain you do—whatever that means." A mischievous look stole across her face. "Pray tell, how did you enjoy your time with Mr. Henry Krinkle?"

Recognition dawned on Nikki. "That was *you*? You made the bogus complaint?"

LOTUS's chief batted her eyes mock-coquettishly. "It needn't always be bombs and bullets, you know. Sometimes government bureaucracy can do one's work quite effectively."

"Not this time," said Hantai Annie, her eyes hot enough to throw off sparks.

"No?" said Mrs. Frost. "Ah, well. Can't blame a girl for trying."

Ebelskeever stepped forward. "Shall we gun them down now, guv'nor?"

The grandmotherly woman tapped a perfectly manicured fingernail against her chin. "Perhaps." Her eyes went to the mind-control device. "Or perhaps we should test our new toy. Let's see . . . whom shall we brainwash first? One of these grubby little orphans?" Mrs. Frost's gaze lingered on Max and Cinnabar. "Or perhaps the legendary Hantai Annie Wong herself?"

Max gulped. He scanned the room for a weapon, a distraction, anything that might help—and his gaze lit on the Coke can, standing forgotten on the table.

"Take me," he said. "Experiment on me."

Mrs. Frost's eyebrows rose. "Really? Are you finally beginning to come around, young Segredo?"

Max nodded.

Cinnabar blurted, "No!" Her body vibrated with anxiety. "Take me instead."

"So eager." Mrs. Frost chuckled. "But I believe I shall give Max a try first. Just wait your turn, my dear."

"Tondemonai!" Hantai Annie burst out. "You cannot experiment on my children!"

A whippet-thin LOTUS agent leveled his rifle at her. "One more word, missus, and you'll be picking lead from your liver."

"Now, now, Mr. Witte." Mrs. Frost held up a calming hand. "There's no call for coarse threats. Mrs. Wong knows perfectly well that she can't do a solitary thing to stop me."

But maybe I can, thought Max.

"I'm ready," he said. "It's only that . . ." He gestured at the Coke can. "I'm a bit thirsty. Do you mind?"

"But that's my—" Wyatt began.

Tremaine dug an elbow into his side. "Don't be a hog, mon. Share your drink with Maxwell." At that, a glint of understanding lit Wyatt's eyes.

"Okay?" Max asked Mrs. Frost. She nodded.

Though his heart was thudding like a trip-hammer, Max maintained a bland expression as he crossed to the table.

Glancing casually about to make sure his team recognized his plan, he picked up the can.

"Well then," said Max with a finger on the pull tab, "bottoms up!"

Quick as a blink, he yanked the tab and tossed the flashbang at Mrs. Frost's feet. Max barely had time to squeeze his eyes shut and plug his ears before the device detonated with a deafening . . .

Ka-TCHOOM!

Crimson bloomed behind Max's closed eyelids, and he stumbled back into the table, reeling from the blast. But through his grimace, he smiled.

Finally, Wyatt had made a gizmo that worked as advertised.

When Max opened his eyes, the scene before him was utter bedlam.

LOTUS agents sprawled on the carpet or lay crumpled against the wall, clutching their ears and rubbing their eyes. A powder burn scorched the plush ivory carpet where the can had landed. Mrs. Frost had toppled a side table when she collapsed, spilling a lamp and a vase of orange lilies onto the floor.

Ebelskeever, too, had fallen, but he still clutched the mind-control device and was even now fumbling for his Beretta, blinking to clear his vision.

Max turned to the team, ears ringing. "Go!" he cried, his

voice all warbly-sounding, like he was speaking underwater. "We've only got five seconds."

"What?" yelled Wyatt.

Max pointed to the exit. "Go!"

Mr. Dobasch, Vespa, and Miss Moorthy had been stunned by the flashbang, but the rest of the crew was relatively unaffected. Tremaine and Mr. V dragged Dobasch to his feet; Max and Wyatt lifted Vespa; Rashid and Nikki took Miss Moorthy, and they all staggered toward the front door, weaving past the downed enemy agents.

On the way, Hantai Annie tried to recover the blue cube, but even half blinded, Ebelskeever fired off a couple of shots at her. She abandoned the attempt.

Spotting the headband thingamabob lying on the carpet, Max snatched it up on impulse, looping it around his neck.

Out the front door they careened, lurching like a catnip-drunk alley cat. The S.P.I.E.S. team tottered down a short flight of stairs. With each step, their coordination improved.

Then they opened the street door and ran smack into another squad of LOTUS operatives.

Everyone tumbled to the ground. Vespa was torn from Max's grasp. A couple of random shots were fired, but friend and foe were so intermingled, the LOTUS agents couldn't shoot for fear of hitting their own people. They grappled hand to hand with the S.P.I.E.S. crew.

Max regained his feet. He aimed a roundhouse kick at

a stubby, swarthy agent. The man dodged away. Sensing a presence behind him, Max spun to find Dijon, the evil super-model, reaching for him. Max ducked into a squat, then took her legs out from underneath her with a sweeping capoeira kick.

Glancing around, he realized that the S.P.I.E.S. team was outnumbered. Also unarmed. It was only a matter of minutes before they were all captured or killed.

Hantai Annie must have reached the same conclusion. She wrested a baton from a fallen spy and clouted the man with it.

"Run!" she cried. "Meet at backup site."

LOTUS agents had already taken Vespa and Miss Moorthy, who were still wobbly from the blast. Though it wrenched him to abandon them, Max knew the director was right.

Time to flee.

He karate-chopped a muscular woman who had pinioned Wyatt's arms. When she released the blond boy, Cinnabar put her on the ground with a spinning back kick.

"Someone's been practicing," said Max.

"Sweet of you to notice," she said. "Now let's move!"

Max, Wyatt, and Cinnabar took off running down the walkway to the street. A hulking LOTUS agent loomed in their path. Peppering him with blows, they dodged past.

At the sidewalk, Max glanced behind him. Tremaine,

Hantai Annie, Dobasch, and Mr. Vazquez were fighting back-to-back, allowing Rashid and Nikki to escape. But the tide of battle was turning against them.

Max wavered, torn.

"Come *on!*" cried Wyatt.

He shook his head, feeling that if he left, he might never see his teachers again.

"Max!" yelled Cinnabar. "Don't be a prat!"

With a frustrated snarl, Max whirled away and dashed after his friends. Down the sidewalk they fled. A light drizzle made the stone slippery.

"Where's the backup meeting site again?" panted Wyatt as they ran.

"Bubbles and Beans Café," said Max and Cinnabar together.

"Right, right," said Wyatt. "I knew that."

Rounding the corner onto a side street, Max skidded on the slick pavement. He pinwheeled his arms and fought for balance, but it didn't help. He blundered into the road.

The black Mercedes screeched to a halt. Max didn't.

The force of his momentum carried him up onto its hood, rolling across it, his world a blur of windscreen, startled faces, and wet metal. Somehow, Max landed on his feet in the middle of the street, the headset still around his neck.

The Mercedes doors blew open, and LOTUS agents flooded out.

"Bugger and blast!" Max swore.

Is there no end to these guys? he thought. They're worse than cockroaches.

"Go!" he shouted to Wyatt and Cinnabar. As his friends sprinted down the sidewalk, Max spun away from the grasp of the driver and into traffic.

Horns blared. Max dodged a hot-pink minicab and juked around a bronze Volvo, making his way to the opposite sidewalk. He glanced back. Two agents were chasing Cinnabar and Wyatt, one was phoning for reinforcements as she climbed back into the car, and two more were coming straight at him.

He ran.

WORST-CHASE SCENARIO

DOWN THE NARROW sidewalk, past tall brick buildings, Max flew. The neighborhood boasted a mix of discreetly upscale shops and blocks of luxury town houses. The street was bare of pedestrians—and this just when he could really use a pack of witnesses, a friendly rugby team, or a couple of surly cops with cannons.

No one to hide him, no one to help him. This would've been a particularly useful time for my father to show up, Max thought. But Simon Segredo was nowhere to be seen.

Max tried a door at random as he passed. Locked.

The enemy agents were gaining.

Now they were close enough for him to make out two powerful, though not particularly athletic looking men—one short and one tall—in dusk-colored suits. Both looked seriously cheesed-off.

"Oi!" yelled Short Spy.

"Stop running, you little git!" cried Tall Spy.

All things considered, Max decided not to take the man's advice. Instead, he cut through a pocket park, down an alleyway, and onto a street lined with brick-and-glass office buildings. These structures stood cheek by jowl—no hidey-holes or alleyways between them.

Up ahead, on the opposite side of the road, Max spotted a coin-operated rack of blue bicycles for rent. Could he hop on a bike and lose his pursuers? A quick slap at his trouser pockets reminded him that he carried only a five-pound note.

Max judged the odds of the LOTUS agents breaking a fiver for him were slim.

He pounded onward.

The pavement turned to gray brick, and suddenly he found he'd entered a tourist zone. The river must be close at hand. Instinct told Max that if he tried seeking help in one of the nearby restaurants or pubs, the two spies would extricate him from it. He'd learned this bitter truth in the foster system: people in authority nearly always believed adults over kids.

A shadowy pedestrian tunnel lit only by violet lights yawned on his right. Ducking into it, Max instantly felt like he was running backward through time. The tunnel gave onto a cramped lane of brick buildings that looked hundreds of years old, crowding together like secondary-school bullies over a potential victim.

But Max had no time for history. His side ached, his lungs burned, and his pursuers were still gaining.

A nook appeared with several café tables, standing empty due to the cold. As he passed, Max snagged the top of a metal chair and flung it behind him. A crash and a curse told him that one of his pursuers had tripped over it.

"You make me run all over this bloody neighborhood, you'll rue it!" shouted Short Spy.

Max had no intention of ruing it. But he did intend to keep running.

The lane opened into a small plaza. On his left, a pub overlooked the river. A few hardy souls laughed and drank at wooden tables under wide purple umbrellas that held off the drizzle. Dead ahead, a three-masted black galleon with red-and-gold trim sat at dock. Clearly a tourist attraction, it was now closed up for the night.

Max longed to stop running.

The galleon would make a perfect hiding place—if the agents on his heels didn't see him hiding. Perhaps he could lose them momentarily. . . .

He checked over his shoulder. Short Spy was only twenty feet behind him, and Tall Spy a little farther back. Panting raggedly, Max dashed through the arched doorway into the pub. A wave of warmth, scrumptious smells, and noisy chatter enfolded him.

"Here now, son," said the hostess, a heavyset, cinnamon-skinned woman. "Are you over fourteen?"

"Absolutely," Max lied between pants, slipping past her and into the low-ceilinged dining room. "I just . . . popped in to . . . look for my mum."

The place was packed. Max wove between the tables, dodging servers who bore platters of fish and chips, meat pies, and sausages. He caught a glimpse of the LOTUS agents at the entrance, coming after him. Fine, let them come.

Hurrying down along one side of the bar, Max faked like he was headed for the men's room. Then he dipped behind a pillar and, keeping his head below bar level, cat-footed his way to the patio door.

A white-haired codger on a stool cackled as Max passed. "Tryin' to duck out on the old lady, eh?" he said.

"Something like that," said Max. "Don't rat on me?"

"She won't hear it from me, lad," said the codger, turning back to his pint.

Max sneaked out the side door and back into the brisk night air. Hiding behind a column, he risked a peek through the window. The two spies were just disappearing into the hall that led to the loo.

A smile twitched at the corners of Max's lips. He hurried down the few steps from the raised patio and dashed across the plaza to the ship. Naturally, the entrance gate was locked. He swung a leg over the railing, clambered around the security cage, and swung himself up onto the gangplank.

A stark spotlight illuminated the ancient sailing ship.

Its bare riggings and masts rose up into darkness, and the entrances to the vessel's cabins were also shrouded in gloom. Crouching behind the gunwale, Max hesitated.

Up or down?

The mental image of being cornered on the crow's nest decided him. Max hustled into the forward cabin. Its ceiling hung low—maybe old-timey sailors were pygmies?—and its bloodred floor was crowded with coiled ropes, wooden chests, and various nautical bits and bobs. A bare bulb cast sinister shadows.

From the plaza, voices carried.

"Where's that little rat got to?" growled a rough male voice.

"Dunno," said another man. "But he'll regret makin' us play hide-and-seek." This last bit was practically shouted, for Max's benefit.

Max got the message. He hunted about for a better hiding place. Five feet away, a dark hatch yawned. The spill of light showed steep wooden steps descending into blackness.

Max crept over to the hatch and down the ladderlike stairs. Fumbling in his pocket for the flashlight, he missed his footing and slipped downward a step.

"Hear that?" said the rough voice.

"He's on the ship!" the other man crowed. "We got him now."

Max cursed silently. He scrambled down to the lower

level and cast about for an escape plan. The ship's wide belly was packed with more trunks and barrels and fake cannons than a road-show version of *Peter Pan*.

Could he hole up inside a trunk? No, only a total cabbage would pick that as an ace hiding place. They'd find him for certain.

Clatters and thumps came from above as the two spies climbed aboard. "Stay here," said the rough voice. "Guard the exit. I'll drive him out."

Max swallowed. Maybe hiding on an old galleon hadn't been such a bright idea after all.

Off in the corner, a flash of red caught his eye—a fire extinguisher. Max pried it from its holder as quietly as possible. Heavy footsteps clomped above. The LOTUS agent had entered the cabin. Max ducked into a dim corner behind the steps, stowed his flashlight, and hefted the heavy metal cylinder.

He waited, heartbeat thudding in his ears like a kick drum. Despite the cold, Max's brow was beaded with sweat.

The spy's footsteps paused at the top of the ladder. "Come out, come out, wherever you are," crooned the man. He took one step down, and then another, his flashlight slicing a swath through the darkness. "Or I'll huff, and I'll puff, and I'll—*ow!*"

A heavy clonk sounded above.

"Gerald?" called the second man. "What's the matter?"

"Bumped my bloody head, that's what's the matter,"

Gerald snarled. "This bloody ship was built for a pack of poxy dwarves."

"I believe they prefer the term 'little people,'" said the second man.

Gerald swore a colorful oath, and as he continued down the steps, Max could tell that this was Tall Spy. The flashlight swept the room as the man neared the bottom of the ladder.

Max's muscles thrummed like steel cables. He raised the fire extinguisher. He'd only have one shot, so he had to make it count.

Gerald stepped onto the lower deck. As he began to turn, Max rushed forward from hiding and clouted him in the temple, hard as he could strike.

With a grunt, the tall spy crumpled. Though sprawled on the floor, he still groaned and stirred, so Max clouted him again. This time, Gerald stayed down.

"Gerald?" Short Spy called. "All right, then?"

Max laid the fire extinguisher beside the unconscious agent and tiptoed over to the other set of steps, following the beam of the man's fallen flashlight. He listened intently.

"What's happening?" said Short Spy. "Jerry? You okay?"

Footsteps thumped along the deck, heading for the same ladder that Gerald had descended. Cautiously, Max crept up the aft steps, watching the forward hatch for Short Spy.

It would be a close thing. . . .

The LOTUS agent's flashlight shone down the trapdoor,

coming to rest on Gerald's feet. Short Spy cursed and began climbing down.

Max eased out the other hatch and into the aft cabin, moving as silently as the memory of fog. When he heard the agent's voice below, he hustled across the deck and onto the gangplank.

"Oi!" the man cried. "Come back here, if you know what's good for you!"

Max knew what was good for him, and it wasn't Short Spy. He vaulted over the rail, swung himself around the cage, and dropped onto the dock. Running flat out, he headed across the plaza toward a well-lighted street.

To his left loomed a tan brick-and-glass monstrosity that looked like someone's idea of a postmodern castle. Ahead lay a majestic old cathedral and the open streets beyond.

"Get him!" cried Short Spy.

Max glanced back to see the agent clambering down from the ship. But to whom had he called out? When Max looked forward again, a female LOTUS spy was running past the cathedral, aiming to cut him off. He whipped a left turn around the corner of the castle, pouring on the speed. The narrow lane wound back away from the church, toward an L-shaped bend in the brick-and-glass building.

His situation felt like déjà vu all over again. If only Max could get out of sight for a moment or two, he could hide somewhere.

If only.

He sprinted down the road, but just as he reached the bend, a midnight-blue SUV jerked to a halt ahead of him. More LOTUS agents poured out.

Honestly, was every other person in this city working for them?

Spies behind him, spies in front of him. Max took the only path available: up a ramp into the castle building. Luckily, the tall glass doors stood unlocked.

He flung them open and found himself in a spacious reception area.

"May I help you?" asked a lean, red-haired woman, her head barely visible above a long counter.

"I seriously doubt it," said Max.

To his right, a pair of elevators waited with doors open. A low, decorative wall with a turnstile, designed for polite, rule-abiding visitors, blocked his way. Through the glass doors, Max could see LOTUS agents pounding up the ramp.

He vaulted the wall and sprinted for the right-hand elevator.

"Hey!" cried the receptionist. "Come back here!"

Max pushed the buttons for all six floors and hopped out again. Then he jumped into the second lift and hit the fourth-floor button. Let the LOTUS agents get their exercise on the stairs.

"I'm calling security!" the woman shouted as the doors closed.

Max shook his head ruefully. Fat lot of good an overweight ex-cop could do against a carload of evil spies. He leaned against the wall to catch his breath.

Above him, the tinny speaker played a cheesy version of some tune that was old when Max's grandfather was still in diapers.

"I hate this song," Max muttered.

He racked his brain, trying to come up with some sort of plan. But after a long day of spying, stealing, running, and fighting, his thoughts were about as lively as raisins in a bowl of porridge.

All he could think was: Find an empty room and hide.

The elevator bell dinged. The doors opened on a long corridor of unlit offices. Max hadn't taken four paces when a deep female voice said, "Hold it right there, sonny-me-lad."

WHERE YOU GONNA RUN TO?

CHAPTER 29

A BEEFY, amber-skinned woman in a blue uniform with SECURITY stitched on the breast pocket stepped between Max and the elevators. A heavy baton dangled from a loop on her belt. Her suspicious squint was well practiced.

Max held up his palms. "It's not what it looks like," he said.

"It never is." The guard took a step toward him. "Come along quietly, and don't make me ring the police."

Max backed away. "No, you don't get it. I'm running from some right dangerous people. I *want* you to call the cops."

A frown furrowed her brow, but the woman kept approaching. "Don't make this any harder on yourself."

"I don't think it *gets* any harder," said Max.

A quick glance down the hallway behind him revealed a green sign that read STAIRS. Max whirled and sprinted for it.

Heavy footfalls clunked down the corridor in pursuit. "Come back here!" cried the woman.

Feeling a bit like the gingerbread man, Max ran, ran, as fast as he could. He slammed through the door without slowing down. Voices and footsteps echoed up the stairwell from the lower level, so Max headed upward.

He skipped the fifth floor, to put some distance between himself and Madame Security Guard. Barreling through the sixth-floor door, Max raced down another corridor like the one below him. He tried a door at random.

Locked. And with a guard on his heels, he had no time to pick it.

A door opened farther down the hall, and a slight, sandy-haired man who looked like a rabbit walking on its hind legs stepped out.

Max ran up to him. "Hide me!" he implored.

Wide-eyed, Rabbit Man clutched his briefcase to his chest. "I should say not," he huffed.

"Stop that boy!" A call rang out from the far end of the hall. Madame Security Guard had arrived.

Rabbit Man popped back into his office and slammed the door.

Bloody marvelous.

Max rolled his eyes. Whatever happened to the milk of human kindness?

Thoroughly knackered, he lurched onward. He had nearly

reached the elevators when one of them dinged. The doors slid open to reveal Ebelskeever, Mrs. Frost, and a pair of truly peeved-looking LOTUS agents.

More good news.

"He's got the headpiece," shouted Ebelskeever.

Max veered left down a short corridor, at the end of which stood another door labeled STAIRS. Thank God for fire regulations, he thought. He burst through it, and again heard footfalls rising up the stairwell.

Lovely. Only one option remained to him.

Max staggered up the last flight, and it ended in a locked steel door.

"Never once the easy way," he muttered.

Fumbling his lockpicks out, Max inserted the torque wrench and began fiddling with his pick, feeling for the tumblers. He reckoned he had maybe ten seconds—more, if the poor security guard tried to detain Mrs. Frost's crew.

So, no pressure there.

Breath ragged, heart thudding, Max tried to calm himself enough to sense the lock's delicate workings. Footsteps hammered below, drawing ever closer. Miracle of miracles, the tumblers aligned, and the door swung open.

He reeled through and slammed it behind him. Two seconds later, a heavy fist battered on the door. "Open up, kid!" boomed a man's voice.

Max hunted around for something to prop up against the

door, but the rooftop stretched as bare and cold as the surface of a frozen lake. To one side rose the complicated jumble of pipes, heating vents, and whatnot that often turns up on rooftops. Along all other sides, the building's crenellations rose against a vista of twinkling city lights, arching bridges, and the dark, dark river that rolled through the city.

It would've been enchanting, thought Max, if not for the whole running-for-your-life bit.

The banging on the door stopped. LOTUS agents were probably picking the lock. Max trotted along the roof's edge, hoping against hope for another rooftop within jumping distance.

No luck. This postmodern castle stood alone.

At last, the door scraped open.

Max turned, his back to the river, his face to the enemy.

Two LOTUS operatives stepped through the door and moved to either side, framing it. Through the portal strolled the petite figure of Mrs. Frost, with the massive Mr. Ebelskeever following at her heels like a pet *T. rex*. She came to a halt about ten feet from Max.

"Well," said Mrs. Frost.

She paused, gloved hands folded in front of her, head slightly cocked, as if she were appraising a rare piece of abstract sculpture.

At that instant, all Max could hear was the keening of the wind, the grumble of distant cars, and the cry of a lonely boat horn. His world shrank to this rooftop, this moment.

He clenched his jaw. No matter what, he wouldn't beg. He wouldn't give them the satisfaction.

"You've led us on a merry chase," said Mrs. Frost, in her perfect, posh tones. "Frightfully resourceful, young man. But now, at long last, the chase is over."

"I'm game for another go if you are," said Max.

LOTUS's chief arched an eyebrow. She shared a meaningful glance with Ebelskeever, who wore his usual evil smirk.

"Set down the headpiece," he growled. "Gently."

Max was fresh out of options, but even though he knew he was beaten, he just couldn't bring himself to comply. Instead, he took a step closer to the parapet. "Not quite yet, I think."

When the gorilla-like spy started toward him, Mrs. Frost put a restraining hand on his arm. "This was all so unnecessary," she said.

"True," said Max. "If only you'd stayed home in bed and given up on the whole taking-over-the-world thing."

Mrs. Frost clucked her tongue in disapproval. "Max Segredo. You've gotten hold of the wrong end of the stick."

"Oh?"

Max stuffed his hands in his jacket pockets, hunching his shoulders against the icy breeze.

LOTUS's chief showed no signs of feeling the cold. "I grant you that Mrs. Wong has the whole noble underdog act going for her," she said, "and she is a capable spymaster, to be sure. But she's out of step with the times."

"Let me guess: you're in step?" Max scoffed.

Mrs. Frost lifted her chin. "Precisely. Max, we're not really enemies, you and I."

"Oh, no?" A bitter chuckle bubbled up. "Friends chase you all over the city, do they?"

"When you're not listening to reason, yes."

Max felt a heat rising from low in his gut, spreading like a wildfire.

"And what is reason?" he shot back.

Mrs. Frost spread her hands. "Your loyalties are misplaced. Join us."

Max looked away, across the glittering jewel box of city lights. He recalled Hantai Annie ordering him to do exactly that, but now that the actual moment had arrived, the words stuck in his craw like a half-chewed sausage.

"Perhaps you're resisting out of loyalty to S.P.I.E.S.," said the grandmotherly woman. "But S.P.I.E.S. is no more."

Max snorted. "Right."

"Oh, it's true," rumbled Ebelskeever. "Even now, our team is burning down your little headquarters, where I spent such a pleasant fortnight."

The big man snapped his fingers, and an agent pulled a computer pad from his bag. Several taps later, the image of a flaming house—Merry Sunshine Orphanage—filled the screen.

"Impossible," said Max. Cold, sudden dread gripped his insides. Where were Jazz and Mr. Stones, and all the others who had stayed behind? Had they gotten out?

"And even now," said Ebelskeever, "our agents have cornered your precious Hantai Annie Wong."

Max pictured the last time he'd seen her, outnumbered, and fighting fiercely outside the safe house. He bit his lip and shook his head, mute. Hot tears blurred his vision.

Taking a couple of leisurely steps closer, Mrs. Frost said, "Perhaps you're resisting out of loyalty to your friends. But one of your friends is, in fact, working for us already."

Anger surged over him like a wave. "Oh, sure," said Max, a protective hand rising to the headpiece around his neck. "And I'm the Queen Mother."

LOTUS's chief turned back to the doorway. "My dear," she called. "Won't you join us?"

A form stepped through the stairwell door and into the harsh glare of the security light. Max couldn't suppress a gasp.

It was Vespa.

Her blond hair was a shaggy mess, and her lovely face wore a miserable expression.

"They caught you, too?" Max asked.

"Not . . . exactly." Vespa winced, avoiding his eyes. She trudged forward to stand beside Mrs. Frost.

"Tell him," the woman commanded, prodding her.

The blond girl hugged her arms and stole a glance at Max. "You remember I said my only relative is an aunt I don't get along with?"

"Yeah . . . ?"

"Well . . ." Her gaze flicked to Mrs. Frost, then down again. "That much was true."

As realization dawned, Max's mouth fell open.

"*She's* your aunt? Mrs. *Frost*?"

Vespa nodded. "She made me go undercover in your school."

Max felt gutted. Several times he tried to speak, his mouth flapping open and closed like a landed flounder's while his mind slotted events into place.

"So . . . the texts from LOTUS, the . . . the hit on Ben Singh, the location of the safe house?" he sputtered.

She shrugged a shoulder. "All me. I told her everything."

"Then . . . you're a liar!" Max spat. "Cinnabar was right: everything about you was a lie."

Vespa gazed up at him, the hurt plain in her toffee-brown eyes. "Not everything," she said. "I do . . . really like you."

Ebelskeever snorted. "Aw, young love. Ain't it grand," he mocked. But the big man fell silent at a sharp look from Mrs. Frost.

Vespa turned her back on them all, shoulders slumped.

"And if your loyalty to S.P.I.E.S. and your friends is misplaced," said Mrs. Frost, "then what shall I say about your loyalty to Simon Segredo, the notorious turncoat?"

"Turncoat?" Max scoffed. "You forced him to help you by threatening to hurt me. You're just sore because he chose me over LOTUS, that night in the mansion."

"Is that what you think?" Mrs. Frost's eyebrows rose.

"Perhaps you wouldn't be so quick to defend your father if you knew the whole truth."

"What truth?" said Max. "That he left my mum and me because he was on the run from you? That even now you're trying to hunt him down and kill him?"

A tolerant half smile appeared on Mrs. Frost's grandmotherly face. Max wanted to wipe it off with something heavy and blunt.

"What do you know about how your mother died?" she asked in a near whisper.

A queasy feeling rippled through Max. "All I need to know," he bluffed.

But in fact, he knew nearly nothing. Only that his mother had died young, only that his father felt he'd failed her.

"Then you've heard the story?" said Mrs. Frost, frowning.

"What story?"

Her eyes read his face. "You don't know, do you? Oh, you poor dear. Max, your father was responsible for her death."

Max reeled, his world crumbling. "No," he whispered. "Never."

"I'm afraid so. He killed her, just as surely as I'm standing here."

He scanned Mrs. Frost's face for signs of lying, but her voice was even, her gaze steady, her body language relaxed.

Max's mind revolted at the thought. Simon killed my mother?

His legs turned to rubber. Dizziness swept through him in a rush. All his hopes, all his daydreams about one day being able to live with his father like a normal son—all gone in an instant.

Poof.

"No." Feeling like he was drowning in the air, Max stumbled backward, gasping. "No. It can't be."

"Careful," said Mrs. Frost. "Come away from there, and give me the headpiece."

Max's legs hit something stony and unyielding. He turned to find himself at the edge of the low wall that bordered the roof. Six floors below him stretched the dark abyss of the broad river. His stomach flip-flopped.

And suddenly it was all too much to take.

Max hopped up onto the parapet.

"Stop him!" barked Mrs. Frost.

"Max, no!" cried Vespa.

And then he jumped.

CHAPTER 30

IN TOO DEEP

THE ACTUAL FALLING isn't so bad, Max had time to think on the way down. It's the landing that gets you.

Bam!

He smacked into the water like a meteorite from a distant galaxy. Icy cold embraced him, and all the breath rushed from his body.

Air, air! his lungs screamed.

No air. He shot down into the filthy river like a bullet.

Surprisingly soon, his feet hit the bottom, folding Max's body into a squat. He pushed off with all his might, flailing his arms like mad, clawing and kicking his way back up.

His head broke the surface. Air rushed back into his lungs with a gasp.

He was alive!

Despite everything, Max laughed aloud from the sheer

wonder of it, getting a mouthful of the foul river water for his pains. He spat and sputtered.

The shock had cleared his mind.

What kind of idiot, he thought, jumps off a building into the river? *This* kind of idiot, he supposed.

Treading water, Max craned his neck and looked up at the castlelike building. Impossibly far above, at the edge of the rooftop, the lights picked out a small white-haired head looking over at him.

Mrs. Frost.

Chills racked his body. Max looked the other way, across the river at the far shore. Idiot he might be, but he wasn't fool enough to try to swim it and escape.

His clothes clung, dragging him down. The headpiece was gone, torn away. Max made his decision and with a strong overhand stroke, swam for the nearby shore. Slick with algae, the sheer concrete embankment stretched a good eight feet above him. No way to climb that.

He swam along until he reached the dock pilings beside the tourist galleon. There, Max clung to a thick loop of rope, catching his breath.

A hand reached down.

Max gripped it and looked up into the triumphant sneer of Mr. Ebelskeever. Through chattering teeth, he said, "What's a b-b-bloke got to do to j-j-join your crew? J-j-jump in the river?"

Ebelskeever's other hand seized Max's arm and, with a powerful heave, dragged him up onto the dock. For a moment, Max lay there, gasping and shuddering with the cold.

And this, he thought, is how it begins.

From the causeway atop a bridge, not a hundred yards distant, Cinnabar and Wyatt watched Max being fished from the river. They witnessed the LOTUS agents bundling him up in a borrowed overcoat and leading him to a black SUV. Even from that distance, they caught Vespa's concern and the victorious strut in Mrs. Frost's stride. "Well, that's that," said Wyatt, slumping against the railing. "They've got Max."

Cinnabar bristled. "That is most definitely *not* that."

"Are you a few crumbs short of a biscuit?" said Wyatt, waving his hands for emphasis. "Max is gone, the bad guys surrounded our backup site, and our whole crew is scattered to the winds—dead or captured, for all we know. Game over. We got creamed. Wipeout."

Cinnabar's mouth tightened. "And you'd let a little thing like that stop you?"

Wyatt regarded her with the kind of look you reserve for someone who tells you they plan to fly to the moon on gossamer wings.

"Little thing?" he said.

"Absolutely," said Cinnabar. "This is no time to wimp out."

"What in the bloody blue blazes are you talking about?"

A gleam came into her golden eyes. "We're going to rescue Max."

From somewhere in the depths of his despair, an incredulous chuckle gurgled out of Wyatt. "What, you and me?"

"Yes."

"Rescue Max?"

"Yes."

"From an insanely powerful spy organization with endless resources and buckets of highly trained agents?"

"Well," Cinnabar considered, "yes."

Wyatt shook his head slowly, marveling. "It's finally happened."

"What?" she asked.

"You're off your rocker."

Cinnabar jabbed a finger at him for emphasis. "If you think I'm going to leave him to the tender mercies of that dyed-blond tartlet, you've got another think coming, Wyatt Jackaroo." She reached down and dragged him to his feet. "Now come on."

"Where are we going?"

Cinnabar eyed the departing SUV. "We've got loads of work to do, and not much time to do it in."

"Well, paint me pink and call me Norma," Wyatt muttered, following her. "You can say that again."

And from the shadows of a nearby building, the tall, lean figure of Simon Segredo emerged, trailing them into the night.

OBSERVATION TRAINING—Spotting a Lie

Everybody lies—particularly spies—but not everyone recognizes when they're being lied to. Nevertheless, that knowledge is hiding in plain sight. When we fib, our bodies give off unconscious signals that the trained observer can read like a book.

Try this experiment: Tell a deliberate lie to someone and make an effort to suppress *all* your body language. Could you do it? Not likely. Even if you kept yourself from making the obvious movements that betray your lie, tiny micro-gestures will still give you away. Responses like dilation of pupils, sweating, and eyeblinks simply cannot be controlled.

Learning to spot those subtle micro-gesture "tells" is part of your advanced training, but here are five of the more common "liar moves" to get you started. As always, you must first observe the subject's normal body language in order to have a baseline to judge by.

1. Covering the Mouth
The hand comes up to cover the mouth, whether as a single finger, several fingers, or a fist. This happens because the brain is subconsciously telling the hand to smother the deceitful words coming from the mouth. Is someone who covers their mouth when speaking always lying? Not always, but this gesture is a good clue that *something* is being withheld.

2. Rubbing the Eye
Just like the "see no evil" monkey, someone who rubs his eye while talking to you may be trying to keep himself from witnessing his deceit. (Or he may have dust in his eye. Don't rush to judgment.) This gesture results from the brain trying to subconsciously shut

out a distasteful sight, like the face of the person you're lying to. The extreme version of this move is looking away while telling the lie.

3. Grabbing the Ear

If you tell someone to meet you at the mall, and they tug on their ear and look away while saying, "Sounds good to me," you might very well be stood up. Ear tugging or drilling a finger into the ear can be the equivalent of a small child clapping both hands over her ears when she wants to block out what's being said. It's the "hear no evil" equivalent of the Eye Rub.

4. Pulling the Collar

Interestingly enough, telling lies can cause a faint tingling sensation in the skin of your neck. This not only explains why people sometimes scratch their neck when fibbing, but also why some liars pull at their collar when they think they might have been found out. Sweat forms on the neck when we think we've been caught in a lie. But this also happens when someone is frustrated or angry, so be sure you understand what's what.

5. Blinking the Eyes

People under pressure—those telling lies, for example—tend to dramatically increase their rate of eye blinking. It's like their brain is trying to block the person they're deceiving from sight. Of course, some people are just blinky, so be sure to make your baseline observations first.

OBSERVATION EXERCISE

How observant are you? In a spy, keen observational abilities can mean the difference between success and failure, between life and death. Try this exercise to sharpen your skills.

Take a blank sheet of paper and, without looking at the room, write down every object in your bedroom. Take your time visualizing the space, and give your list as much detail as possible.

When you've finished, take a look around the room and check how accurate you were. You'll probably be surprised to notice that many things you see every day are missing from your list.

Fear not. If you keep up this exercise for several days, you'll find the number of missing objects diminishing as you go.

Extra credit:
The next time you're in a public place—a shopping center, a library, or a school—imagine that you're standing at a crime scene. Notice every detail and every "suspect" around you, paying particular attention to the people, how they look and how they're dressed.

Then remove yourself from that setting and try to write down all those details. Can you describe the people the way you'd describe suspects to a police sketch artist? The more often you do this, the stronger your powers of observation will grow.

Excerpted from:
Survival Skills for the Modern Spy, 3rd Edition
By Giacomo Fleming, Belle Maclean, and S. Gromonowitz

**For more spy information and activities,
please visit www.school4spies.com.**

ACKNOWLEDGMENTS

ONCE AGAIN, it took a small village to write a book, and I'm grateful for the generous assistance of so many friends and acquaintances. Thanks to Peter Selvaggio for patiently explaining the ins and outs of security systems, and how to make break-ins even harder for my juvenile spies. Thanks to Mick Guinn for insights on computer hacking. And a major mahalo to my international consultants, who helped me with the dialogue of characters from outside the United States: Annie Sung Bernstein and Janette Cross (Japanese), Carol Bond (Aussie-isms), and Terry Sheldon (Brit-speak). I greatly appreciate your time and efforts. Any errors that found their way into the book are purely the result of my own uncontrollable bent for fiction.

And of course, I couldn't have written this book without the loving support of my wife, Janette, who always offers this spy a place to come in from the cold.